TIMELESS DESIRE

THE DESIRE SERIES BOOK 9

BARBARA DONLON BRADLEY

ONE

Heather sat between Storm's legs as she watched her son climb the advanced rock wall Bert had created for him. Her heart stopped when he walked out on a thin wire ten feet above the ground. He acted like he was on the ground and it frightened Heather. He did a flip in the air then landed back on it. Heather ducked her head then looked through her fingers to be sure he was okay. He gave her a big grin.

"My heart, you must show him your belief in his ability. Hiding is sending the opposite message," Storm said softly next to her ear.

"I know." She tilted her head so she could look up at her mate. "But the thought of our son getting hurt scares me. I can't help but worry."

"I am fine, Mommy. Uncle Bert says I have the best agility he's ever seen for someone my age." Terrick leaped off the wire, landed on the ground, and ran to her side.

Heather wrapped her arms around her son. "That was breathtaking to watch."

"It scared you a little, huh?" He gave her a quick kiss then sat in her lap.

"It did, but it's okay. I'll do better next time." Heather ruffled his hair. "You were wonderful."

"Thank you." He rested his head against her collarbone.

"We need to head back to Vespia, son," said Storm. They were on Bert's compound, orbiting Vespia. "Your older sister and her mate will be coming a few hours after we leave to spend time with you two."

"Oh, good. I like Skye."

"We do too," said Heather when Storm remained quiet. "And we're taking Bert with us. He wishes to add some upgrades to our computer system."

"When will you be back?" He lifted his face to look at her.

"In a few days." She hugged him. "Why don't you get your sister and walk us to our ship?"

"Okay, Mommy."

———

Their ship landed in one of the caves that ran beneath Vespia that they used as their tarmac. Fridon stepped up to them the moment they disembarked.

"Reasta has attacked another one of our posts." He led them to the main computer room, where everything that had been going on was up and viewable. "We keep moving them and she keeps finding them."

"How many people have we lost?" asked Heather as she studied the data.

"Five so far."

Heather swore under her breath. She hated losing their soldiers. "And her people are still attacking?"

"Yes, we can't stop them."

Heather turned to Bert. "I'm sorry, but you're sort of trapped here until we can stop her."

"Then let me see what I can do to help you end this."

"Thank you." Heather turned to her mate. "Storm, each person we lose—"

———

"What the hell?" Skye ran his hands over the control panel, trying to get a response. Any response. All the power went out on the ship for a second before it powered back up. Now everything worked fine. He wondered what caused that.

"That was odd." Sam ran a few tests. She looked at him. "Everything seems to be fine now."

Skye slowed their ship down as they got close to Vespian space. Protocol needed to be followed, and he knew who would be the one yelling at him if he didn't follow it. He sent the proper message and waited for clearance. They'd figure out what happened to the ship once they landed. "I wish I knew what caused that. I've never had any trouble with this ship before."

"We'll check with Bert once we're through." Sam sat in the copilot's seat. She pressed a few buttons and cupped her ear. "Skye, security is contacting us."

"That's odd." He activated the communication system. "This is Skye Latimer."

"What is the purpose for your visit?"

"Purpose?" He looked at Sam. Why were they asking that? "We're returning home."

"We have no record of your citizenship." And they cut the line.

"What are they talking about?" Sam leaned forward. "I'll get them back."

"Wait." He reached out and took her hand in his. "I don't want to end up in jail while we try to figure out what happened. Let's leave like we're supposed to, and once we're out of their radar, we'll come back and use the ship's cloaking device to go to Bert's ship. He'll have the answers for us."

———

They floated in Vespian space staring at their screen.

"Where is Bert's ship?" asked Sam.

"I'm not sure. It should be right here." Skye hit a few buttons. He sat back and stared at the empty part of space in front of them. Something crazy was going on and they needed to figure out what had happened. "We need to listen to the communiqués from Vespia and see if we can get any answers."

"What are we looking for?" Sam glanced at him as she opened the communication system so they could listen in.

"I don't know. Let's focus on anything about your family."

It didn't take them long to figure out what part of the problem was.

"My dad is mated to another woman? Who is Susan?" Sam asked.

"I think they're talking about Susan Harris. She was involved with Heather's kidnapping when she was pregnant with the twins."

"While I was still with Ialog? The one who wanted to replace Mom? I remember her." Sam sat back in her chair and clasped her hands together, trying to hide her fear. She turned to look at him again. "How did this happen? And where is Mom?"

"I don't know. We need to find Bert and talk to him."

"And how do you think you're going to do that?" Her voice was sharp. Skye knew she was frightened.

"I'm going to go to the last place he was before he moved to Vespia." Skye set the ship on autopilot out of Vespian space then he released his straps and went to her side. "It's going to be okay, Sam. We will figure this out."

"Do you think we're in an alternate reality?"

"Or something changed the timeline to one we don't recognize." Skye climbed back into his seat and headed to the planet where he knew Bert had lived. Sam was very quiet during the trip. "You okay?"

"I don't really exist, do I?"

"I wish I could answer that, but I don't know." Skye looked over at her to see how she was doing. He wanted to console her but didn't know how. She wanted the truth, and he would never lie just to keep her happy. If he could, he'd take her in his arms, but they were in a busy part of space where using autopilot made him uneasy. He would do it if she needed him, but she sat there staring out the screen, so he stayed in his chair.

"Why weren't we affected by this?" Sam's voice was soft.

"This ship is shielded from temporal shifts. Bert told me he had used it to time travel. I think we were protected because of it."

"What happens if we leave the ship?"

"Well, we could have one of two things happen. We'd be fine and our memories of the other timeline remain intact since the change has already happened, or the moment we step out of the ship we are altered to fit in this timeline, forget everything, and live out our lives without each other."

"I don't like that second one at all."

"Me either." He pointed to the planet Fevirs. The last

place he knew Bert had been before he came to Vespia. "We're here." Skye opened the communication system. "Bert, this is Skye Latimer. We need to talk."

"You think he's going to answer?" asked Sam after a few seconds. Bert normally responded immediately.

"May I help you?" Bert's face filled the screen.

"Yes. Clearance green, four two six nine."

"Okay. So you know my clearance codes. I must assume you know me?"

"This is not the time to play games, Bert. We've either been thrown into another dimension, or the timeline has changed around us." His comment didn't seem to faze Bert.

"I see." He studied them for a moment. "What do you remember?"

"For one you had a ship that was in orbit around Vespia. Then there is my bondmate, Sam. Her parents are Storm and Heather, except we've learned that Storm is now mated to some woman named Susan and Sam's mother has never been to Vespia."

"So we're not sure if I even exist right now," added Sam.

"Have you two been out of that ship?" Bert didn't comment, but Skye did see the slight brow movement that showed his interest.

"No. Not sure if that was a smart idea so we stayed put."

"I'm going to send something over. You need to wear them before you leave your ship."

Skye turned to the pad and watched as two necklaces appeared. He picked his up and slipped it around his neck then handed Sam hers.

"You have them on?"

"Yes."

"Make sure they are under your shirts so they can sink into your body. I'm sending the coordinates for you to land now, and I'll meet you there."

Skye followed Bert's directions, even though he knew these coordinates from the original timeline, and they landed next to his old complex. "We need to see where the shift happened so we can correct it."

"It might not be that easy." Bert escorted them inside. "I have been tracing little frizzons all day. Whoever did this was very sloppy. They've had to go back and continue to make corrections."

"Then you remember, too."

"Sadly, no. I must have been out of the compound when it happened. I only know because of that." He pointed to one of many screens in the room. Red bars blinked on several. "Each one shows a major shift when the timeline changed."

"Then we can fix it."

"I need to know what the timeline should be like first. Bert studied Sam. "Like your girlfriend here. If her parents haven't met, then she probably doesn't exist. At least not in this form."

"What?" Sam rubbed her arms at the thought. Skye wrapped his arms around her to give her some moral support.

"The timeline will always try to adjust itself. That is one of the reasons technology hasn't created something that can alter time permanently. It won't work because of the way time flows. There are natural alterations to keep time flowing but trying to change it never works." He looked at Skye. "You said you had something that shows the original timeline?"

Skye nodded and held up his handheld. He was grateful it was protected against the timeline change. Another one of Fridon's creations.

"Perfect." Bert looked at it for a moment. "Is this protected properly?"

"Yes."

"Excellent. This will let me figure out what changes were made so we can repair them to get the timeline back. You also need to go out there and find out just how far off it is."

"Are you going to keep this?" He handed it over.

"No. You should have it with you so can compare your data to what you find. I just need a minute to get what I need from it." Bert took Skye's handheld and downloaded all the data from it. "This will give me a starting point to work from. I'll keep in touch as needed, but you need to find this Heather and Storm and see what their life is like now. See what it will take to bring this timeline together again."

"Where do we start?" asked Sam.

"Earth. That's where Heather should be." Skye looked at Bert. "Can you give me any data on what my life has been like? It would help me behave properly."

"I can pull your file, but you should be able to access the memories of the Skye from this timeline as well. That way, when you're faced with a situation you're not sure about, or how you might have handled it in the past, the right memory should pop into your head and allow you to behave properly."

"How is that possible?"

"There are two of you here right now. The device I gave you will keep you slightly out of sync so you won't wreak havoc with the timeline, but still allow you to share your other self's memories."

"Great." Skye didn't want to deal with this craziness, but he'd do whatever he needed to get the proper timeline back. He turned Sam in his arms so he could look at her. "Let's go find your mother."

———

Heather Drexel stood in front of her commanding officer and took notes on what was needed for the upcoming function. She hated the tediousness of some of the things her job required her to do, but she had worked too hard to get this position to complain. Dian, her aunt, had recommended she try for the position when it opened. It would look good on her record and allow her to learn about other races that she wouldn't have been able to do as a security guard. Knowing some of the more boring things she would have to do, she had been hesitant, but Dian kept suggesting she try so she did and landed the job. If it hadn't been for her aunt, she wouldn't have met *him*, and he made it all worthwhile.

She enjoyed being Admiral Barrington's assistant but couldn't help but feel like something was missing from her life from time to time. At least she had something to look forward to at this function. The man that made her heart flutter every time she saw him would be there.

"You with me, captain?" asked Bear.

"Yes, sir." She straightened her shoulders and held her pad against her chest. "This function will run smoothly, sir. Just like all the other ones."

——

Skye landed their ship in a secluded spot on Earth. Not an easy thing to do when most of the planet was populated now. The Ancient cloaking technology on the ship was more advanced than anything Earth could detect, so all he needed to do was find a place to set it down. He ended up landing in the territory once known as Washington state. So much had been preserved hundreds of years ago it was about the only place he could land in seclusion.

"You realized this is very close to where Ialog had his

compound." Sam brushed a stray piece of hair from her eyes.

"This is where you grew up?" He looked around as if he could see her there as a child.

She nodded.

"You know you've never spoken about it."

She shrugged. "What is there to say?"

"You were rapidly aged and given a computer insert to cope with it all." He stopped her and turned her toward him. Her closed-off look bothered him. How did she come to mean so much to him that he would want to wipe away the sadness he could see? Skye Latimer, the man who never got close to anyone, allowed this woman inside his armor and he was happy he did. He touched her face. "You never got a chance to be a child, grow up, get into trouble the way everyone else did. You're younger than the twins yet are now old enough to have your own. How does it make you feel?"

"Have you become a psychiatrist now?" She stepped around him and started walking.

"No, but I know you better than you know yourself. You have never shown any emotion when anyone spoke about it. In fact, it's one of the times when you lock yourself away from everyone."

"I don't know how to talk about it. It was a year of my very short life. It seemed very normal when I was going through it. It's everyone else telling me it wasn't normal that bothers me."

"Sam." He caught up to her and wrapped his arms around her. "Look at me."

"Please don't patronize me." She kept her gaze down.

"Have I ever done that?" Skye hooked a finger under her chin and lifted it until she was looking at him. "In fact, have

I ever given you sad eyes when you talked about your rapid aging?"

"No, Mom is great at it though."

"Sam, your mom didn't have a normal childhood either." He shifted his hold and got them walking again. "She was a ward of the government and had the weird contraption in her back. People shunned her because they didn't know how to handle her. Then she met your father and learned she wasn't human but part of a race that had disappeared and had abilities she didn't want. Then she was kidnapped by Ialog twice and now has to battle Reasta. The one thing she wanted for all her children was to have what she didn't, a normal life."

"It still bothers me that she is upset over something that she couldn't control."

"And how would you feel if the roles were reversed?"

"When did you become such a fan of my family? I thought you didn't trust my parents."

Skye checked his handheld for directions then pointed. They made their way quickly through the wooded area near the ship. "I spent time with them when Heather changed the memories of everyone on Vespia. I got to see them in a way no one else did. Your mom also gave me her file when we first met so I had her history."

"They let you leave with it?"

"No, but you've learned how I can retain info. Between the two things I realized my mistrust was misplaced."

"Wow. I never thought I'd hear you say that." They found the road and headed to the closest platform for massive transit.

"I know, just like you never thought you'd hear me ask you to go through the mating ceremony. I never got an answer by the way."

"Skye, you don't have to do this." She looked at him as

they continued to walk. "I know you hated it when my dad sort of pushed you to do the bonding because I marked you. I don't want you to feel obligated to do what is expected."

"Sam, I want to do this. I admire what your parents have, the joy they share. We deserve the same."

"Are you sure?"

"Very much."

"Then I would be happy to mate with you." The smile she gave him made his heart skip a beat.

He drew her to him and captured her lips with his. His tongue begged for entrance then dived in when she gave it. Pulling her close, his hands roamed as he explored her body. Finally, he broke the kiss and rested his head against hers. "How adventurous are you?"

"Why?" She frowned as she pulled back to look at him.

"Because there is a clear-cut path right there and I'd love to find us a place to celebrate."

"Through there, really? You sure we'll find something suitable?"

"I do. I have the schematics of this place in here." He touched the side of his head. "There is a nice little cove just a few hundred feet ahead."

Sam smiled. "Then let's go."

They made their way to the small cove he saw on his screen. Trees blocked their view until they were almost upon it.

"It's beautiful." Sam found the small cove endearing. The grass was thick and soft, and the trees covered the area so they shouldn't be spotted easily. All of a sudden, she acted shy.

"Nervous?" She didn't have too many inhibitions because of her rapid aging. Why was she acting this way?

"A little." She looked at him and gave him a smile. "I guess this means more to me than I realize."

"But we've been bonded. It's like being engaged on Earth." He took her hand and pulled her close.

"I know." She rested her hand on his chest. "I do know I love you."

"And I love you. You're all I want, Sam. I might have told you when we first met that I could walk away at any time but that's not true anymore."

Sam laughed. "My father gave you plenty of reasons to leave. I might have worried about that in the beginning, but not now."

"Good, because you're going to have a hard time getting rid of me." He opened the seal of her blouse. They knew their Vespian uniforms would draw too much unwanted attention so they had replicated Earth clothing so they could blend in better.

Sam worked on his top as well. They helped each other undress, but before they could lie down Skye grabbed his handheld and scanned the area. "Are you looking for something?"

"Yeah, rocks, or manmade items to make us uncomfortable." He smiled as he ran his spare hand up and down her back. "I don't want you arching against me and later find out it was from pain instead of pleasure."

She laughed as she took his hand and went to the center of the small glade. "Of all the things we have tried we've never been intimate outside before."

"There was that one time when you worked for Mason. Out on the balcony." He knelt and urged her to join him.

"It was, but I meant like this." She knelt in front of him. "With nature surrounding us. I see why my father likes his grotto so much."

Skye wrapped his arms around her, cradling her close as he claimed her lips with his. He eased her to the ground, making sure she was comfortable on the grass. His hands glided over her skin, feeding her need. Sam wrapped her legs around his waist, silently signaling what she wanted.

Skye laughed as he entered her. "No foreplay?"

"Not this time." She sighed as she felt him fill her. "With everything that is going on I want this, now. You have always been there for me and this mission will test us. I want to show you how much this means to me. How much you mean to me." Tears filled her eyes as she looked up at him.

"Sam." Skye brushed the tears away. "We will be successful."

"Show me how much you love me, Skye. Right now, here."

Skye started to move inside her, long, deep strokes. The kind that she loved. Her mind relaxed enough so she could enjoy their intimacy. He pressed soft kisses to her eyes, her cheeks, her throat. The last set of kisses brought more tears to her eyes. It made her think of her parents.

"Sam."

"I'm fine, Skye." She touched his face as she gave him a smile. "Maybe we need to switch things up a little." She rolled them over so she was on top.

"You do like it on top."

She ignored him as she whipped her hair behind her and closed her eyes. She needed to block everything out. Time to only feel. Skye's hands glided over her thighs then her hips as she started to move up and down. Her muscles tightened around him, causing a wonderful friction. Each time she slid down his length she felt the delicious sensations that made her lose control. She started moving faster, racing toward the free-fall sensation she was working for.

It was close. Sam could feel it. Each movement brought her closer to the release she craved, making her get lost in the euphoria blossoming inside her. Her body wanted more.

Skye reached up and wrapped his arms around her as he flipped them over, allowing her to give up control and get lost in her orgasm.

Sam felt it unfurl in her stomach, leaving her with the blissful moment only Skye could give her. It flowed through her, filling her body with joy and allowing the world and her fears to fall away for a moment.

———

As they approached the main security building Skye wondered what they would encounter. Bert gave him the files on Heather and Storm from this timeline so he would have an idea of what to expect when he interacted with them. He wasn't really surprised to find out that Storm happened to be on Earth. In their timeline, he made frequent journeys there with his mate. It seems things hadn't changed with his marriage to Susan. According to the files, Skye was part of Heather's staff. It should prove interesting.

Skye had located his apartment and changed into his uniform. Sam still wore her civilian clothing, but he could see she wasn't quite as comfortable as she should be. Part of it was because they were going to meet her mother, but he wondered if part was because she was used to wearing uniforms as well and just felt a little out of sorts being the only one in casual clothes.

He took her hand, and they headed into the building. Skye wanted to pull her into his arms as they rode the elevator to the floor where Heather's office was but knew he needed to be the man of this timeline. The only support he could give was a gentle squeeze of his hand. The smile she gave him showed she understood and appreciated what he could do.

Heather was shocked to see him. "Latimer? I thought you were sent on a mission."

So Bert must have gotten him out of the way. "It was a quick one."

"And who do you have with you?" Heather looked at Sam, who stood behind him. "Was she cleared?"

"I wouldn't have brought her if she hadn't been cleared." Skye gestured for Sam to step up. "She's interested in security."

"When did you become a bleeding-heart helping strangers interested in joining security?" Heather went back to what she was working on when they first stepped into the office.

"I know her parents."

That seemed to mollify her. "You know we don't have time to babysit people."

"I won't get underfoot," Sam spoke quietly. He knew she did it because she sounded like her mother, but to Heather, she came across as shy.

Heather arched a brow at him. "Well, I'm glad you're back. The ambassador from Vespia has arrived and we are to attend the function this evening. The president will be there as well as Admiral Barrister."

Skye nodded. "Anything you need me to do?"

"No." She looked at Sam for a moment before looking back at him. "I was able to take care of everything this time."

"Who else is attending?" He watched as she picked up a tablet and handed it to him.

"The basics, dignitaries, those high on the social ladder. It's all in there." She sat back in her chair. "Since I thought you were going to be gone during this, I assigned someone else as my second, but I'll put you back on right now. I'm more comfortable with you at my side."

He nodded. "Can you make sure Sam is on the list? This will give her the perfect chance to see some of the boring things we get to do."

"Is that wise?"

"I'll take any reprimand if she does something wrong."

She hesitated like she wanted to argue with him, but then she shrugged. "Alright but know I'm against it."

"Yes ma'am." He wondered why she gave in. That wasn't like Heather. If she thought something was wrong, she showed her stubbornness when arguing against it. Of course, this Heather hadn't gone through the same things that made her the Heather he knew. This was going to be complicated.

———

Heather looked from Skye to Sam, who looked familiar. Did she know the girl's parents? If she did know her parents, it seemed that neither wanted to use it as leverage to allow her to join them. Skye must believe in her a lot. And Latimer. Since when did he start protecting young women? She noticed how he stepped toward Sam when she questioned him. The color of the young woman's eyes didn't go unnoticed either. Very few had her eye color. Probably color augmentation, but why did she have to pick violet? Skye would know how much that irritated her.

All she knew was the girl better not get underfoot this evening or there would be hell to pay.

———

Now in his dress uniform, Skye stood in line with Heather and Sam. Heather had fabricated Sam a cadet uniform to wear so people would know she was in training. They stood

17

close to the wall, at attention, as the president passed them with his personal bodyguards. Once he passed by, they fell into step with those guards.

Heather was now a captain in security and Bear's assistant. She was also in charge of assigning guards to the president, depending on the function. It looked like in this timeline she wasn't the woman to break the rules if she thought her way was better. She was the one to enforce them.

They slowly made their way through the line. Sam stayed at his side.

"This is very strange," she whispered.

He grabbed her hand and gave it a squeeze. She was used to being part of the party, not part of those who came to show their respect. Having her mother in the line instead of at her father's side was the most unnerving thing for her.

They worked their way through the Vespian council. Sam remained quiet, showing proper respect, but not saying much. Susan was standing next to Storm, enjoying all the attention, but when she spotted Heather, her whole demeanor changed. She stiffened and became standoffish. Her words became clipped. It was obvious she didn't like Heather.

Heather faced Susan. "So, how's married life?"

Heather didn't seem to care for her either. She was trying to antagonize her.

"Why are you here, Heather?"

"Doing my job." She looked at the president, making sure he was out of earshot before looking back at Susan. "How about you, got that treaty signed yet?"

"Captain, nice to see you again." Storm clasped her hand and gently urged her to stand in front of him. Skye was happy he was trying to defuse the tension.

Skye also noticed Storm lingered a little longer with

Heather than he should. Then Storm took his hand and smiled. "Lt. Latimer. Good to see you again. I had heard you wouldn't be attending."

"I was able to finish my mission early." How did Storm know he wasn't going to be there? As he thought about it, he realized it was probably on the list of attendees, which would have been altered to add him and Sam.

"Good to hear." He spotted Sam. "And who do we have here?" He turned his smile on Sam as he grasped her hand. If he wasn't her father Skye would be very angry at the smile he gave her.

Skye sure didn't want Sam to make a scene so he said the first thing that popped into his head. "She's my fiancé."

"Really?" Storm looked at him. Skye felt Sam turn to look at him too, but he had already said it. There was no way to take it back.

"Yes. Something our parents set up for us." Skye knew Heather had turned toward him as well. It wasn't something they discussed so he knew what he said caught her off guard. "My last mission was to bring her here."

"Interesting."

Toki was next. She was polite to the president, Bear and Heather, but honed in on them. "Mr. Latimer, right?"

"Yes, ma'am." He offered her his hand which she ignored.

"Sorry, I don't follow your earth custom." She then turned to Sam. Skye found it interesting that she took one of Sam's hands in hers. He knew she didn't touch people because of her visions. They could overpower her at any time. "You're new though. You don't quite belong here, do you? And you have Vespian blood."

Sam pulled her hand from Toki's before she could pick up anything else from her. She touched Skye's arm, not knowing how to answer.

"I wish to speak to you two later." She smiled at them then dismissed them.

Skye bowed his head before they moved on. Toki was the last person they had to pay respects to so when they finished with her, they headed to the bar. He wondered how much Heather heard. The comment about Vespian blood would raise questions.

"Fiancé? Really? You could have warned me," grumbled Heather. She signaled the bartender.

"Sorry. I was on the spot and that was the first thing that popped into my head." Skye fought the frown threatening to crease his brow. He knew he couldn't react, but what was she doing? She was on duty.

"Well, you two better sell it because I'm sure it will come back up." The bartender set a tray with three drinks on it. Heather pulled out a scanner, and ran them over the drinks, then slipped a small chip under one of them. "And don't ignore the Vespian religious leader. If she wants to talk to you, she will make it happen."

He nodded, happy Heather hadn't said anything about Sam's Vespian blood. Hopefully, she thought Toki was a little crazy and chose to ignore it. As far as their relationship, it was real so selling it wouldn't be hard, but talking to Toki might not be a smart idea. She knew things she shouldn't and that could get them in trouble.

Heather turned on her heel and headed back toward the president. She carried the tray above her head so she wouldn't spill anything as she weaved her way through the crowd. Once she was at the side of the president, she lowered the tray and held it out.

"Captain, you don't have to play waitress for me." He nodded at her as he picked up one of the drinks.

"Yes, sir. I know, sir, but I also know you feel more comfortable when I do this for you." She turned the tray to

Bear, who took the second drink then she offered the third one with the chip beneath it to Storm, who had been standing with the president talking.

Heather then stepped back to a guard position and watched the crowd.

As the three men moved so did they. Skye stayed behind Heather and did what was expected. Sam did the same thing. No one could approach the three men without one of them blocking their way and making sure they were cleared.

"Admiral, every time we're together at a function like this I always ask for Heather to be part of my security, yet you always say no."

"I'm sorry, Mr. President, but she worked hard to become my second. I don't think I can find a better person for that position." Bear smiled. "If she were to want to leave, I'd have to fight you for her."

The president turned to Heather. "Remember, Captain, my door is always open."

"Thank you, Mr. President."

Skye watched the interplay and wondered why Heather had taken the position of Bear's second. It was a lot of administration work, and he knew she hated that. It didn't quite make sense to him.

Storm had been quiet and sipped at the drink he held. While the president and Bear were verbally fighting over Heather, he discreetly pulled the chip from under the glass and slipped it inside his outfit.

The lighting changed, alerting them it was time for the meal. Storm went to the dais where Susan and his family waited.

They took their places against the wall while the rest of the dignitaries took their seats.

———

There was something wrong with Skye. Heather was sure of it. He had always had her back, but since he showed up with that young woman, he wasn't acting like himself. Could she still trust him?

Everything could be jeopardized if she couldn't.

She tried to maintain her training as she kept an eye on the guests and waited for time to go by.

He was here. So close yet untouchable. Her heart pounded in her chest at the thought of being with him again.

She wasn't one to get involved with married men. It just sort of happened because of her favorite comb. One night at one of these functions she lost it. Storm had found it and brought it to her apartment. One thing led to another, and she found herself in bed with the man having the best orgasm of her life. Heather hadn't planned on being with him again, but when he came back to Earth, he sought her out. She was all he could think about, and he wanted more.

Heather sighed. She wanted the night to end so they could be together. He was a wonderful lover, always making sure she was satisfied. Something she hadn't experienced with other men. She couldn't give him up now even if she wanted to. Her need was like an addiction.

Storm looked up at her and gave her a bone-melting smile and she felt it to her toes. It didn't matter who he was married to, she wanted to be with him. She did pause. As much as she hated Susan, was she with Storm to get back at her? She rubbed her hands on her uniform. Heather knew better.

She was pretty sure she wouldn't have gotten involved with the ambassador if he had married any other woman, but there was so much animosity there and all from Susan she wasn't worried about hurting the woman's feelings. It wasn't a real wedding anyway. Susan was only married to Storm to get a treaty signed. The moment she completed her task she would be sent back to Earth.

Storm didn't even really know the woman. She lived in a small apartment the Vespian Council had given her, while Storm lived in his own place when he was on Vespia. Even here at the embassy, he had his own room. They never used it but being in security gave her access to the floor plans.

The meal ended and the guests started moving around. Heather followed the president and Bear. Skye fell into step with her. Very soon she'd know if Skye was still going to help out.

———

Skye wanted to get his hands on the chip Heather gave Storm. If would give him more information to work with. He noticed the smoldering looks Storm gave her while they were guarding the dining area. He also saw the hateful looks Susan kept shooting her.

In their timeline, Susan had been up for the position to be with Storm, but Heather won out because she fit all the criteria. So how did this happen? Did Ialog have a hand in putting Susan with Storm? If so, why didn't he take Heather the way he wanted? Or did he already have what he needed from her? Then again was all this Susan's doing?

He needed to see *this* Heather's file too.

Skye focused on their job when he realized the president was leaving. As Storm said his goodbyes, he handed Skye the glass he held in his hand. The chip was on the bottom once again. He discretely pulled it off the bottom and palmed it. Now he needed to know if he was supposed to give this back to Heather or just destroy it.

Not knowing what his other self did had him second-guessing.

Once the president left, most of the guards were relieved, but as long as Bear stayed so did Heather and Skye. When he got a moment, he slipped the chip into his handheld and viewed the data. It was directions to an apartment. An apartment? Then it dawned on him.

Bert said the timeline would try to repair itself.

Sam gave him a questioning look when he smiled.

"It looks like your parents are lovers," he whispered next to her ear.

Sam smiled at that one. She noticed Toki coming at them. "Looks like it's time to have that talk with my aunt."

He looked up and saw her walking towards them. How bad could it be? "I'm ready."

"You've never dealt with my aunt on a one-on-one have you?"

"No."

"Be prepared. You'll find she has insights most don't." Sam gave her the proper bow.

"You know our ways." She gestured for them to follow her.

Skye looked at Heather, who gave him a slight nod, giving her permission to speak to Toki. He pressed his hand against the small of Sam's back, urging her to move.

"Yes."

"We don't teach our ways to outsiders." She looked at Sam.

"I know." Sam smiled.

"Then you are saying you are Vespian." They had made their way outside to the gardens where they could have a little more privacy.

"As are my parents."

"Yet as the religious leader, I know the families, but I don't know you."

"But you do." Sam laid a hand on her arm. "Don't you."

She looked at Sam and nodded. "Let me have your hand, child."

"Let's sit." Sam gestured for them to sit on a bench surrounded by bushes. It would keep them away from prying eyes. She turned to her aunt and offered her hand.

Taking her hand, Toki's eyes rolled into the back of her head.

"Skye?"

"On it." He grabbed Toki before she could slump to the ground. "Does everyone in this family have visions?"

"The visions are part of the job for her. Mom has them naturally." She smiled at her aunt as she came back around.

"You don't belong here."

"That's not quite true, Toki. This," and she gestured to their surroundings. "Is all wrong, but you know that."

"I saw my brother when I touched you."

Sam nodded.

"And the captain is in there as well." She looked at Sam. "In fact, you have her eyes with the Vespian ring."

Sam just brightened her smile.

"And you are here to fix what went wrong?"

"That is our goal, Aunt Toki."

"Come, let us walk some more." She headed deeper into the garden. "I am fortunate that the guards cannot record me. My visions and conversations fall under the protection of my position. Since we came to Earth I have had visions. Ones that show a different life for so many of us. I see a man with brown hair and gold eyes with a violet ring."

"That would be Kuarto." Sam hesitated.

"He means something to me, doesn't he?"

"He is your mate."

"My mate? But I am not allowed to mate."

"Where we're from you met your mate just before you became the religious leader and changed the laws so some of the more archaic rules could be abolished."

"Sam."

She knew he felt she shouldn't be giving her this information. "We need the help, Skye. I want my parents back."

"I know, but I don't want to make whoever did this aware we know what has happened and are trying to fix it," Skye said under his breath.

"You think someone that close to us did this?"

"I think it was done by the woman who is in the wrong place right now, but she couldn't have done it by herself and that is what is causing me to be cautious," said Skye. He looked at Toki. "You might not remember our enemies, but they are dangerous."

"We also know who we can trust. If we have their help our chances of being successful go up." She touched Toki's arm again. "What have you seen?"

"Shadows of things that do not always make sense. My brother carrying a small boy. He and the captain dancing. A wedding portrait of her that is beautiful, and erotic. A man with blonde hair and a woman with snake eyes." She paused for a moment. "And my father."

"Toki, we need help. We need to know what has happened since the council decided to sign the treaty. How Susan ended up being the one making sure the treaty goes through."

"I also need to see your brother's files as well as the captains," added Skye.

Toki smiled. "Let me see what I can do."

———

Heather wondered why Vespia's religious leader had singled out Skye and Sam. Sam was new, but Toki knew Skye. The woman had spoken to him on numerous occasions. Did the woman really believe this Sam was Vespian?

"You seem deep in thought."

The deep timbre of his voice filled her, making her wish they were alone instead of standing in the middle of the ballroom as the admiral said his goodbyes to the Vespian council and the remaining dignitaries.

"Curious as to why your religious leader is interested in two of my people." She looked up into his golden eyes and felt her heart start to flutter.

"We have learned not to question our religious leader." He glanced outside where his sister had taken off with Skye and Sam. "There is always a purpose, and it is always for the good of Vespia."

She wished she could have such faith. "Did the president push about the treaty?"

"Of course, and his anger was directed at Susan as usual. He spoke to Anseri at length about it and tracked Susan down after that."

"I'm surprised she isn't clinging to your side. She doesn't like me talking to you."

"Anseri insisted that she retire." He became quiet when the admiral stepped up to talk to Heather.

"Captain, you are to stay and make sure our remaining guests behave themselves."

Heather nodded. She expected that. Vespian's exuded a pheromone that affected humans. Most wore a chip to keep them calm, the rest had shots to allow them to enjoy the evening. It either stopped the people from throwing themselves at one of the Vespians, or starting a fight, but the meds and devices were known to wear off or break down as the evening went on. That was when security worked the hardest.

She was the only one immune, although she wasn't sure about that. All she wanted to do was find a quiet corner and throw herself at Storm. Instead, she had to play baby-sitter to a bunch of dignitaries.

"So you will be staying?" asked Storm.

"Yes. Admiral's orders."

Storm gave her that smile that turned her insides to jelly.

———

Skye was grateful for Toki's help. She was able to get him the files he needed within minutes, which gave him the chance to compare Heather and Storm's files to the ones he had in his mind. He found where the change happened. He didn't know why yet, but at least he had something to start with. The next thing he needed to do was confront Heather and he really wasn't looking forward to that. How was he going to convince her of what had happened when she had no memory of the change?

A lot of the guests had left, including the admiral. Thank goodness for Toki's position or they'd be in the brig about now for abandoning their posts. Heather was watching, but this time Storm stood beside her. They spoke quietly as she kept an eye on the crowd. If someone stepped out of line, she signaled one of the guards still on duty that was closest to take care of the problem.

She kept looking at him but remained quiet. What was she expecting? Did she want him to go out amongst the crowd like the rest? It would give her time alone with Storm, which was something he was pretty sure she wanted because their need practically rolled off them in waves.

But it wouldn't give them the privacy. Oh. How dumb could he be? His name was on that chip that Storm gave him. He helped secure the room they hoped to get to. Skye bet his counterpart helped them keep their relationship private. Time to find out. "Captain, you haven't had a break yet. I can cover for you."

A flash of shock filled her face before she schooled her features and smiled. Was that out of character for him, or had she started to suspect that he wasn't acting like his old self?

A memory from this timeline popped into his head, showing Heather responding to this scenario the same way time after time. It shocked the hell out of him. Having a memory that wasn't his own was a little disconcerting, but now he had what he needed so he wasn't going to complain.

"I'm fine."

"You say that every time. The admiral has a standing order to make sure you take a break. You haven't had anything to eat since we left the office earlier." He repeated the same words he had in the past.

Heather played along a little longer before she gave in. She headed toward the gardens. Storm stood beside Skye for a few minutes longer then mumbled something about checking on security and took off. Sam slipped her hand in his.

"What have you figured out so far?"

"The timeline changed back when Heather first arrived. Dian was there to claim her. She raised Heather, sent her to the academy. That change might be what caused all of this."

———

They had used the alcove before. Fear and excitement filled Heather as they came up on it. The chance of getting caught was high. This was a busy corridor and Susan suspected something was going on, so they needed to be careful.

Storm opened the door, checked their surroundings once more before pulling her in behind him. He sealed the door and wrapped his arms around her. His lips claimed hers, his tongue brushing against the seam of her lips, begging for entrance. The moment she gave it, he deepened the kiss, his tongue searched for hers, drawing it into the dance that took their breath away. They worked on the seals of each other's clothes, exposing the skin they needed to touch.

Once the barriers were removed Storm lifted her, pressed her against a wall, centered himself, and drove into her. He broke the kiss and watched as she reacted to him filling her. She cried out at the exquisite invasion. There was something about him that made her throw caution out the window. She was on duty for God's sake. Then he started to move inside her and her thoughts shattered. It didn't matter. All that mattered was the way he made her feel. Each stroke brought her closer and closer to her release.

Heather clung to Storm as they raced toward their climaxes. Her muscles clamped down on him, meeting him thrust for thrust, causing him to groan in pleasure. He shifted his pace and drew a moan from her.

"So close," she whispered. Then it happened. Her climax filled her, starting at her core and racing through her blood, sending her to a place where her euphoria controlled her.

"So beautiful." Storm brushed his fingers along her jaw. "I wish we had more time."

"We have the apartment."

"And I can't wait to take my time with you," he gave her that wonderful bone-melting smile.

"You keep smiling like that and we'll never get out of here."

"Is that a bad thing?" He started to nibble on her throat.

"I have to get back to work. You know that." She practically sighed her words. Heather didn't want to leave any more than he did, but they had to.

Storm helped her get dressed. "Once I make sure the corridor is clear I'll let you out. I'll follow as soon as I'm sure it is safe."

———

Skye saw an angry-looking Susan as she searched the room. This would be a good chance to see if she was the one who changed the timeline. She did gain the most and her anger might make her say something she shouldn't.

"Looking for something, Susan?"

"My husband." She jammed her hands on her hips. "He's with that woman, isn't he?"

"He said something about checking in with security." Skye wasn't about to have that anger directed at him.

"And your captain?"

"I sent her on a break. She headed out into the garden."

"Right. She's with my husband. I know it."

"Susan, Heather would never jeopardize her position by doing what you're insinuating. What do you have against her?"

"You wouldn't understand." She hesitated. "I can't seem to keep them apart."

"Why does it bother you anyway? You are only married to the ambassador because of the treaty. Once you have that completed you will come back to Earth."

"She didn't."

"Who?" So Susan was aware of the original timeline. The

only way she could possibly know that would be if she was the one who caused it. The question was how?

"Never mind."

"You're not making any sense, Susan. Who didn't have to come back? You think the Vespians will want to keep you? They aren't known for accepting strangers into their ranks. What have you done to make them want to allow you to stay after the treaty is done?"

She glared at him.

Storm came back into the ballroom and spotted Susan talking to him. He stepped up to her side and grabbed her arm. "I thought the council told you to retire."

"Well, I couldn't sleep." She glared up at him.

"You know Anseri doesn't like it when you go against her requests. Hasn't she already threatened to replace you?"

Susan's color faded. Skye could tell she didn't like the threat. Heather came in from the garden. The moment Susan saw her she started all over again. "You need to stay away from him."

Heather sighed. "Susan, I'm just doing my job and right now that is make sure all of your guests leave the embassy. How about you? You got that treaty signed yet?"

"I hate you!" She stomped away from them and toward her room.

"Well, that was fun," Sam commented.

"She's always that way." Heather brushed a hand down her uniform. "I still don't understand why she hasn't gotten that treaty signed yet. It's been four years."

Skye looked at Sam. Heather had the treaty signed in less than a year.

The rest of the evening went relatively smoothly. There were a few people they had to escort out because their chip or shot wore out, but overall, it was a quiet night. Heather released the last of the guards when the last guest left.

"You're relieved as well, Latimer."

He nodded. "You coming?"

"Yes." Heather looked at Storm. "Thank you, Ambassador."

"Thank you, Captain."

She headed out with Skye and Sam. Heather cast one last look over her shoulder before they stepped out into the warm night. "Good night, Latimer. We'll go over the data from the function tomorrow instead of tonight."

"See you tomorrow then." Skye watched her head off. She was probably on her way to the apartment. He wondered how she would feel when they showed up later.

————

Heather opened the door to the apartment then leaned back against the door once it closed. Excitement filled her at the thought of what would happen here when Storm arrived. Yet she hated it. How did she get into this situation? He was from Vespia, and that race was known for having lots of sex partners. She was nothing more than a dalliance to him.

She pushed herself away from the door. When did she fall in love with him? That wasn't supposed to happen. It was supposed to be fun. A night of hot sex when he came into town. A way to get back at Susan for all her rude comments throughout the years.

Susan wanted Storm to be her bed partner, but from what Storm told Heather he had no interest in Susan. Humans were too weak and couldn't put up with his libido.

But Heather could, and it was the best sex she ever had. In fact, after being with Storm, other men paled in comparison. She didn't even look for another partner anymore. She just waited for Storm.

She understood it could be hours before he showed up

so knew better than to wait up for him. She took a quick shower then climbed into bed. Besides, she loved the way he always woke her up.

————

Storm pressed his hand against the panel of the apartment Heather had rented. He had wanted to get here earlier but his mother had other plans. She wanted Susan gone. The woman wasn't doing the job and the people of Vespia didn't understand why she was still on the planet.

He agreed with his mother. Susan was a bane in his side, and he didn't want her around either. Storm wanted Heather. So much so that he told his mother he wanted to mate with her and if the council went against it, he would leave Vespia and live with her on Earth. That silenced his mother which surprised him.

Now he had to wait to hear what the council had to say. He wasn't sure what made him reveal his heart's desire, but he knew he wouldn't be happy with any other woman. He just wasn't sure how Heather would feel.

The door opened for him, and he stepped inside. The lights were low, but he didn't expect to find Heather awake at this hour. The door closed behind him, sealing them away from the rest of the galaxy for as long as they wanted. She always requested time off after big functions like theirs so they would have several days before they would have to surface.

He walked into the bedroom and found her curled up on her side, sleeping. The soft cover hid her from his view. She was so beautiful. There was something about her that had him wanting more. Had him wanting her at his side all the time. Storm wasn't sure why, but he knew this woman was more to him than just a sex partner.

Quietly he peeled off his clothes and climbed in beside her. Using gentle fingers, he slipped them inside the cover then brushed them along her side. Storm continued down over her hip before brushing against the outside of her thigh.

Her lashes fluttered before those beautiful violet eyes opened and looked up at him. The sexy smile she gave him stopped his heart for a moment.

"What time is it?"

"Late, but I have cleared my schedule to be with you."

"Me too." Her smile softened.

He wanted to talk to her but the cover she had draped over her body had slipped, revealing the soft flesh he ached to touch. His fingers had a mind of their own as he brushed them against her throat then slid them down to one pert nipple. He forgot all about explaining anything at that point.

Heather shifted so he could touch her wherever he wanted.

Storm laid beside her as his hands continued to travel her body, dipping into her belly button, brushing across a thigh. "You are so beautiful."

She blushed. Heather never knew how to take such compliments. She never saw herself like that.

He knew he had to get her past this moment, so he leaned forward and captured her lips with his. Storm pulled her into his embrace as he deepened the kiss, drawing her tongue to dance with his. When he broke the kiss he worked his way down to her throat, pulling the gentle tissue into his mouth. His hands weren't idle, working their way down to her core, stroking her and drawing sighs out of her as she opened her legs to give him better access.

The desire to taste her drove him to move down her body until he was at her core and lathing her. The moan she emitted was music to his ears. He couldn't wait any longer and climbed back up her body. He drove in deep, emitting his own moan when her muscles clamped down on him.

He set a nice slow pace, enjoying the way her sheath tightened against him. It made him shake. Storm picked up the pace, pulling them into a wonderful cocoon of desire and need. Heather met him thrust for thrust. They raced each other toward their release. One particular stroke drew another moan from Heather. He kept trying to hit that one spot, being successful most of the time. She shook in his arms.

Her breath came out in short pants as she tried to take control, but he wouldn't let her. He changed their pace once again, denying either of them their release.

"Storm." Her voice soft.

"We have all night." He continued to drive in and out of her.

"Please."

How could he deny her? He changed the pace again, giving her just what she wanted. Each stroke was deep, quick, and took their breath away. He pumped into her, reveling in the way her muscles caressed him as he moved in and out of her. Storm wanted it to go on forever.

Heather's breath hitched as she clamped down on him. She started to vibrate in his arms as her orgasm crashed through her. The sound he hoped for started deep inside her before the scream he loved to hear broke through and filled the room.

He felt his orgasm start to wash over him just as she turned boneless in his arms. He pressed a kiss against her forehead. "You are phenomenal."

"Each time we're together is phenomenal," she breathed. Her words were barely a whisper.

———

"You sure this is wise?" asked Sam.

"No, but we have to talk to them." Skye checked his handheld to make sure they weren't engaged. "No one else can be around. Trying to convince them what happened will be hard enough without an audience."

"I don't feel good about this."

"I just hope your father doesn't walk around naked as we try to explain everything." He touched her face. "You ready?"

Sam nodded.

Skye hit the sensor to alert Heather and Storm they had company.

"Latimer? Go away," Heather said through the apartment com.

"We need to talk, now."

"I'm not opening the door for you."

"Then I'll override the lock you have on this door and come in anyway."

"I am ordering you to go away, Latimer."

"We're not on duty right now, Drexel. Open the door before I make a scene."

She swore. "Fine. You get five minutes."

The door opened for them as Heather and Storm came out of the room. Heather had a wrap around her that didn't hide much. Storm had a pair of soft pants on.

"What do you want?" Heather's voice held her anger at being interrupted.

Sam was the one who spoke first. "Do I look familiar to the two of you?"

"A little." Heather sighed. "Look, what is this all about?"

"There has been a shift in the timeline."

"What are you talking about?" asked Storm.

"This, you two, Susan being the one in charge of doing the treaty is all wrong." Sam gestured for them to sit.

"Something happened in your past to change the timeline I'm from. If we hadn't been inside a temporal ship I wouldn't exist right now."

"Why not?"

"Because I'm your daughter."

TWO

Heather stared at her in disbelief. "I'm sterile."

"I know and so is Da—Storm, yet you had three children before someone messed with the timeline. That device in your back hides the fact that you are fertile."

"You're crazy."

"Check my DNA."

Heather stared at her. "Okay." She got up and got her handheld. "Hair fiber?"

Sam ran her fingers through her hair, found several loose ones, and handed them to her. Heather looked at the hairs in her hand for a second before she reached out and pulled one from Sam's head. She set it on her screen. "Computer, analyze the DNA here and compare it to Heather Drexel."

It took only seconds. "DNA is a match."

Storm pulled a hair and handed it to Heather.

A few seconds later they heard the same four words.

"How is this possible?"

"In my timeline, you were ordered to guard Storm. During that mission, you were assigned to get the treaty with Vespia signed and there is only one way you can step foot on Vespian soil."

"Of course. I'd have to marry a Vespian. That's what Susan had to do." Heather didn't sound convinced.

"Yes, but you two did more than marry by Earth laws, you mated the way Vespians do. Toki was mad as hell. But uncle presided over the ceremony and Toki witnessed it."

"You know about uncle?" Storm asked.

"Yes, he retired when Toki turned fifty and she became religious leader."

"You seem to know a lot about us. How does the mating ceremony go?"

"It is a very intimate affair. The couple being mated wear nothing but a ceremonial robe. The religious leader presides as the couple are intimate, with close friends and family members witnessing their union." Sam smiled. As she sat there a strange bruise filled Heather's neck. "Once the ceremony has been blessed the partners end up with a mark. They are identical. Sometimes though, one marks the other before the mating ceremony."

"That is very rare."

"Yet that is what you have done." She pointed to Heather's throat. It was faint, but it was there.

Storm brushed his fingers along it. "I did that? How? Only a Vespian would bear the mark of her or his mate."

"Heather is Vespian." Sam touched her chest. "So am I."

"I was born here."

"You were found in a field of heather. That is how you got your name. In my timeline, you had no family and were raised by the planet. A ward trained to work in security."

"My aunt raised me."

"That is the first change in the timeline," Skye said. "You didn't meet Dian until after the birth of Sam and the twins. She warned us of what was to come."

40

"You want to explain that?"

"We don't have the time. Our main goal is to fix this timeline. If we can do that explaining how Dian came into your life won't matter."

"Is this why my sister wanted to talk to the two of you?" asked Storm. "She has this uncanny way of knowing the truth."

"Yes. So much has changed, yet the timeline is trying to fix itself." Skye took Sam's hand. "You and Heather are a perfect example."

"We know you have questions, and as we talk, we're going to raise more, but we don't have the time to explain everything." Sam leaned forward, cutting off Skye. "We need to get the timeline back. Too much is at stake."

"We'll give you two a little time to think about this." Skye stood. "We'll be back in a few hours."

———

Heather didn't know what to think. She got up and looked at the mark now prominent on her neck in the mirror. Storm came up behind her. She touched it as she looked at his reflection. "You marked me?"

"I spoke to my mother tonight." He wrapped his arms around her, not answering her question. "I told her I wanted to mate with you. That if the council said no, I would stay here to be with you."

"But you're the future leader of the planet." She turned in his arms. He was willing to give it all up because of her? Why? "I won't be the reason you step away from that."

She tried to move around him, but he moved quickly and pinned her to the wall.

"And what type of leader would I be if I didn't have the one thing I want the most at my side? Latimer told us we belong together. That Susan is the reason we're not." He brushed his fingers along the mark he gave her. "When I'm away from you, you are all I think about."

"What about your other partners? I don't think they'll be very happy if you bring an off-worlder to your planet."

"Once we became intimate, I found other partners didn't excite me the way you do. I haven't been with anyone else in months." He brushed his fingers along her jaw.

"Me either." He hadn't been with anyone? A thrill raced through her at the thought.

"And I don't care about anything but being with you. Do you know how hard it was for me not to drag you into my arms and kiss you until you were senseless at the function tonight?"

"Storm."

"Heather, I care for you so much. I'll do anything to be with you, including offering my services to your government."

She didn't know what to think. The thought of him giving up everything for her humbled her. How could he do this?

"If you don't care for me the way I care for you say so and I'll walk out the door."

She looked up into those golden eyes that held her spellbound. "I don't want to start a war between our planets."

"Let me worry about that."

"I have to worry about that. I'm in Earth's security. I'd be slapped in a brig, court-martialed, and possibly shot if they believed I caused this." She touched his face. "I can't let you do this."

He stepped back from her. "And what if Latimer is telling the truth? That we're mates? With children?"

"Okay. If Latimer is right, then we need to work with him to fix everything." She stepped up to him. "I love you,

Storm, and I want a life with you, but not at the price we have to pay right now."

"And if I wasn't the next leader of Vespia?"

"I'd quit and we'd find a nice quiet little planet to spend the rest of our lives together on."

The smile he gave her filled her with joy. "Then I want to start the rest of our lives right now." He wrapped his arms around her and captured her lips with his. Keeping one arm around her, he slid the other under her knees and lifted her feet off the floor. He carried her into the bedroom and placed her gently on the bed before joining her.

"I have a question."

"What?" she looked up at his face only inches from hers.

"The word love doesn't translate into Vespian. We understand affection, but not the real meaning of love."

"Love is that wonderful feeling when the person you care for walks into a room. The way your heart starts to beat faster when you see them."

"That I understand." He pressed an ear between her breasts. "Like your heart is doing right now."

"Yes." She felt the heat of his breath brush against one nipple and felt it pucker.

"What else?" He rubbed the pad of a finger across the pert tip.

"Um, the way you worry about him or her when they are away." She was having trouble focusing. "Especially if you know they could be in harm's way."

"Like the way I feel when I'm away from you. What could happen if you were sent on a mission." He propped his head up to look at her.

Heather nodded.

Storm moved his head and closed his mouth over the nipple he had been playing with. He sucked on it for a few moments before he realized she had stopped talking. "Did I interrupt you?"

"I can't think when you do that."

"Really?" He gave her the smile that melted her bones. "What about when I do this?"

He slipped two fingers inside her as he went back to her breast. Her answer was a moan.

Her head dropped back on the bed. "I can only think of how badly I want you inside me right now."

"That I can do." He climbed back up her body. "But you still haven't explained love to me. Why do you use it for so many things?"

"Love is a hard word to describe." Her voice came out soft.

"I know one thing that is hard right now." He centered himself and slid in deep.

Heather's muscles settled around his erection as her body accepted him in. The idea of thought didn't register.

"So why do you use it as a noun?" He set a nice slow pace.

"What?" She had forgotten what they were talking about. All she wanted to do was enjoy the intimacy of the moment.

"The word love?"

She just looked at him.

He chuckled. "You're always so quiet when we're intimate."

"I can't help it. All I can focus on is what my body feels when we're together like this." She arched up against him when he hit a sensitive spot.

"Then I won't tax you right now." He dipped his head to nibble on her neck.

"Storm, you're not..." Her words trailed off as he hit the

spot again and drew a moan out of her. Her muscles tightened around him.

Storm picked up the pace, driving into her faster and she met him thrust for thrust. They raced for the same goal which was just out of their reach. Each time he filled her Heather's breath hitched. Her hands clutched at him, wanting the thing that still eluded her. She felt it slowly build inside her, filling her with a warmth that relaxed her. As the wave of her orgasm overtook her, she felt the warmth become a heat that sparked an out-of-body experience.

She never found this with another man. Storm had a way with her body that she had never experienced before. She was addicted.

"And think we can do that for the rest of our lives."

———

Skye sat on the couch of the room his other self had been assigned to and went through the data on his handheld. He and Sam had changed into civilian clothing and were waiting for the right time to head back to the apartment Heather and Storm were now occupying.

"You've been staring at that screen for hours." Sam stood in front of him.

"I know. I just want to be sure if we go back and stop Dian from raising Heather that the timeline will repair itself."

She cleared her throat, which made him look up. She stood there in a wispy short gown that shimmered as she shifted on her feet.

He sat his device on the table and stood. "Decided I needed a break?"

"Yes." She gave him a sultry smile. "You are a little

hyper-focused right now and I thought I'd try to take your mind off of things."

He stepped up to her and ran his hands over her shoulders before dipping them down to her waist. "You just want that hyper-focus on you."

"I love it when I'm the center of your attention." She released the seal on his shirt so she could run her fingers over his chest.

"I feel the same way." He eased the gown off her shoulders, allowing it to whisper its way down her body to the floor.

She opened the seal on his pants and helped them to the floor as well. "So you see the logic of taking a break?"

"Yes, I do." He wrapped his arms around her and pulled her close. "Have you been planning this for a while?"

"You know how my mind works when I have nothing to do." She urged him back toward the couch. "Are you asking that because you want to know if you can be in control?"

"I have learned the longer you have time to think about something like this the more you want to dominate the situation." He sat and waited for her to climb on his lap. Sam straddled him then flicked her hair back off her face. Skye grabbed several pillows and stuffed them behind his back so he could be closer to the edge of the couch for Sam. That way her legs wouldn't be spread so wide. He helped her center herself so she could slide down his shaft.

"You make me sound like my father." She touched his face with soft fingers. "Right now, I'll take that as a compliment."

Sam set a strong pace for them, taking him as deep as she could each time. Her muscles tightened against him, creating an exquisite sensation he didn't want to end.

He wanted to take control but knew she needed to have

this one. With everything spinning out of control he would give her whatever she needed to feel a little more secure. Skye ran his hands up her back then moved them around to cup her breasts. Using the pad of his thumbs he brushed them against her nipples as she rode him. Each caress had her tightening her muscles against him. She started to lose control.

Sam braced her hands on his chest, helping her keep control until she hit her climax. All he needed to hear was the two little words. She said it almost every time.

"Oh, God."

There they were. Sam dropped her head back as her orgasm took her over. He could tell by her breathing, the way her body swayed above him, and the exquisite tightening of her muscles surrounding him.

He moved his hands to her hips to help her keep up the pace she was desperately trying to maintain. Her body clenched around him, sending her through an orgasm that took his breath away.

She collapsed on top of him once her release was finished. "I'm sorry. Skye."

"Sorry?" He brushed a few wet tendrils out of her eyes.

"You didn't climax."

"Sam." He shifted them so she was lying on the couch beneath him. "Since when has that been a problem? All it means is you get to have another orgasm."

She gave him a brilliant smile. "It does, doesn't it?"

———

True to their word, Skye and Sam had given Heather and Storm a few hours and now sat with them in their room.

Sam was happy to see her parents curled up around each other like they had in her past.

"So how do you plan on fixing this timeline?" asked Storm.

"First, we need to look at your past. I need to know all the little changes that have happened. One big one I know is that Heather had a guardian growing up."

"I didn't have one in your timeline? What did I do for a living?"

"You worked in security, like you do now, but you were a ward of the planet as a child. You never had family to worry about, so you always volunteered for all the worst missions. You've been demoted a few times during those missions as well because you went against protocol from time to time to make those missions successful."

"And when I met Storm?"

"You were a lieutenant."

Her eyes widened. "How many times was I demoted?"

"Your records show three times."

"Sounds like you were a bit of a hellion." Storm pressed a kiss against her forehead.

"I've compared your two lives and have found a lot of similarities. There were several key things missing that shouldn't be." He rested his elbows on his knees and leaned toward them. "Have you ever heard of a man named Ialog?"

Heather stiffened. "How do you know that name?"

"Because in my timeline he has been after you since you met Storm. He's the reason Sam is an adult instead of a child."

What?" Storm's brow crinkled.

"It's a long story." Skye sat back. "Your records show you were in a coma for almost a year and a specialist worked on you. His name was stricken from the records, and no details were given about what happened during that time so I'm going to make a guess."

Heather sat up and crossed her arms over her chest.

"You lived during that coma. Met a man and fell in love, became pregnant but lost the baby just before you woke up. Knowing you were sterile, you pretended nothing happened and you didn't tell anyone what you dreamed because you knew you'd be in for months, if not years, of psych evaluations. Something you didn't want to face."

"How the hell did you know that?" Heather stood. "I told no one, no one!"

"I know that because that was what Ialog tried to do in our timeline. He had you drugged and tried to keep you in a world he created in your mind."

"But Dad rescued you," Sam interjected. "He saved you and my twin siblings. Because you met him before Ialog could get his hands on you, you were already pregnant with the twins. Ialog was desperate for a child from you so found a way to force you to fertilize an egg and I'm the result."

"You see why this is so complicated?" Skye looked over at Sam for a moment before focusing on Heather and Storm once again. "Our past isn't yours right now and we need to work together to bring back the timeline intact."

"We will help you."

Skye smiled.

———

Skye's first goal was to find the machine Susan had to be using. What caused Dian to raise Heather was a mystery, but that wouldn't have altered the timeline this much. Dian knew who she was supposed to end up with and would have done what was needed to make it happen. Heather's background might be different, but she still would have ended up with Storm.

Everything still pointed to Susan as the one who altered

the timeline, but where did she get the machine and learn how to use it? She must have gotten it from someone because she didn't have the training to make one, but who? It didn't make sense that Ialog would have given it to her. He didn't need her to achieve his goal. Reasta had no idea who Susan was and probably would have kept it for herself. He needed to figure this out and fast.

He and Sam were on their way back to the embassy to see if they could find the machine. Skye assumed it had to be somewhere handy so Susan could make the changes as she needed. The embassy was where he assumed it was at.

"So do you think there is another me out there?" asked Sam.

"I'm sure there is," replied Skye. "Ialog wanted a child from Heather. He told her what he had wanted to do when he kidnapped her the first time. This time it is possible he was able to make it happen. She really could have had the child he was after."

"I wonder if she is like me."

"That I can't answer. I love the woman you are." Skye wanted to put his arm around her shoulder and bring her to his side, but they had just gotten clearance to land at the embassy and he had to do that manually. "But I'm sure it's something we won't have to worry about. We're going to fix this."

"I'm not worried, just curious."

But he knew better. This whole time change really bothered her.

They landed at the embassy and requested a meeting with Toki. She would be the one who would help them the most. She met them at the main entrance.

"I've been expecting you." She gestured for them to follow her. "You have spoken to my brother."

"Yes." Skye took Sam's hand in his.

"Thought so. He has told the council he wants to make Captain Drexel his mate and if they refused his request, he was going to give up his right to secession to be with her."

"What?" Sam touched Skye's arm. "When did he have time to do that?"

"He did it last night after the last of our guests left." Toki looked at them. "When did you speak to him?"

"This morning."

"Then he made this decision on his own." She led them into a candle-lit room. "Here we may speak freely."

"What exactly did Storm say?" asked Skye.

"I wasn't privy to the conversation." She looked at him from under her lashes. "And as a Vespian you would know this. You look Vespian but haven't been raised on our planet, have you?"

The comment shocked Skye. Very few people knew he was Vespian. The Toki from their original timeline knew it, but there was no way anyone knew it in this one. How did she figure it out? "How the hell do you know that?"

"You forget that I have my ways?" She shook her head. "You are knowledgeable of our ways. I have seen you show respect the way it's supposed to be done."

"And I apologize for my rash question, but I do have one I must ask."

She nodded.

"Does Susan know about this request?"

"No. The council is still discussing it. She does know they are in session, but not the subject."

"Do they know why you're talking to us?" He wanted to know how much they knew about him and Sam.

"No. I only tell them what I feel they need to know." She looked at him. "You are an enigma to me so have kept this information to myself."

"Let's sit." Sam gestured to the soft pillows placed

around the room. This was Toki's meditation room. It resembled the one on their home planet. "What we have to tell you is a long story."

———

They explained everything to Toki. They needed the council's backing to scan for the machine they thought was in the embassy. If they had to search room to room, it would take them too long and they could be stopped before they found it.

Toki came back into the meditation room. "They wish to speak to you two."

Skye looked at Sam. "You need to talk to them."

"Me? What are you going to do?"

"I'll be with you, but you know how to speak to them. We need their help." He touched her arm. "I could make a real mess of everything."

They followed Toki to where the council waited.

Sam gave the proper bow and waited for Anseri to speak first.

"Our religious leader requested we speak to you, why?"

"We have a request." Sam looked at the council. "But first I wish to explain why we have that request."

"Go on." Anseri and the rest of the council showed no emotion, even though Sam knew they had to be curious.

"My name is Samistwitha. I have Vespian and Ancient blood." She heard them murmuring amongst themselves at her statement. "I am also from a different timeline. Someone altered it and we need your help to fix it."

"And how do we know this is true?"

"Test my blood."

Anseri nodded and one of their doctors approached her.

Once he was done, he brought the readings to Anseri. She looked at Sam once she saw the readings.

"Now compare it to DNA you have on file. I recommend you check the family of the future leader first."

She looked up quickly when something matched. "You have my family blood."

Sam nodded. "I am your granddaughter."

That brought more murmurings.

"How is that possible?"

"Because in the timeline I'm from Susan wasn't the one who was in charge of the treaty. It was Heather Drexel. She not only married your son she mated with him," Sam said. "We believe Susan is behind the time change and believe she has a machine here that made those changes."

"That's not possible. Everything brought in has to be inspected. She hasn't brought anything to the embassy that had to go through any screening."

"So she couldn't have snuck it in?" She felt Skye's hand on her arm. She gestured for him to speak. He didn't want to, but after her urging he finally spoke.

"We don't know what we're looking for, only the signature it leaves. It could be something small enough to fit in a pocket."

"And who are you?"

"My mate." Sam reached her hand toward him and he took it before stepping to her side.

"I am Skye Latimer. I have learned through your people that I am from the family that was banned from the planet."

"Then you are Vespian."

"Yes, ma'am."

"And you feel that is enough for us to believe you?"

Skye grinned. "No ma'am, but I hope it is enough to understand that things aren't right. I know you need to check out what we say. But time is of the essence. I fear the timeline could change again before we can stop the culprit."

"And you believe such a machine is here?"

"I do."

Sam and Skye waited as the council spoke amongst themselves. If they didn't agree Sam and Skye would have to find another way to get the scan done.

Anseri nodded at something someone said to her then looked at Skye. "Fridon will escort you to our security. Run your scans."

Skye smiled. "Thank you."

———

Storm heard his communication device go off. He tried to reach it without disturbing the beautiful woman curled up against him, but he couldn't reach it without waking her, so he settled back against the pillows and held her close.

Her lashes fluttered before she opened her eyes to look at him. "Your answer?"

"It can wait." He brushed a few strains of hair out of her face.

She shifted then sat up. "Go on. No need to put it off."

He leaned over and picked up the device. Taking a deep breath, he answered.

"We have discussed your request."

Storm waited for his mother to continue.

"We have approved it. You have permission to contact the UCE and request Heather Drexel as our new liaison."

"Thank you, Anseri." He closed communications and turned to Heather. "I know what I'm asking is a lot from you. To give up your life here and be my mate, but I can't see my life without you."

"Are you asking me to marry you, Storm? What about Susan?"

"Marriage is an Earth thing. We mate. It goes deeper than your ceremonies that can be broken with a signature. We only have one mate, and once the ceremony has been consummated there is no going back."

"You still haven't said anything about Susan."

"Why does she bother you?" Storm moved toward her and pinned her to the bed. "She will be left here when we head to Vespia in a few days. The contract I have with her will be nullified when I replace her with you. Your government wants this treaty so they will go along with my suggestions."

"But what about what Latimer spoke about?" She looked up into his eyes. "If she has some sort of machine that can alter the timeline, don't you think something like this will make her try to change things again?"

"I will handle her later, right now I believe I asked you a question."

"Actually, you didn't." She grinned at him. "A girl only mates once and you need to do it right."

"You're right." He pressed a kiss to her lips. "I do need to do this right." He pressed a kiss against the new mark that had appeared on her throat. "I want to do this right."

Storm shifted his weight so he could move down her body a little. He kissed a wet trail down to a breast. Using his tongue, he circled the tip, which pebbled under his ministrations. Once he was happy with what he caused, he paid the same amount of attention to her other breast.

"Storm." Heather's voice came out soft.

"There is a reason I'm doing this, I promise." He continued to work his way down her body, planting kisses along the way.

"Please."

Storm grinned against her skin. He wanted to be sure she was ready before he entered her body. Climbing back up her, he centered himself and drove into her. The sweetest sound of a moan reached his ears, he captured her lips with his, drawing her tongue to dance with his. It took him some time to break the kiss, her response filled him with such joy.

"Heather Drexel, I want to spend the rest of my life with you and I don't care where." He started moving inside her. "Will you be my mate?"

———

She looked up at him. He was serious. What if Earth refused to go along with it and she was banned? She wouldn't be able to go to Vespia with him. If she did, she could start a war between the two planets. "Even if we live in some hovel on the edge of the galaxy?"

"I don't care where I am as long as I'm with you." Gentle fingers caressed her face. "You are my heart."

He hit a sensitive spot inside her, causing her to arch up against him. When she spoke, it was barely above a whisper. To have him to herself would be a dream come true. "And we can do this again?"

He chuckled. "Any time you want."

"I love you and would be proud to be your mate."

His lips captured hers. His tongue danced and dipped with hers, when he released her mouth, a sigh escaped her. He wrapped his arms around her and flipped them over. Heather rose above him like a goddess.

She started to ride him, licking her lips when she felt the beginning of her orgasm start to blossom inside her. Picking up the pace, she reached for the elusive euphoria she found in his arms. So close. Then it filled her, flinging her out of her body to float among the clouds.

Susan wasn't going to be happy.

———

Storm stood in front of the door to Susan's room. Behind him stood the council and Toki, as well as a handful of guards, to make sure she did as she was told.

She spun around when the doors opened to reveal him and his entourage.

"I wish to speak to you."

"Of course, Storm." She looked at Toki then the council as they filed into her room. A frown puckered her brow. "Why is the council with you?"

"We are not happy with the way the treaty is proceeding." He crossed his arms over his chest. "I have spoken to your UCE, and it is in both planets' best interest to cancel the contract with you and go with another. You are to pack your things and leave the embassy in one hour, or I will have you escorted to our holding cells until one of Earth's security can come and collect you."

"What?" All the color drained from her face. "Why?"

"You have been sabotaging the treaty, Susan. You were only invited to my planet to get it signed, and you have abused that situation. It should have been signed years ago."

"Who is replacing me?"

"Your superiors haven't given me a name yet."

Her gaze darted around the room like she was trying to find a way past them. If she was going to be a problem, he would lock her up right now and let his men take care of her things. He had brought guards with him to watch her gather her things when he and the council stepped away, but it might be better to let them go through her things by hand than to scan them anyway.

She mumbled to herself, and she started pulling out her travel bags. "It's Heather Drexel, isn't it? That bitch!"

"What grievance do you have with her?" He didn't bother to answer her question as he watched her in amusement while she started haphazardly shoving clothing into her bags.

She looked at him. "You wouldn't understand."

Storm watched as she slipped something into her pocket. He didn't say a word just held out his hand.

"What?"

"I'll take whatever that was."

"It's nothing."

"Susan, you know the Vespian rule. We get to inspect everything before you leave the premises, so you either give it to me now, or I'll have you searched before you leave the embassy."

She sighed as she fished into her pocket and pulled out a small flat disk.

It didn't look like much, but he could tell at a glance it was an advanced piece of technology. He palmed it.

"That is mine. It goes with my bracelet." She held out her wrist to show the bracelet with a marble-shaped crystal.

"And you'll get it back once we clear it." He signaled two of the guards to step forward. "These two men will help you pack." Then he turned on his heel and went to security. Skye Latimer waited for him. "My men are helping her pack to make sure she doesn't have this machine you are looking for, but she did try to slip this into her pocket. It's not Vespian."

Skye took the cylinder from him. "It's a calibrator. She probably uses it to adjust the timelines. She can still make the adjustments. This just makes it easier."

"No reason to make any of this easier for her." Storm grinned. "What now?"

"We follow her and see where the machine is."

———

Susan wanted to scream. Somehow, it fell apart fast. She thought she had changed everything she needed to so she could get what she wanted. It didn't matter. A few more tweaks and she could fix this problem. Storm might have taken her calibrator, and she had no way to get it back, but she could still do what she needed to do.

The Vespian guards brought her to the gates of the embassy.

"The ambassador will have your items sent to the address UCE has on file. If you wish them to go to another location you need to contact your government."

She nodded. It didn't matter where her stuff went. She planned on changing everything as soon as she could. All she had to do was dump the guard who was suddenly following her.

———

Skye sat in his ship with Sam. Storm was having Susan followed while they were on their way back to Bert's compound.

"Why didn't we bring extra medallions with us?" Sam asked.

Skye turned to Sam and gave her a rueful smile. "I didn't think we'd need it. I had no idea who made the time change when we first came here so had hoped we'd be able to fix it quickly and be done with it."

"And now?"

"Now, knowing Susan is the one altering everything, plus the fact that we haven't found the machine, gives her the chance to keep making changes every time she gets caught until we can stop her. We'll get the medallions as soon as we can. I don't want to waste time having to explain everything to Heather and Storm over and over. Bert's medallions will allow them to be aware of the timeline change and remember what our goal is."

He landed the ship near the compound. Bert met them at the end of the gangplank. "What did you learn?"

"That it's not any of our enemies. I'm pretty sure it's a woman named Susan, who doesn't have the science back-ground to do this right." Skye stepped onto the tarmac. "And she has hidden it so she can make changes any time she wants."

"That will make the timeline break down faster." He gestured for them to follow him. "I might have what you need to pinpoint the location of the equipment. After I make a few alterations, you should be able to see all the changes so you can correct them once you gain control of the machine."

"Good, we'll be happy when we get our timeline back."

THREE

Skye and Sam headed back to Earth. He wanted to give Heather and Storm their medallions before they went after Susan. Then all the power went out in the ship.

"Damn it!" Power came back on. And the quiet section of space they were in was suddenly crowded with ships. "We're too late."

———

Storm sat in his office, reading the file his mother forwarded him. Fridon came in and stood in front of his desk.

"The team is ready for inspection, sir."

"Thank you, Fridon." He didn't look up.

"Your little human is asking to speak to you as well. I told her you were in meetings most of the morning then you had to handle inspections."

"She is a bit annoying, isn't she?" Storm looked up. "Anseri wants me to be nice to her because of this treaty, but it is becoming more and more difficult."

"We could go on the mission." Fridon grinned.

"You have already been through the file?"

"Yes, sir. There is a small colony of humans under attack on an outpost. We are the closest to them. It could keep us away for a few days."

"And will keep the humans happy since we are trying to negotiate this treaty with them. I'm not really sure why, though. They have nothing we want but our religious leader said it was important so now I have an annoying human as my partner." He looked up at Fridon. "A break would be nice. You are very sure of your team?"

Fridon crossed his arms over his chest the way Storm had done thousands of times and smiled. "Yes, sir."

"I will speak to the council."

———

Heather Drexel checked her ammo. Each shot had to count. Those damn lizard people just kept coming. They had killed hundreds of them. One would think that they had put a dent in their numbers, but every time there were more and more.

Her shoulder hurt and she was exhausted, but she refused to give up. She would fight to her dying breath. Heather allowed her weapon to drop as she surveyed the area. Their enemy had stopped their attack for the moment, giving them a small respite.

"Captain."

She turned to the male voice. What was his name? Rogers? "Yes?"

"Three more wounded. Two dead."

She nodded. Heather wanted to cry, but she was their leader. Showing her emotions was out of the question. Her job was to focus on the people who were relying on her to keep them alive, which wasn't easy with what they had to work with.

Their supplies were low. They didn't have enough food to feed everyone for much longer and they had nothing in medical supplies. Sometimes being dead was better than the suffering some of their people had gone through before dying anyway.

She asked the question she knew would hurt the most. "Who?"

"Rodriguez, and Allen are dead. Capa'i, Smith and Henry are wounded."

She nodded again. "How many did we get?"

"Seven."

"How close are they?"

"Four are pretty close."

"Then cover me."

"Captain, you can't go out there. They've already kidnapped you once."

"Our ammo is getting too low. We need their weapons if we want to continue to fight."

"Let one of the other men go."

"No." She shook her head. "They won't kill me, they want me too badly."

When she started for their safety border he grabbed her arm. "I can't let you do this."

"And we can't afford to lose any more people." Heather moved around him and continued to the border. They sent a message off when this first started, but since then their communication system had been down so they didn't know if their message had ever been received. All she knew was that reinforcements had better get there soon or they were all doomed.

———

Storm stood in front of the council. He wanted to go on this mission with Fridon's team but knew the council could deny him the chance if they felt he was needed at home.

"You have read the files?" asked Anseri.

"Yes, ma'am. Since we are trying to sign a treaty with Earth, I recommend we rescue this outpost. It is only a few days from here and their closest ship is still weeks away."

"We agree."

"The team has been picked, and I wish to join them."

"You are the future leader of this planet, and this mission is very dangerous. Why would you want to risk your life this way?"

"I have gone on missions worse than this and came back home. I feel my presence will help the team be more successful. They need my tactical knowledge."

His mother looked at him. "And what about your bride?"

He sighed. His mother knew him too well. "Permission to speak freely?" At her nod, he continued. "That is one of the reasons I wish to go. Mother, she is driving me crazy. Constantly interrupting meetings, demanding time I don't have to give. Perhaps if I were gone for a while she would learn to interact with our people instead of hiding away in her apartment all the time and making demands of me."

His mother didn't answer right away. "Granted, but you are to stay out of harm's way."

"Of course." He grinned. This mission was going to feel like a vacation after dealing with Susan for so long.

———

Skye and Sam's ship was halted and boarded before they could get out of sight. Skye found himself in front of an angry Admiral Barrington in the cargo area of his ship.

"How the hell did you get away? And why didn't you bring the rest of the outpost with you? This ship looks big enough to house everyone."

"Sir?" He had no idea what was going on. They didn't have time to check the timeline before they were boarded. In his timeline, Bear had seen the ship several times.

"Answer me or you're going in the brig for abandoning your post."

"Permission to speak freely." He looked at the guards around them. "Alone."

"And give you the chance to escape?"

"Sir, you know me." Skye normally would have kept everything to himself and landed up in the brig, but they didn't have time for that. He had to tell him the truth and hope for the best. "Have I ever given you a reason to not trust me?"

"Until now, no, but we're at war and I've seen too many of my best officers cloned."

Cloned? He had to come clean to get to the bottom of this. "I have no weapon. Your people have control of my ship. Sam is being held. I can't harm you or anyone else."

"You are one of the best at hand-to-hand."

"And you are the one who trained me, sir. I'm not a clone and you can test me if that would give me a chance to explain myself."

Bear nodded to the doctor standing nearby. He ran a scan. "He's the real Latimer, sir. Everything lines up."

"Alright, I give you one minute, and the guards will be right outside this room." They filed out. Once the room was empty, he looked at Skye. "The clock is ticking."

"This timeline is wrong."

"What? What are you talking about?" Bear pulled a weapon on Skye.

"Sir, hear me out. The woman I'm with, her name is Sam,

and we were in this ship when the timeline changed, twice. This ship has a temporal device that keeps us from being affected by the timeline changes. I don't know what is going on, but I can prove what I'm saying is true. I have a device on my bridge that will show you what has happened."

"And how did you get this so-called machine."

"You know those special assignments I have gone on from time to time? The man behind them is named Bert. This is his ship as well."

"Never heard of him." Bear crossed his arms over his chest.

"I didn't think you had, sir, but you never know. On my bridge is the equipment you need to see. If you humor me long enough to let me show it to you, everything should make sense."

"So you want me to go to your bridge, without any backup, to look at some machine?" He shook his head. "I don't have time for this, Latimer."

"I know my story sounds farfetched, sir, and I'm not sure if I have anything on me that will prove my story, but my goal here is to fix the timeline and get everything back the way it should be."

One of the guards came into the room. "Sorry, sir, but the woman demanded she speak to Latimer."

"You people can't control her?"

"She hasn't tried to escape, but she took out two of my men to get her point across. Moves only one person would ever do. Heather Drexel. She also used your signature move, sir."

He glared at Skye. "Bring her in."

Sam dashed into the room and grabbed Skye by the arms. "My link is back."

"What?" He was too busy dealing with the admiral to understand her.

"My mental connection with my mother. I can feel it. It's different, but I can feel it. Mom's in trouble. She's on some outpost and surrounded by Reasta's people." She gripped the sleeves of his shirt. "We have to rescue her."

"Nice show," Bear said angrily. "But I'm not buying it."

Sam turned to him. She knew they didn't have time for this. "You don't know me, but I know you. You're Admiral Archibald Barrister. You trained Heather Drexel, and if the timeline hasn't changed that much my mother was the one who kept figuring out the training scenarios before you could implement them. She is one of your best students. So is Skye. In my timeline, you have one sister, are a widow and sort of adopted my mother while she was training. You and a gentleman by the name of Henry took care of her while she was in the academy. And Heather is the only one who can call you Bear."

"Your mother?"

Sam nodded.

"How do you know all of this?" He studied her like he wasn't sure what to think of her.

"Because in the proper timeline, you are friends with my parents. I actually trained with you. You are respected and trusted by my family." She turned back to Skye. "Reasta can't win, Skye. We have to save her."

"We will, Sam. One step at a time." He looked at the Admiral.

"Who is Reasta?" asked Bear.

"A woman with snake-like eyes who wants to build an army from my mother's offspring." Sam snapped. "Look, every minute we stand here talking is precious. What will it take to convince you we are telling the truth?"

"Do you know what this Reasta looks like?"

"Yes. Will that do it?"

"Here's some images I want you to go through." Bear handed her a tablet.

Sam flipped through them until she came across Reasta's picture. "That is her and the man behind her is her second in command."

"And how do I know you two aren't working for her?"

Sam glared at him. "You don't."

He studied her for a moment before turning to Skye. "Show me this machine, Latimer."

Skye nodded. He led their small entourage toward the bridge.

"Skye, Sam. I see you have guests," said the voice of the computer.

"Yes, and they have clearance. The first is Admiral Barrister. He will name the guards who will be accompanying us."

"Interesting computer, Laitmer. If you try anything my men have orders to take you out."

"Sir, if you understood what was really going on you'd understand why your threat is hollow to us." They walked to the bridge where Bert had installed the timeline reader. Lights flashed as a steady stream of data flowed across the screen showing all the errors that had happened.

"Damn, Susan created an ugly mess this time." Skye moved some of the data to the main screen. He studied all the data that centered around Storm and Heather. When this change happened, Heather's position changed. Instead of her being Bear's assistant she was sent into deep space and got caught in an attack on the outpost she was sent to inspect. And Reasta was at war with the entire galaxy instead of just Vespia.

"One small change caused all of this?" asked Sam.

"If you don't know what you're doing, yeah." He looked at Sam. "We have to stop Susan."

"We have to save my mother, first."

"Sam, if we can stop Susan, we can switch the timeline back to the way it should be." Skye wrapped his hands around her arms. "None of this would have happened."

"But I'll know we abandoned her."

The sad look in Sam's eyes got to him. She was right. They needed to save Heather then stop Susan. "It depends on what the Admiral will allow us to do."

"So you're now remembering I'm in the room?" he asked. "This Susan you are talking about. Is it Susan Harris?"

"Yes, the one assigned to get the treaty signed. In our timeline Heather was assigned to do that and she got it done in a few months. The grain you want from Vespia has been shipping to Earth for more than three years."

"Months? We can't seem to get the treaty signed."

"I know. Susan has kept them from signing the treaty."

"Why?"

"She wanted to be the wife of an ambassador. Now that she has it, she doesn't want it to end."

"People are dying because we don't have that treaty yet." Bear looked at the data. "And you believe if we can figure out how Susan has made these changes the timeline you came from will reappear?"

"Yes, sir."

"Are we at war in your timeline?"

"No, sir. Reasta is a threat, but she wants Heather. Since Heather ended up on Vespia that is where she is focusing her attention. I'm assuming that since Heather never went to Vespia the only way for Reasta to get her is to fight Earth and any planet willing to help our planet."

"You go and get Captain Drexel and we'll try to figure out how Susan did this and stop her."

"You believe us?"

"For now."

"Thank you, sir."

———

Storm's ship came close to the planet where the outpost was.

His communications officer loaded readings he felt Storm should see to the main screen. "Sir, there is a massive ship in orbit around the planet."

"Have they spotted us?" asked Storm as he stepped up behind the soldier running navigation.

"No."

"Evasive maneuvers. Keep us hidden."

The ship slid behind a moon and security brought their shields up, turning on their cloaking device. The navigator brought the ship into a close orbit around the moon. "Transporting will be tricky. We will have to do it while we're behind the moon so we can drop the shields."

"What is happening on the surface?"

"They are under fire right now. I detect fourteen life forms within the ruins of the outpost fighting and fifty outside firing on them."

"Then we need to get down there now." Storm rested a hand on the chair the navigator sat in. "Can you contact them?"

"No, sir. Their system is down. No communication, no security grid." He pressed a few buttons. "We'll have a window in fifteen. I've notified your team. We'll transport you behind those attacking."

"Good." He headed to where the rest of the team waited. He entered the transportation area, and another soldier approached them.

"Sir, the council has called us back."

"What?" That didn't make sense. "Show me."

It was the council's signature, but his mother would have been on the screen giving him a reason for the withdrawal. Instead, it was one of the other council members demanding they come back. He contacted the woman who would be in charge of the ship while he would be gone.

"What are your orders, sir?"

"We're going down."

"And what do I tell the council?"

"I have a feeling if you were to contact them you would find the council confused about a message they didn't send."

"Sir?"

"What would you do if a ship came into the space where you were?"

"You'd shoot at them."

"Or trick them into leaving the area." Storm wanted to laugh. He had been known for doing that when needed. He picked up his helmet and walked to where the rest of the team waited. "Once we've secured the area, I'll signal you to send down the supplies needed to get their systems back up. Then I want you to head back to Vespia. Make that other ship think we heeded the message from the council. Once you are out of their radar range double back with the cloak on and set a stationary orbit around this moon. It shouldn't take you more than three days. We'll have everything ready for your return."

"Yes, sir."

Storm turned to the team. "Commander, we're ready."

"The data on what we're going into has been loaded into your helmets. Use your camouflage mode. We need to eliminate the target before we can see what the status is with the humans." Storm snapped his helmet on. "Let's go."

———

"How many more?" Heather shouted to be heard over exploding rocks and shrapnel falling all around her.

"Too many to count."

This was it then. Their final assault. Well, they weren't going to get her without a fight. Heather stood from her vantage point and shot. One by one she watched her enemy fall. Good, the more damage she did before she turned her weapon on herself the happier she'd be.

"Captain! Get down," said Rogers. He had stepped up to be her second when they lost Latimer.

"No. If this is it, I'm going down fighting. Remember your promise."

"Yes, ma'am."

Heather had better accuracy standing up. She watched as their enemy came at them. Suddenly, they were dropping like flies. Soldiers further away were dropping to the ground before the ones right in front of them. She frowned. Were they shooting their own men?

She couldn't see anything but knew to be on guard. The last of their enemies fell, and silence filled the air.

"Captain Drexel? Don't shoot. We're your reinforcements."

The male voice was nice, but she had been through too much to believe anything so easily. "Prove it."

———

The female warrior was gorgeous. He noticed her the moment she stood, not caring if she could be hit and started firing with a determination he hadn't seen in a while. Her white hair flowed about her face and those beautiful violet eyes looked haunted yet filled with determination when she was fighting her enemy.

He could tell by her eyes that she had demons. Big ones.

Storm released the seals on his helmet, breaking the camouflage and coming into view. He tucked it under his arm and waited for the female to accept them. His men followed suit until all eleven soldiers appeared in front of her.

"Vespians," she spat. "I thought we lowly humans were below your race."

"We're signing a treaty with your planet."

"Right, like Susan Harris wants to leave the cushy job of being an ambassador's wife." Heather signaled several of her people to stand watch as she spoke to the Vespian.

Storm grinned. That was what he thought, too. The treaty should have been signed a long time ago but the little human was finding things to keep the treaty from completion so he could send her back to her planet. He was tired of her whining and wanted her gone.

"Nevertheless, we are here." He pulled his gloves off.

"And how do I know this is true? You still haven't given me proof."

He held out a small pad he had hidden in his suit. The woman nodded to one of her other men who came out and took it from him.

"The admiral's personal code is on this, Captain."

She studied him for a moment before she finally dropped her weapon. She gave another signal, and her men came out and started taking weapons from the bodies littering the ground.

"Are we cleared to join you?"

"Yes." She stepped out and approached him. She stuck her hand out in the Earth greeting. "Heather Drexel."

"Storm." A beautiful shade of pink filled her cheeks as they clasped hands.

"The ambassador? What are you doing here? Aren't you afraid to get your suit dirty?" She let go quickly then gestured for him to follow her back to their ruined compound. Her men fell in behind the rest of his team, watching for enemy stragglers as they retreated.

"I am head of Vespian security as well as the ambassador to Earth."

"Multi-tasker. Good for you."

Her snarky comment drew a laugh out of him. "And this suit is quite durable."

She shot him a glare. Most human females were all over him, but she wasn't. This woman was all business. He found her intriguing. "Your admiral received your message but had no idea what happened. Who does that ship in orbit belong to?"

"We don't know. Never saw the race before, but they have snake eyes."

Rogers came up to her. "Two more wounded."

Heather sighed. "And dead?"

"This time we were lucky."

She nodded. They stepped behind the crumbling walls to what he thought was anarchy. Heather started shouting out orders and everyone scurried to do as she commanded.

The wounded were moved to another location. The room held dozens of people. No wonder there were only fourteen fighting, at least twice as many were wounded. Storm signaled the medic he brought who nodded before grabbing his med-pack and worked with the people in their makeshift medlab.

Storm wanted to know more about the captain.

Her second in command came up to stand beside him. "Thank you."

"For the doctor?"

"For showing up when you did. We wouldn't have been able to fight them off this time." He watched the medic work with different patients.

"Why are they after you?"

"We don't know. They showed up right after the Captain arrived to inspect our outpost. That was six months ago."

"You have been fighting them that long?"

"Yes, it was an annoyance in the beginning, but they were able to take out our power. No grid to keep them at bay. When we lost the grid, we lost access to the rest of the compound."

"And your Captain?"

"Has kept us alive. She fought beside us instead of giving orders and staying in the background." He turned to look at Storm. "But something happened a few weeks ago. They got her. Had her for almost a day. We don't know how she escaped, but she did and came back changed. There's a haunted look in her eyes that wasn't there before."

He had noticed that haunted look too. What caused it?

Heather walked up to them. She spoke to her second. "Make sure the wounded get fed first."

"Yes, ma'am."

She looked at Storm for a moment before heading off to talk with his medic.

———

What was wrong with her? Her job was to protect these people, not be distracted by a handsome man. His jet-black hair and golden eyes called to her. She wished she hadn't touched him. The simple contact brought an erotic image of her caught in the middle of an orgasm that she wished she hadn't seen. If she wasn't careful, it would come true, and she didn't need the complication.

Someone handed her a ration when she wasn't hungry, but because her people were watching her, she took a few bites. They couldn't afford to waste food, and she felt her people deserved to eat before she did. She was the reason they were in this mess.

Heather had no clue why the aliens wanted her, but when she had been kidnapped, she found out she was the target. The guards who took her just had no idea who they had. The only thing that worked in her favor. One complained loud enough to give her the information she needed, and she knew she had to get away from them before they realized just whom they had captured. Their attack came late in the day and once the sun set the temperatures dropped to a dangerous level, so they had planned on camping that night before heading to the small scout ship they had landed a few miles back. Heather knew she would rather die because of the cold than let them drag her to the main ship. She waited until they slept to get away. It was easy for her to escape. She had to take out a half dozen guards before she was free, but they didn't expect her to fight them. They were no match for her.

Once she returned to the outpost, she had planned on fighting until her last breath and killing herself before they could get their hands on her again, but the presence of the Vespians complicated things. Especially their leader. What was the ambassador doing here anyway?

"You're not eating." Storm's voice washed over her. It made her feel safe and secure.

"Not hungry."

"You need to keep your energy up."

"Not you, too." She was tired of people trying to babysit her. "I'm fine. I don't need anyone to watch over me."

"All right." He watched her. "I need a landing place for the supplies we brought, and if you show my second to your power source, he will do his best to get it up and running."

"Sure." A nice safe conversation. The way he was looking at her gave her the distinct impression he wanted to devour her. "How far into the compound can your system transport?" She took him to a room near the medical area that they weren't using.

"This won't be a problem." He pressed a button on his collar, and she heard other voices.

"Sir, we're ready to transport the supplies."

"Triangulate on my signal." He gave them the dimensions, ignoring her and giving her a chance to study him without him noticing.

She had to hand it to the Vespians they were all a good-looking lot, but this one, wow. He was stuff of fantasies. And that smile. It could melt the clothes off of women. She looked down at what was left of her uniform and grinned. There wasn't a lot of hers left. Another one of the reasons those aliens didn't know who she was. That was like ice water on her thoughts, and she turned on her heels and left.

———

Storm watched as the supplies appeared in front of them. Food, medicine, clothing, bedding, weapons and ammo. All the real basics they needed to fight until the ship came back.

His team started unpacking everything. Food was placed against one wall. Medicine was brought to the makeshift medlab, and so were some of the uniforms. Those that were seriously injured were sealed in the suits to put them into stasis until the ship could come back and they could be worked on in a real medlab.

Storm grabbed one of the uniforms and went in search of Heather. What she had on exposed more than it covered and although he did enjoy the view, what she wore wouldn't protect her the way one of their uniforms would. He also knew she had a death wish and would probably fight him on wearing it.

He found her staring out at the carnage they caused. One by one the bodies just disappeared.

"She's teleporting them up. Then she recycles them and sends them back." Heather didn't look at him. "I know this because I've seen some of those faces over and over. We kill them and she brings them back to life to be killed all over again."

He had thought about just throwing the uniform at her and demanding she wear it, but perhaps he should let her talk.

"How? How does she do this? Why does she do this? They kill my people, and we've lost them forever."

"And you blame yourself."

She didn't answer, just continued to stare.

"You are a visiting dignitary. Why should you care?" He knew what he said was cruel, but whatever she was keeping to herself needed to come out.

"You wouldn't understand."

Her silhouette drew him. He wanted to take her in his arms and ease away the pain she felt. "Try me."

"Why? You don't know me." She turned to look at him.

"I have had people die under my command. Doing things I ordered them to do. It hurts. But keeping it inside you isn't right."

"And exactly who am I supposed to talk to?"

"Me." He stepped as close as he could.

"No." she went to step around him, but he grabbed her arm.

The man who was her second came up to them. He noted the hold Storm had on Heather but didn't comment. "We have communications back."

"Any word from Latimer?"

"No ma'am."

She looked up at him then her arm. He let go, but not before slapping the uniform against her chest. Heather looked down at it, wrapped it around one hand then let it drop to the floor.

———

"Who is this Latimer? A lover?" asked Storm as Heather moved away, and the man remained at his side.

"Not that I'm aware of. He was her assistant. Went after her when she disappeared." He looked at Storm. "They came here to do an inspection and got caught by those lizards. They could have isolated themselves and tried to get off the planet, but they jumped right in to help. When the commander of the station was killed, she became our commanding officer. No one had to beg her and between the two of them, they kept us alive. The captain kept to herself when she wasn't giving orders or fighting. Some of our people thought of her as an ice princess. All business."

"And he is still missing?" Storm picked up the uniform she dropped on the ground.

"Yeah. Another thing she's not happy about, but she won't talk about what happened. We don't know if he found her and got caught himself, was killed trying to free her, or if she never saw him. Nothing. The fact that she asked if we heard from him tells me she doesn't know what happened to him either."

One of his guards walked close enough to catch his attention. He followed him to where Fridon worked.

"I can get partial power to the security grid. Focusing on the medical area, the border, and a few other rooms if you want a staging area and sleeping quarters."

"Do it." Storm clasped a hand on his shoulder. "What about the food processors, and ammo reloads?"

"It will take a little more work, but I should have them up soon."

"What about running water?" Heather's soft voice filled him with desire. He didn't realize she was behind them.

"That should be up in a few minutes," Fridon answered her question.

Storm turned to look at her. She stood there with her arms wrapped around herself. He had a strong urge to take her in his arms. Why, he didn't know. There was something about this woman that touched him like no other. Perhaps it was because of the circumstances.

"Good. If we ration it everyone could be able to get cleaned."

"Captain, the water comes from the core of the planet. Hot and cold, there is plenty, you just couldn't access it once the system went down." Fridon looked up at her.

"Thank you. I'll let everyone know." She smiled for the first time, and it took Storm's breath away. The way it lit up her face for just a moment. Something so simple made her happy and he wanted to see her happy a lot.

Heather took off and Storm missed her presence.

"I'll have their tactical computer up in a few hours, sir." Fridon then switched to Vespian so no one could understand him. "She is quite pretty."

Storm knew what Fridon was getting at but refused to acknowledge it. "Who?"

"Right. I've noticed the way you've been watching her, sir. We all have. Isn't she a bit damaged for you? Most of your conquests have been much easier. There are other women here who would be quite happy to satisfy you."

He had noticed a few of the other females trying to catch his attention, but for some reason, he wasn't interested. "Let it go, Fridon."

"Of course." He turned back to the panel he had been working on. "May I say one more thing on the subject then I won't bring it back up?"

"Fridon."

"You aren't the only one interested in the human leader. You need to make your move soon before someone beats you to it."

———

Hot water danced across her skin, drawing a sigh out of her. God, she needed this. She almost felt human. The showers were in the old gym so that five could use them at a time. Guards watched since the grid didn't cover this area yet, but she didn't care. To get the grime off her body for the first time in months was close to a miracle.

It started as a niggling sensation. Someone was watching her. When she focused, she noticed none of the other showers were running anymore, but she allowed the rest of the outpost to shower before her. It was the least she could do. Who was watching her? Focusing her thoughts, she sensed his presence so didn't turn around.

"I sure hope you are enjoying the view."

"I am."

The deep baritone voice shook her to the core. The one person she didn't need to see her naked was the culprit.

"Did you need something, ambassador?" She pretended his presence didn't bother her. Using the last of the soap she had, she washed her hair then used the suds to rinse the rest of her body one last time.

"Night is coming, and I was sent to find out how you wish to arrange guard duty. Finding you still in the shower was just an added bonus."

"I always take first watch." She turned the water off. The thought of climbing back in her tattered uniform made her insides crawl but having him watch her as she put on the Vespian uniform he made sure she had with her when she came here didn't sit well either. Pride had her grabbing her old uniform.

"You put that on, and I will wrestle you to the ground, rip it off you, and physically dress you in the uniform I gave you. Now if you can handle that then go ahead and try to prove a point by putting on your old uniform."

A frown crossed her face. Either she could keep her pride and be manhandled by a man that made her body scream for things it hadn't wanted in a long time, give in and watch the knowing smile that would spread across his face when he got his way, or she could just stand there naked and not give him the satisfaction of either. That last option was the most dangerous of the three. She needed clothing to protect her from his gaze. She could tell he liked what he saw, and she feared if he decided to take advantage of her state of dress she wouldn't fight him.

"You are an asshole." Saying it made her feel better.

"A human term of endearment?"

She wanted to laugh. Instead, she gave him her best glare and took the Vespian uniform. The thought of him touching her in such an intimate fashion had her heart beating faster than normal. That was dangerous.

She closed the seals and found him watching. No knowing smile. The look in his eyes showed respect. He understood.

"I will take the watch after you."

"Fine." If she woke him. The stims she took helped keep her awake. She hated sleeping. The nightmares were too horrible for her to want to sleep.

She ran her hands through her wet hair as she passed him. Time to stand watch. It would help cleanse her of any wayward thoughts.

———

He shouldn't have seen her naked. It just made matters worse. His desire for her escalated the moment he saw her body. Although a little too thin, it was flawless in his eyes. A slight pink hue covered her fair skin. He found it beautiful and that pushed him to want to touch her. Was all that creamy skin as soft as it looked? Storm shook his head. Did she know how she affected him?

Night was falling and the temperature started to drop. Those who hadn't gotten a Vespian suit were feeling it. Heather looked at him. "It might be warm during the day, but it gets pretty cold at night. You might want to cover up."

"No need. Our suits will keep our temperature regulated. It works up to one hundred fifty degrees below zero Earth standard."

"I'll take first watch." She chose to ignore his comment. "You can rest with everyone else until your shift."

"No need. I brought a roll to use while I wait, but we Vespians don't need the amount of sleep you humans are used to." He placed a small cube on the floor and using his foot, put a little pressure on it. It inflated quickly. "I'll probably be awake before my shift starts."

Storm could tell by her face it wasn't something she wanted to hear. He chose to lie down close to where she stood guard and closed his eyes. Sleep might not come, but this would give him time to relax. It also gave him time to study her without her knowing it.

Her second was a bit of a talker which wasn't the Vespian way, but Storm was grateful for the information. It allowed him to be aware of things that he wouldn't have been able to find out otherwise, like the fact that she refused to sleep and took stims to keep her awake. That was deadly. The body could only put up with that for a few weeks before it started to shut down. She was at that point now. He was aware that she had just used one, but when her shift ended, he would make sure she couldn't do it again. Even if he had to wrap himself around her to stop her.

He grinned. That actually sounded like fun. Being intimate with her was something he wanted to experience, but he knew humans were shy and she would more than likely fight him if he tried to seduce her. This little human didn't understand Vespians, but she would by the time he was done with her.

———

Heather found it hard to concentrate. He was right there behind her. All she had to do was tilt her head and she would be able to watch him while she kept an eye on the perimeter. A sigh escaped her. Why was she attracted to this man? Was it because he was a stranger, someone she could use and then forget when he went back home?

There wasn't much known about Vespians other than they had very loose morals when it came to sex. Friends told her they had orgies in the streets and people could constantly see couples having sex in public. When she asked her friends where they got this information, they didn't have an answer so she didn't know how true it was, but Earth was the worst when it came to learning about other planets. Old habits die hard. If they didn't understand it, they feared it.

The Vespians with them were respectful. She grinned. No wild orgies happening here.

She slid her hands against her stomach. No pockets. It sort of drove her crazy. A slight noise put her on alert before she felt him at her back, his breath brushing against the nape of her neck. His hand slid against her hip before they took hers and showed her that the suit did indeed have pockets.

"The suit is quite versatile. Just press your fingers along your hip bone to make them appear or disappear." His deep baritone voice heightened the desire she was feeling for him. "There are others up at the top near the seams."

His hands moved up her body, sparking a desire to turn in his arms and let him have his way with her.

"And no more stims." He held the one she had hidden in her uniform.

"Please, I need that."

"How long have you been taking them, Heather? You know these can kill you. We can break your addiction."

"I wish that was all it was." She spoke softly. "I'm not addicted. In fact, I wish I could step away from them."

"Then why don't you?"

She looked up at him. The compassion she saw in his eyes broke her. Heather hadn't told anyone what had happened when she was captured, or about the night-mares that started when she came back. The fact that she could read most people's thoughts, including his. Espe-cially his. He would be safe to talk to and she needed to talk.

"I have nightmares."

"That's not unusual after what you went through."

"Okay, first I'm going to hurt my second in command for

talking too much, and second, my nightmares become reality. I can't face what I keep seeing."

"Then you have visions while you sleep."

"No." Then she thought about it. It did make sense. "Yes, maybe. I don't know."

"Visions shouldn't be ignored."

"Why do you say that?" She thought he would scoff at her comment.

"My sister is our religious leader, and she has visions. I learned from her what happens when you ignore your visions." He touched her face. A soft, gentle slide along her cheek. "Perhaps you should face them and see what they are trying to tell you."

"There is so much blood." She shook her head. She didn't want to think about what she saw in her dreams. That was why she was avoiding sleep in the first place.

"You may take the bed while I take my shift."

"Not really tired."

"Then if you wish you can stay with me."

Anything would be better than pretending she was asleep.

They talked about nothing really, just things that popped into their heads, but Heather found Storm easy to talk to. She was sad when Fridon came to take his turn. Storm gestured to the bed. "Time to sleep."

She stifled a yawn. "I'm fine."

"Come, you need to rest." He took her hand and walked her to the bed.

Heather shook her head.

"I'll stay with you and wake you if you start having a nightmare."

She looked at him, knowing it wasn't a good idea. His thoughts were filled with all kinds of erotic thoughts. There was a high possibility that they wouldn't get much sleep. "I'm not tired."

"You are a liar. You can barely keep your eyes open right now. If you'd rather sleep in the main room I don't care, as long as you sleep."

Heather knew he was sincere. As much as he wanted her, he was concerned about her welfare. If she slept with everyone else, she might be safer, but they wouldn't. Her screams woke everyone the last time. If it happened again at least she'd only wake Storm.

He took her hesitancy as a yes as he sat then pulled her down beside him.

Good Lord, this was awkward. She didn't know what to do with herself. Heather wasn't used to sleeping with men. It showed one of her weaknesses and she hated it. She stared up at the ceiling, wanting to crawl away and find some corner to hide in, but if she didn't face this now, she would have to in the light of day, and probably with an audience.

"Get comfortable, Heather. I don't bite, only nibble."

Just the thought of what he could nibble on had her blood boiling. She lay there, mentally debating with herself until she finally gave in and curled up against him.

———

Storm felt like he won a major battle with her when he felt her shift and rest her head on his chest. Her lean body snuggled against his and he wanted to shout for joy. He wrapped his arms around her shoulders and closed his eyes. Sleep might evade him because there were other things he'd much rather be doing with this woman, but tonight she needed to sleep. The stims she had been taking could have wreaked havoc with her system and would make it next to impossible to sleep. If she dozed off like she seemed to be doing, then she hadn't done that much damage yet.

She sighed as she settled intimately against him then slipped into a light sleep. Good. He opened his eyes and looked for Fridon who had already moved to a discreet distance. The man knew to give them some privacy. Whether he thought it was for sex or not didn't matter to Storm. If Heather did have a nightmare, she wouldn't want any witnesses either. She wouldn't have been taking stims if she could handle them.

Her almost white hair stood out in stark contrast to his black uniform. She kept it cropped like her position required, but in the six months she had been here it had started to grow. That was probably why she kept it back in a braid. He wanted to release it, run his fingers through it.

He wondered how angry would she be with him if he did.

———

Heather found herself in a beautiful garden. She wore some sort of form-fitting gown that she found very comfortable. Beautiful colors and wonderful aromas filled her. A fleeting thought of how vivid the dream was floated through her head before she fell into it full force.

Flowers from all over the galaxy grew there. Anseri went to great pains to make sure they all thrived. It was her pride and joy, and she had gardeners to care for it when she couldn't work on it.

Warm, strong arms wrapped around Heather. "I see I found you. I told you what would happen if I caught you before you got back to our rooms."

She laughed as she turned in Storm's arms. "I do believe that was the last time I was here. This time your mother is supposed to join me for lunch." Heather pointed to the small table set with two place settings.

"Ah." He pressed a quick kiss against her lips. "Or perhaps I talked my mother into letting me have that lunch with you since my father just got back and I thought she should spend some time with her mate."

"So you could spend time with yours?"

"Of course." He touched her face tenderly. "But I have a different venue than the table and chairs."

"Oh? You don't want to sit in the garden and eat?"

"Our lunch will be in the garden, my heart, but the table and chairs are not something I'd care to utilize. I have a better idea." He shifted his hold on her and led her to a blanket nearby. Behind it was a brightly colored lien-to. On the blanket, one of the servers had added several pillows for comfort. A little further back was a small tent. The last thing placed was a basket before the servers stepped back to a discreet distance. "I know how much you love mother's garden and didn't think you'd be happy anywhere else."

"That is very sweet of you." She linked arms with him. "And the tent?"

"Ah, well, I thought you'd like to change your clothes."

"Really?" What was he up to?

"I want you to be comfortable."

"You want easy access to my body."

"Of course I do, but I also know you find the dress cumbersome when you're on the floor with the twins. You'll have the same problem here."

"And what did you have in mind for me to wear."

"It's in the tent." He pulled her close and gave her another quick kiss. "You go change and I'll get everything ready."

She wondered what he had planned as she walked to the tent. She turned and found him pulling his uniform off. A knowing smile spread across her face as she allowed the flap to fall back down. He gave her a choice from his favorite lingerie as well as a silk wrap because he knew she'd be shy about doing this with people around, even if they were at a discreet distance. She changed into what she knew he hoped to see and pulled the wrap around her. When she opened the flap Storm stood at the entrance.

"You afraid I wouldn't come out?"

He laughed. "I guess I was just a little excited about having the afternoon with you and thought about helping you but knew you wouldn't be happy with me if I pushed too hard."

"So you were standing out here, deliberating on what to do?" She pressed her hand to his heart. He had shed his uniform for a pair of soft pants. Heather couldn't help but smile at the fact he was still partially dressed. He walked around in their rooms naked all the time, but when people were expected, or they were someplace like this he had started wearing something to cover up and she knew he did it for her. He didn't care who saw him naked.

He took her hand and led her to the blanket covered with pillows.

"What have you planned for us?" She brushed a hair behind her ear as she sat down. "Finger food?"

"You know me well." He sat beside her before lying on his side so he could face her. He reached behind the pillows and brought out a tray laden with fruit, cheeses, and small bites of meat. All things they both liked, but Heather knew by the look in his eyes they wouldn't get much eating done.

He offered her a small piece of cheese. A smile spread across his lips when her mouth closed over his fingers.

She picked up a piece of his favorite fruit and started to offer it to him. The shocked look he gave her made her laugh before she put it between her teeth and offered it the way he wanted.

"Much better." He ran his fingers down her jaw to rest them on her throat before he claimed the fruit and her lips. Storm pressed her back into the pillows as his tongue dipped into her mouth, caressing her and drawing a sigh from her. Those never-idle hands of his skimmed across her skin, brushing along her hip, dipping into her belly button, all the places he knew helped escalate her desire.

Breaking the kiss, he worked his way down her throat, drawing the soft tissue of her mark into his mouth before spreading kisses across her collarbone and down to one of her breasts. His tongue slipped inside the lace covering her nipple for a quick caress before he moved to the other one and did the same thing.

She felt it to her toes.

Hot wet kisses continued to mark his passage down her body until he reached her core. When his mouth covered it, she sucked in her breath.

Heather opened her eyes. Her heart pounded in her chest. What a time to wake up. What was that anyway? So erotic. She had never fantasized like that before. She lifted her head to look at the man in the middle of her fantasy and found him wide awake and looking at her.

"So beautiful." He rolled over and trapped her body under his. "I have never experienced anything like that."

Storm's head dipped to hers, capturing her lips with his. Just like in the dream his tongue swirled inside her mouth, exciting her and drawing a sigh from her.

"Wait." She pushed against his chest until he lifted up so she could look at him.

"You deny me after we shared something like that?" He looked heartbroken.

"You experienced it too?" She had never shared a dream with anyone before. How did he have the same dream?

"It felt like I lived it." He lowered his head to hers, capturing her lips once again.

Need unfurled inside her. She felt his hands working on the seals of her uniform, exposing her body to his touch. Her hands did the same thing. A thrill raced through her when she could feel his skin against hers. Their uniforms ended up in a pile on the floor in their hurry to be flesh to flesh. Storm pulled up a cover to shield them from prying eyes.

He pressed his lips to the spot on her throat where she had felt her desire escalate each time he touched it in the dream then brushed his fingers against the soft skin. "You don't know what that mark on your throat was, do you?"

"I just know that every time you touched it in that dream, I felt it to my toes." She looked up at him. His beautiful golden eyes held her captive.

"It is a mark that a couple gets when they mate."

"You mean I'll have one once we have sex?"

"No." He smiled. "It's like when you humans marry. You sign a contract stating you're married, yes?"

She nodded.

"The mark is our contract. We only mate once in our lives and the mark proves which couple belongs together."

"That is what I saw on your chest, then. Is that what mine looked like?"

"They are identical." He touched her throat again. "But I don't know how I was able to mark you. It is something only my race gets."

"It was only a dream." She shifted under him and allowed him to sit intimately between her legs. The beat of her heart picked up speed when she felt his hardness trapped between them.

"Have you ever been to Vespia?" He braced himself up on his elbows so he could look into her eyes.

"No, but I've read a lot of the missives sent."

"Then how did you know what my mother's garden looks like? Or the finger foods? The mark? I don't know how, but that was real."

"Could I have pulled it from your mind?" The moment she said it she wished she hadn't.

"What do you mean?"

"Nothing." She dropped her gaze. How could she explain her question without having him look at her like she lost her mind?

"You have not lied to me yet, why do you want to try now?" His fingers shifted from her throat to her jaw, holding it so she had to look him in the face.

"Because I don't know what to tell you." Fear filled her. She didn't know what was happening to her. How could she explain it to a stranger?

"I'm not a stranger. Your dream showed we should have a life together."

How did he know what she was thinking?

"Trust this." He eased himself into her, allowing her muscles time to adjust to his invasion. He set a nice slow pace that had her body humming. Each stroke was perfect. It took her breath away. Heather couldn't think, all she could do was feel. Each time he filled her it was completely. Her muscles wrapped around him, intensifying everything she was feeling.

Her orgasm started slowly, like a slow-burning flame. The flames climbed higher and higher until she was consumed by the euphoria that wrapped around her, flinging her out to the stars. She couldn't talk, couldn't think anything past she never felt this before.

She had other lovers, but they never satisfied her. Not like this.

Storm touched her face with gentle fingers. "So beautiful. You see why I believe that was real? What just happened between us was magnificent. You can't deny that."

"And I don't want to. I've never experienced anything like that before, but what did we see? Something we both created because it's what we want?"

"You still don't believe we belong together?"

"How?" She knew this wasn't the time to talk about this, but he did ask. "I'm human and you're Vespian. The ambassador to Earth with a human wife. You think our governments are going to allow this because we have great sex together?"

"I know my planet understands things aren't always as they seem. They would hear us out and if our religious leader agreed they wouldn't stand in our way." He grinned. "But I am glad you enjoyed what we shared as much as I did."

She felt a blush fill her cheeks. "Earth wouldn't be so forgiving. They want this treaty to go through. That is all they care about."

"Then I would think they would agree to any demands my planet gave them, including switching the liaison from Earth."

"Storm, I am nothing. Just a captain in security. Why would they think I'd be a better choice?"

"Because I think you are."

She frowned. This was getting her nowhere.

"Sleep. We still have several hours before everyone rises." He pulled her into his arms once again.

Heather rested her head on his chest. He wanted her badly enough to start a war? Was he crazy?

FOUR

Skye and Sam's ship entered the solar system where the outpost was, and they found something they didn't want to see.

"Is that Reasta's ship?" asked Sam. She stared at the screen in fear.

"I'm afraid it is." Skye reached over to take her hand. He was grateful that the cloak on the ship kept them from detection by Reasta's equipment. If he had used it before the timeline changed, they never would have been stopped by Earth's security and could have gotten here earlier.

"She can't get my mother, Skye." Sam took his hand and held it tight.

"Sam, I promise your mother is fine. I'm picking up readings from the planet she's with the people of the outpost. Reasta hasn't gotten her." Skye squeezed her hand before he let it go so he could bring up the readings. He highlighted Heather's so Sam could see it. She was in close proximity to someone else. Who was the question. "Hmm."

"Are those Vespian readings?" Sam pointed to the other signatures they were picking up.

"Yes." Skye used the system to pinpoint. "No matter what Susan does they end up together. This one is your father, and that one is Fridon. The rest are the elite team Heather worked with."

"And that's mom?" Sam tilted her head as she looked at the readings. "Where is she?"

"In bed with your father."

Sam grinned. "They really can't stay away from each other, can they?"

"Nope." He smiled back. "But now comes the fun part. We need to talk to them and get them to understand what happened. Again."

———

Heather climbed back into her new uniform, wondering how everything changed so fast. Yesterday they were strangers. It only took one dream. One dream and now he was talking about taking her back to Vespia with him. That dream made them lovers, several times over. That was pretty much all they did. Storm would tell her to rest only to wake her up again because his desire became too much for him to bear.

She closed the seals. That was a first, too. No one else ever found her that desirable. Normally, her partners left her yawning. There was no second or third time. But with Storm, wow, the man was insatiable, and she found out she was just as bad.

Yet once he donned his uniform there was no evidence of the passionate man who had brought her to heights she didn't know she could reach.

"Captain."

She looked up. "Yes?"

"It's Latimer."

That was all the man had to say to get her moving. She walked quickly to the communication bay so she could talk to him. "Latimer?"

"Captain." He was quiet for a moment. "I'm glad you're okay. We need to talk."

"Where are you?"

"Coming in, but I have a guest. Is the grid up?"

"Yes. We have guests as well. Vespians. They are helping us get everything back online." She looked up when Storm walked in.

"Good to hear you have reinforcements. We'll be approaching the outpost in a few minutes."

"We'll be there to meet you." Heather turned on her heel and walked to the border. We? Had he brought reinforcements too? The moment she spotted Skye she had one of the guards use the remote to drop the shield long enough for them to enter. She frowned. Where was his uniform? Weapon in hand she stopped him with a gesture. "Change of clothes?"

"Yes." He didn't back down from her question. "Got them from my ship."

"They look a lot like the Vespian uniform."

"They should. That's who we got them from." Sam stepped forward and confronted her mother. She knew she couldn't raise too much suspicion so went with the answer that made the most sense. "We met them on our way here."

———

"Her?" Heather recognized the young woman from the communiqués they received from the snaked-eyed woman when that ship first arrived. She was always in the background, but Heather knew it was the same girl. "Latimer are you crazy? From what we have learned Old Snake Eyes wouldn't let her out of her sight. And you decide to rescue her and bring her here? Is that where you've been all this time?"

He just looked at her. "Like I said we need to talk. Privately."

"I don't think so." She leveled her weapon on him. The young woman watched her. Frowning at something, but Heather had no clue what.

"Then you've seen me before?" The young woman sighed in relief when Heather nodded. "Where is the ambassador?"

"What?"

"You have Vespians here and he's never far from you."

"Sam." Skye turned to the young woman. He was acting like he knew her. What was going on here?

"Sorry, Skye." Sam shook her head. "But we don't have time to play games." She looked back at Heather. "Reasta will be coming, and if she catches us, we're all dead."

Storm came up and stood behind Heather. A thrill filled her when he bent down to whisper in her ear. "She looks like you. Sounds like you, too."

What Heather noticed was she had her violet eyes with the Vespian ring around the iris and the shape and size reminded her of Storm's. They did have the same basic build, even though the young woman was a little taller than she was.

Sam pulled the necklace she always wore out of the uniform. Pulling it off, she held it out. "My parents gave this to me."

"Careful, Sam, if you lose contact with that it could disappear."

"Why?" asked Storm, curiosity on his face.

"Because it's not from this timeline," said Sam, as she let

the chain drop so it swung from her fingers. "Neither are we."

"Everybody inside." Heather didn't lower her weapon, but she did relax her stance. This was what Storm hinted at when they talked about the dream they shared. Could it be possible?

Skye took the hand of the young woman and led her inside. They looked around like they'd never been there before. Skye was the one who helped her set up the place. It brought her thoughts back to that timeline comment. Could it be true?

They followed her to the room they had converted into a staging area. She cleared the room so they could talk privately. "Explain."

"I am really Skye Latimer not some clone of Reasta's doing."

"Clone? Is that why those things keep coming? She's cloning them?" God that made so much sense. No wonder why she seemed to have an endless supply of soldiers. She had seen the same faces over and over but Heather assumed their enemy had a way to repair them so they could fight again.

"That is what she has done before," said Skye.

"Then how can I prove you're the real Latimer and not some clone."

"Test my blood." He held out his arm.

"In case you haven't noticed we're without a lot right now. That includes a medlab. Everything we're doing is from portable medpacks. We don't have a way to test for clones. We can't even heal everyone at the moment."

"What about me?" asked Sam. "You can still check DNA, can't you?"

Heather wasn't sure. She stepped out and asked for the head of their so-called medical team. She started asking questions the moment he walked in. "Can you test our female guest's DNA? Tell us who she is?"

"If she's in our data base I can."

"Good." Sam nodded. "Then take a sample of my blood and compare it to Heather and Storms."

The doctor stepped forward and took a sample then did the same with Heather and Storm. He didn't say anything when he handed Heather the results. She looked at the readings then held out the pad the data was on. "This shows we're related. How?"

"I'm your daughter."

Heather looked at the young woman. Her sterility aside, she would have remembered being pregnant. Unbidden, she thought about the time she spent in a coma. There she had been pregnant, but that wasn't real. "There is no way you're my daughter."

"But I am. In my timeline, you had to rescue me from a man called Ialog or Al. He used an advanced aging technique on me so I'd mature within a year instead of the way I should have aged. Here I'm betting you were in a coma for almost a year. While in that coma you were pregnant but didn't come to term."

"How could you possibly know that?" Heather wrapped her arms around herself. This couldn't be real, yet this woman knew things she shouldn't. She had kept everything she dreamed to herself when she came out of the coma. If the girl was guessing, she was amazing.

"Because Ialog tried that in our timeline. His problem was you had already met Storm so he wasn't successful. He ended up tricking you into a different way to produce me." Sam crossed her arms over her chest in frustration, mimicking Heather. "Look, there is so much to explain, but we don't have a lot of time. Susan could switch the timeline at any time. Especially when she learns you two are together again."

"Susan Harris?" asked Heather.

"You mean that little human working on the treaty?" asked Storm at the same time.

"Yes. You three are the focal point, but in the last time-line she seemed to know what was going on where you two didn't."

Heather looked at Storm. Should she tell them? Should she trust them?

————

Sam sensed a hesitancy in her mother. She knew her mind was expanding in this timeline. Perhaps because of the danger she was in the device had started to disintegrate. She needed to keep pushing. "Your device? Is it still intact?"

Heather's eyes widened at her question. She looked at Storm again before looking back at Sam. "What are you talking about?"

Hmm, if Dian raised her maybe she never got the device, or if she did Dian had a way of shielding it from everyone, including her. Or maybe she didn't want to say anything in front of her dad. Time to try a different tactic.

Can you hear me?

Heather took a step back, but Storm braced his hands on her, blocking any further movement.

This is crazy.

No, it's not. You have a bond with all your children. You also have one with your mate. Whether you want to hear this or not you have a very powerful mind. In my timeline, you were raised as a ward of the planet. Trained from the beginning to work for the government. You had a device inside you that no one from Earth could explain. It hid your true identity from people like Ialog.

Made you read human. When you met Storm, it started to disintegrate, allowing your mind to grow.

Where was this device placed?

The small of your back.

When I joined security, Dian gave me this necklace. She said it would help protect me and to never take it off. It was destroyed during one of the attacks. Since then, I've been able to read some people's thoughts. Have had some very strange dreams and the nightmares have been the worst I've ever had.

"Is there someplace where we can talk a little more privately?" asked Sam.

Heather nodded. She looked at the doctor, who picked up his kit and headed back out.

"Ambassador, would it be possible for Fridon to join us?" Sam gave him a bright smile.

Storm nodded. "How do you know the name of my second?"

"Because he is best friends with my mother." Sam took one of the seats. When Fridon entered she spoke to him. "You are the tech of the elite squad. Do you have your adaptable tool?"

"How do you know about that?" He looked at Storm, who shook his head.

"Because you created one for me." Skye held up his. When Fridon went to reach for it he pulled it back. "Understand it is from another timeline the data I have on it could cause trouble with yours."

"What makes you say that?" asked Storm as Fridon opened the screen.

"It now holds three timelines."

"Three?" Storm looked at him. "How is that possible? If what you say is true you should have been assimilated into this timeline.

"We're wearing a device that is keeping us and everything touching us between the two timelines. We remember everything the way it should be and can still interact in this timeline."

"Can I see it?" Fridon's voice held a note of excitement.

Sam smiled. He always got that way when he learned of something new.

Skye reached behind him and pulled the necklace out of his skin.

"This is Ancient in design." Fridon turned it in his hands. "And what would happen if the timeline were to change right now?"

"I don't know for sure, but since you're touching it I would assume it would cover you as well."

Fridon grinned as he pressed his little device against it. Pulling the screen up, he downloaded the data into it. Once he was done, he let go and Skye put it back around his neck.

"And now that I have a copy will it protect me as well?"

"That I don't know," said Skye.

"If it does then you will have one more person to help you."

Sam nodded. Her parents were the ones they had to protect but the more help they got the happier she'd be.

"We have one for you and Storm." Skye pulled the two Bert had created in the last timeline out of his pocket. "It is already set so I know they won't disappear the moment I hand them to you."

"You want us to wear them?"

"Each time the timeline changes you don't remember your life before and we have to explain what has happened to you over and over. This medallion will allow you to remember. To recognize that changes have taken place." Skye set them on the table they sat at. "We need your help to stop the changes and get the proper timeline back. Susan wants what Heather had. We thought we could fix it easily, but she's already changed the timeline once on us. Having to explain what has happened every time she changes it will burn time we don't have."

"Will this make us like you?" Storm turned it over in his hand. "We'll remember the past timeline as well as this one?"

"It will allow you to remember this timeline if it changes again," said Skye. "The only way for you to remember the original timeline is to get it back."

"And how are we to do that?"

"We need to find the machine doing this. I believe it's in Susan's possession. In the last timeline, we were able to scan the Vespian embassy on Earth and found nothing."

"What is the proper timeline?" asked Storm.

"You and Heather are mated and live on Vespia. Mom is part of the elder council. Fridon is also mated." Sam left out that her father's sister is mated since he believed that she should have waited until she fulfilled her role as their religious leader. "And then there are the twins."

"Twins?"

"Yes." Sam smiled. "Your twins. They're about four now. Everyone dotes on them."

"I'm sterile." The look on her mother's face showed she was having trouble believing any of this.

"So am I," said Storm.

"I know. Yet I sit before you proof that you do have children." Sam clasped her hands in front of her.

"Captain!"

Heather looked like she wanted to say something but the voice coming from the hallway made her turn around instead.

"We're under attack!"

That got everyone moving. Heather was the first one

there, but only by a second. Her weapon was out and firing before she could settle in a particular spot.

"Sam, remember what we learned."

She nodded. In their time while battling Reasta, they learned that the clones were her hardest to maintain. If they hit them just right, it took more power to regenerate them. Sometimes that could be worse than just creating new ones. The death blow had to aimed just right so the clones couldn't fight anymore yet where alive enough for Reasta to try to recycle them.

One by one the enemy dropped, and they kept coming.

"Each time there is more and more," complained Heather. She shot three more before her weapon was out of ammo. Someone handed her a new one and she fired again and again.

Bodies piled up outside their compound. The stench was nauseating.

Then they stopped. Those still standing disappeared from sight.

Heather wiped her brow. "Stand down."

Everyone stopped firing. Those that were wounded headed to the medical area. Two more were dead.

Heather knelt by the bodies, trying not to cry.

"It's not your fault," Storm said softly in her ear.

"Yes, it is." She looked up at him while tears ran down her cheeks. "It's me they're after."

Skye crouched down beside her. "And it's you she can't get."

———

Storm wanted to know more. He spoke to Skye while Heather checked on the wounded. "Why is that woman after Heather?"

"She wants to live forever and believes Heather is the key."

"And there is more to that than you are saying."

"Storm, without the knowledge from your proper time-line you're going to think I am crazy." Skye looked at him. "My ship will give you all this information."

"So now, you not only want us to trust you without telling us everything, you want us to leave these people and go to your ship to get the answers we seek?"

"I know I'm asking a lot. Trust is very hard for me as well. If you say no, I'll understand, but if you want those answers then you'll have to trust me."

"Our life together. Was it good?"

Skye smiled. "A picture speaks a thousand words." He pulled out his handheld and pulled up the picture that they had released to all of Vespia. Heather caught in a middle of an orgasm, head back, eyes closed, mouth slightly opened.

"So beautiful." Storm brushed his fingers against the image. He had seen the real thing, and the image just made him want to experience it again. He looked at Heather. She still knelt next to the two who had died. Seeing her hurting like this bothered him. The desire to wipe away the pain was a palpable thing. "We need time."

"The one thing we don't have."

———

Storm touched Heather's arm. "Come, walk with me."

He could tell she didn't want to, but there wasn't anything she could do in the medlab. The rest of the place had been cleaned up and guards were in place.

Heather finally nodded. After saying her goodbyes to the person she spoke to, she stood and followed him out of the room.

"This man Skye, how well do you trust him?" They headed to the section Fridon had just returned power to.

"Before I was kidnapped? I trusted him with my life, but with all this talk about a time shift I'm not sure what to think."

"You don't believe him?" He slipped his arm around her waist. The desire building in him drove him to touch her.

"I don't know what to believe." She looked up at him. "You really think that dream was part of the other reality?"

"There were too many things in that dream you couldn't know about." He was quiet for a moment. He itched to bare some skin but wasn't sure how this little human would respond. They needed to get further away from everyone before he allowed his libido to take control. "You made a comment earlier about taking it from my mind. What did you mean?"

"I've been able to read minds recently."

"What? Really?" He stopped them from walking and turned her to face him. "Can you read mine right now?"

"You're taking this awfully well."

"On my planet, we have a religious leader who has abilities no one can explain, but we have learned over the years to never question them. They have never been wrong in their leadership." He touched her face. "This ability is a lot like that."

"Then it doesn't frighten you?"

"What frightens me is this all-encompassing need I have for you. When I am on missions I remain a soldier. But with you, all I can think of is what we shared." His fingers traced the spot where her mark had been in their shared dream. "And how much I want to share that with you again."

That pretty pink hue filled her cheeks again.

"This color that fills your cheeks from time to time is

lovely." He brushed a thumb across it. "Why does it do that?"

"It's a blush and it shows up when we're embarrassed."

"I have embarrassed you?"

"No, well, the thought of the great sex we had caused this." She pressed her hands on her cheeks. "I get a little flushed when I get aroused."

"Really?" Storm smiled, knowing she was as affected as he was. The smile that spread across his face expressed his happiness at her comment. "Then you want this as badly as I do."

He backed her up against a nearby wall. Before she could argue with him, he captured her lips with his. His hands worked on the seals of her uniform, easing it off her once he opened the right ones. It took her a few seconds, but she started doing the same thing, pushing it off his body when she had enough open to remove it.

He slid his fingers into her folds and found she was ready so he centered himself and drove into her. As much as he wanted to arouse her properly, neither needed it right now. She broke the kiss and sucked in her breath as he slid in deep. "Are you okay?"

"Oh, yes." Her hands closed around his derriere, pulling him closer.

That silent piece of communication was all he needed to set a strong pace. She felt so good, the way her body hugged him had him shaking in no time. The intimacy between them was powerful. He knew no other lover would hold a candle to what they shared here.

His lips worked their way down to her throat. The desire to mark her like she had been in the dream was strong, but he didn't want to do that without her understanding what it meant. He wasn't sure she was ready for that. Yet her throat called to him. Storm pressed his lips to her neck. The soft tissue warmed with the brief touch of his lips.

Heather moaned her pleasure, and he latched onto the delicate tissue, not thinking of anything more than to make her moan again.

Her muscles tightened against him. He felt them ripple against his shaft as she got closer to her orgasm. The exquisite sensation had him pumping into her faster. This was something he wanted all the time. He switched to long deep strokes and at first Heather didn't seem to be happy about it, but then he heard her breath catch. Suddenly she moved with him, meeting him thrust for thrust. There was a spot he hit that had her vibrating in his arms. He shifted his penetration, looking for the tale-tell signs that he found the sensitive spot again. When he did he was greeted with another moan and her release.

She clutched at him when it started. He could almost see it spread through her body as it flowed through her and took over. Her head dropped back, her eyes closed, the faint flush she spoke about filled her cheeks and it reminded him of the image Skye showed him. So beautiful. So passionate.

Her body clenched around him, and it was all it took to send him over the edge as well. It filled him with euphoria. The intensity overpowering him for a moment.

Their breath came out in short pants as they tried to regain control.

Storm didn't want to let go of her. She was almost bone-less once she relaxed against him. He held her as long as she let him.

"Wow." She opened her eyes and looked up at him. The softness of her gaze made his heart skip a beat.

"Do you still question that we belong together?" He brushed a few stray hairs from her face. "Because what we just shared tells me we do. We have a destiny. Maybe the timeline did change, but if it has, it is still trying to bring us together."

"I know." She looked away for a moment.

"You do?"

"Sam and I have a mind link. One I've been trying to ignore. She keeps pushing images at me. Ones that have meaning to her. Every one of them shows us together. Including a few where you're growling at Skye because you feel he's taking advantage of your daughter. Your over-protectiveness is quite endearing."

"I protect what is mine." He let her down so they could get dressed. "What about the medallions? Are you ready to wear yours?"

"I think so."

He held it out to her. "It sinks beneath the skin like Skye's did."

"Is that where yours is?" She took the necklace from him.

He nodded. Storm smiled when she slipped it around her neck and allowed it to sink into her skin.

"What now?"

"I believe we go speak to Skye and see what the next step is."

———

"My people need to be safe." Storm growled as he crossed his arms over his chest.

"They will be," said Skye. He fought a smile. That was the man he knew. "In my timeline, your smaller scout ships can outrun her large ship. I also don't think she's going to attack your people. She wants Heather and will not take the chance of harming her. If she follows her basic traits she'll wait until Heather has been returned to Earth where she'd have a better chance of grabbing her."

"How do you plan on tricking her into thinking Heather is on our ship?" asked Fridon.

"It will take some work, but I know she can't detect my ship. Once yours returns we'll have to boost your shields so she can't see inside your ship. The technology I have in this ship is more advanced and we'll make it look like everyone from the planet transported to your ship. It will take perfect timing, and our transporting must be exact, but we can make this work."

"And if she decides not to wait for Heather to go to Earth and boards the ship anyway to get her?" Storm didn't look happy with his plan.

"I'm hoping we'll have gotten to Susan and fixed the timeline by that point."

"Tell me more about this woman, Reasta." Heather had been quiet up until that point.

"She went to war to get you." Sam touched her mother's hand. "She sees you as the answer to her prayers."

"Why? I'm just a security officer."

"Skye, can I see your pad?" Sam held out her hand, not giving him a chance to say no. Once he handed it over, she tapped against the screen until she got what she wanted. She turned it so Heather could see it. "Can you read this please?"

"Joy of love, life, family is the key."

"That is a Vespian saying," commented Storm.

"Good, then you recognized it." She turned the small pad toward him. "Tell me what language this is."

He looked at it and sat back. Looking at Heather he replied, "That is the Ancient language."

"What? No." She pulled the pad back toward her. "It's Earth English..."

Weird symbols filled the small screen. Heather pushed it away. "That can't be right."

"Mom, sorry. Heather, you are Vespian and can read, speak and understand Ancient." Sam touched her hand again as she spoke. "We don't have time to work through this like we should. You have to accept and move on because the longer you refuse to believe us the less time we have to stop Susan."

Heather stood. "You are asking a lot."

"I know." Sam stood as well. "Yet we lived it. You have to trust us, or we'll never get the timeline right."

"Why me?"

"Because you are the center. It's not something you want, I know, but Susan wanted the job you ended up with. Now she is the one doing the treaty and she refuses to get it signed. She doesn't want to go back to Earth, she wants what you and Dad have—had." She rubbed a hand on her face. "This is so hard. How do you think I feel, being here, knowing you see me as a stranger instead of your daughter?"

"Perhaps we should take a break?" Skye stood as well. Sam was visibly upset, and he needed to calm her down.

"Yes," agreed Storm. He got up and ushered Heather away from the table.

Skye turned Sam to face him. "You okay?"

"Now I know how Mom felt being alone all those years." She took a deep breath. "I'll be okay in a minute. It's just I can hear her thoughts, and she doesn't want to believe any of this."

"Imagine how you would feel if I came to you and said we were bonded if you didn't know the timeline had changed." He brushed a strand of hair out of her face.

"I know and I keep reminding myself of that, but it's still hard. They're my parents, Skye. I want them back."

"And we'll get them back. I promise."

———

"So, what are the Ancients?" Heather had her arms crossed over her chest because she didn't know what to do with her hands.

"They were a race that lived on my planet thousands of years ago." He rested a hand on her arm. "You seem distracted."

"So no one has been around talking the language I could understand in a while, huh?"

Storm watched her. What was he expecting? For her to grow a second head? "We have historians."

"Historians? Great. I'm not a big enough of a freak."

"You are not a freak." Storm grabbed her by the arms. "You are special. The ability to read the Ancient language is very rare and those that have that ability are revered on my planet. If Sam is right and you can read, speak, and understand it you are the only one."

"How can I speak a language from a race I've never heard of before?"

"Perhaps that is a question for Sam and Skye. They seem to have all the answers."

"And that is just a little too convenient for me." She stepped away from him.

"Why are you fighting this so hard?"

"I don't have religious leaders who are never questioned. Ours are quite fallible." She glared at him. "To me, you are taking this too well."

"I don't question every little thing because I know how to trust and don't give me that haughty smile. We Vespians don't trust easily. You know our history."

"Then why do you trust them?" She watched his face. "Because of the dream?"

"You want to deny what we shared?"

"I—" Heather gripped his arms as her eyes rolled into the back of her head. Storm grabbed her before she slid to the floor.

———

Sam staggered against Skye. "I feel—"

Her eyes rolled up into the back of her head and she slumped to the ground. Skye caught her before she hit the floor.

"Damn it, Heather. Not again." He remembered this happened before when Reasta first showed up on the planet. Heather had created a special place in her mind where she felt safe. Whenever she pulled anyone in with her, they normally passed out like this.

Storm came running in with Heather in his arms. "Her too? Do we need a medic?"

"No. We just need a quiet place and give them time."

———

Sam found herself in a white room, although it really wasn't a room. It reminded her of the place Skye had tried to describe when he went into Heather's mind. When Reasta first showed up Heather used her mental abilities to work on a plan to defeat that horrible woman. Skye said they had gone deep into her mind, where Heather felt it was safe. She had never seen that part of her mother's mind, but her bond with her family came from a different level of her mind. She wondered why they went so deep this time if this was the same place.

"Hello?"

"Sam?" Heather appeared in front of her. "Where are we?"

"I believe we're in your mind." She looked around. "Not sure where though."

"And why do I keep getting flashes of these images?" Behind her pictures appeared. Some from the last timeline and some from their timeline.

The moment one appeared that Sam recognized, she touched it, halting to progression of images.

Heather laughed. "That tickled."

"Does this look familiar to you?" Sam would have to be careful if just touching a memory would make her mom laugh.

"No." Heather shook her head. "Should it?"

"It is the day you gave birth to the twins." Sam wished she knew how to make her relive it. What if they tried to step through the picture? Grabbing Heather's hand, she pulled her along as Sam tried to enter the picture. At first, it resisted, but like a thin veil, when she put enough pressure it tore, allowing them to pass through.

———

Heather sat up in bed and held their brand-new daughter in her arms, touching her tiny fingers with awe. "Twins, Storm, they are so beautiful."

"Just like their mother." Storm cradled her against his chest as he reclined on the same bed.

Sam held onto Heather's hand as they watched they scene unfold. "I was there that day. I watched you give birth to my brother and sister."

"Then the infant isn't you?"

"No."

"Why not?"

Sam didn't want to answer because she feared it would change the image. "It will become clear as we watch."

Kuarto came over with another small bundle. "Storm, are you ready for your son?"

He shifted a little so he could take the child while still supporting Heather's back. Kuarto gently laid the infant in his arms. He held his son close. "My heart."

Heather looked up at him with a big grin. "Softie."

"Ha. You are just as bad. I saw that tear when your brother handed you our daughter."

Kuarto came back in a few minutes later. "You have a visitor."

"Sam!" Heather smiled at her daughter. "Come and meet your sister and brother."

Kuarto brought a chair for Sam then left the room. She came up and gave her mom a hug then gave her dad the same thing. Sam stood for a few minutes, cooing at her sister and brother, offering a finger for them to grasp. "They are beautiful, Mom."

"Would you like to hold your sister?"

"Of course." Sam took her sister and sat in the chair left for her.

She watched herself and noticed the slight sadness fill her face.

"I'm sorry, Sam," Heather said.

"Mom, this wasn't your doing."

"I thought we'd get you back in time. I never suspected that Ialog would rapid age you." She touched her knee. "You're younger than the twins yet are full grown. I never wanted that."

Sam took her hand. "I know, but we can't change what happened. I don't want you to blame yourself over something that was out of our control."

"You went through a rapid age process?" Heather turned toward her. "I remember. This was when you asked me to wipe your mind. Allow you to go to Earth and find your way. That was when you met Skye."

Sam found herself floating away from Heather. "Mom?"

"The timeline memories are coming too fast, Sam. I can't hold you here anymore."

She opened her eyes and realized she was back in the ruins of the outpost. Sitting up, she found Skye at her side. The moment Storm saw her awake he moved to her as well.

"Is she okay?"

"She's fine." Sam smiled at Storm. "It takes a little getting used to, but this is normal for her from time to time."

"What is going on?" asked Skye.

"She's regaining her memories from both timelines. At least that's what I think is happening."

"How did she get her memories back?" asked Storm.

"I'm afraid it's my fault." Sam gave him an apologetic smile. "When I met her in her mind there were images nearby. I recognized one of them from when the twins were born, and I brought her into it so she could relive it. I think I created a tear that caused all the memories to escape."

"Is that possible?"

Sam looked at her father. She didn't know how to answer that question. It shouldn't be, but it was happening. "Bert kept saying Mom's mind was very powerful. He'd be the one to ask. He might not remember the other timelines, but I bet this wouldn't surprise him."

Heather opened her eyes.

"Are you alright?" Storm was at her side, brushing his fingers through the hair on the side of her face.

"I'm fine, my heart." She touched his face and smiled.

He moved back as she sat up. Heather looked at her daughter and opened her arms. "Sam."

"Oh, Mom, I'm so glad to have you back." She sat next to her and welcomed her hug. Resting her head on her shoulder, Sam sighed. The moment her mother looked at her, Sam saw the recognition that had been missing.

"Oh, sweetheart, I can't imagine what you have gone through." Heather held her close. "I don't understand how all this happened."

"We've already discussed this, but you should remember that." Skye narrowed his eyes at her.

"I do. I remember what you told us the last time too, but none of this makes sense. How did Susan get the machine? Who gave it to her? Reasta makes the most sense, but she said she didn't have any more energy to run another time-line shift so if she found another way why would she give it to Susan instead of using it herself?"

"Yep, you're back. Look, I've thought the same thing."

"Have you seen this machine she has?"

"No." Skye shook his head. "Never got the chance."

"What about Bert?"

"He was affected like you." Skye looked at her then Storm. "Bert wasn't in his compound when the original timeline was changed."

"But you spoke to him in the last timeline? He would have put on one of these medallions as well and could be working on how to fix the timeline."

"We need to gain control of whatever is causing this before we can fix everything."

"We start with Susan."

———

"This is how you were kept from being affected by the changes?" Heather looked around the small ship Skye commanded. She remembered Bert lending it to Skye on many occasions. "I never realized it had those options."

"I'm grateful it did have those options, if it hadn't, none of us would be aware of what had happened." Skye sat in his command chair and programmed the preflight checks to prepare for flight.

Heather wondered if the ship Storm got from Bert had it as well.

"This ship is Ancient in design." Storm touched several panels with Ancient writing on it only to have Skye slap his hand.

"Please don't touch anything. You never know what you might accidentally activate."

Storm glared at him. "I have been in command of enough ships to know what not to touch. This is not part of your bridge."

"Actually, it is." Skye pressed a few keys on the panel Storm had just stroked. "The design of this bridge is a lot different than a Vespian ship. I want to be sure we're properly cloaked before Reasta figures out there are two ships here, not one. We can't let her attack the other ship."

"And if she does?"

"Then we'll have to reveal ourselves." Skye sat back. "Why don't you let Sam show you to your room? I'll call if there's trouble."

Heather took Storm's hand and urged him to follow Sam.

"It's not the biggest room, but it should be comfortable enough for you."

"Thank you, sweetheart." Heather touched her forehead to her daughters. "I'm going to try to free your father's memories."

"You really think you can?" Sam backed up from her mom and hit the panel to open the door to their room.

"I won't know until I try."

The door opened.

"I have been quite insistent." Storm wrapped his arms around Heather as he smiled at Sam. "It's not fair that everyone but me remembers."

"Yes, he has been, and he's right. If he can regain his memory, then all of us will be able to push harder to regain the right timeline." Heather turned so she could run her fingers along his jaw. "But I don't know how difficult this will be, so I wanted to wait until we were safe on this ship to work on it."

Sam nodded. "Good luck. I love you, Mom."

"Love you too, sweetheart." Heather turned to her mate as the door sealed them in.

"What now?"

Heather pressed her palm against his heart. "We get undressed."

"Oh, I like this already." He opened the seals of his uniform. "Why do we need to get undressed?"

"Because our mental connection is the strongest when we climax. That's when our bond first started. I've never tried what I'm about to do and I want to give us every chance to make this work." Heather removed her uniform. She felt the heat of his hand on the side of her throat before she removed the last part.

"In that dream we shared your mark was right here." He brushed his fingers against the spot. "Is that where I marked you?"

"Yes." She smiled at him as she stepped out of the outfit and into his arms. "You gave it to me before we were mated. Your sister wasn't very happy with you when she saw it, but we've never done much of anything the normal Vespian way. My mark is something I'm very proud of. It's also very sensitive to your touch."

"My touch? Really?" He touched the spot again. "Do you think it will appear now that you have broken the veil between timelines?"

"I don't see how." Heather moved to the bed. "You haven't given it to me yet."

"I wish to." Storm followed her. "The desire to mark you has been overpowering."

"You've been fighting it?" She sat on the bed and pulled him with her.

"I couldn't give it to you without you understanding what it meant. The mark is our way of picking our mate. What if you didn't want that? What if my people decide my mate must be Vespian?" He sat next to her before easing her to the mattress. "But now I know we're supposed to be together. We're mated in another timeline."

"You said once that nothing can separate us. This proves it." She touched his face as he moved to cover her body with his.

"I wish to arouse you, show you how much I enjoy being with you, but my need to feel your muscles surround me is as overpowering as my desire to mark you." He centered himself and drove into her. He pressed soft kisses against her forehead as he allowed her body to adjust to his invasion.

"There have been many times when we barely made it out of our clothes, my heart. I love it when you lose control." She brushed a bit of hair out of his face as she shifted her legs to wrap them around his waist.

He started to move, Heather could tell he wanted to take his time, but the sensations they were feeling wouldn't let him. He set a nice strong pace that she picked up pretty quickly. Slow wasn't going to work right now. She tilted her hips to give him better penetration. Storm wrapped his arms around her, drawing her into his embrace, before pulling them up into a seated position. She grinned. It was her favorite position. She started to move against him, intensifying those exquisite sensations and drawing a moan from him. His lips captured hers, his tongue demanding entrance, which she gladly gave. Their tongues danced together, heightening their desire for each other.

He broke the kiss after a while, pressing his lips across her cheek then down her throat. She felt him pull the soft tissue where her mark should be into his mouth. It was her turn to moan.

Heather knew she needed to connect with his mind so when they climaxed their minds should flow together. Soft gentle brushes against his thoughts had him sucking in his breath.

"Is that you?"

"Yes, my heart." She ran her hands up his back, caressing his muscles along the way.

"I have never felt anything so erotic." He pumped into her faster. "It is like silk weaving through my thoughts."

She loved every stroke. Each one went deep and glided against a sensitive spot. It wasn't long before she could feel her release inching its way through her. It started slowly, deep inside, blossoming up, then it raced through her blood, filling her with joy and flinging her to the stars.

Her mind opened and brushed against his. She could feel his desire then release as their minds bonded once more.

"Where are we?" asked Storm.

"Your mind, my heart." The moment they hit their orgasm, and their minds entwined she allowed him to draw them into his memories.

"Do you know what to look for?"

"Yes." She pressed her hand against his heart. "I have been here before. Your mind is very neat, like a computer. Now, I need you to think about our life together. Whatever you wish to remember."

A screen popped up beside them. His files were neatly lined up with different colors for different people. His mother was always a royal blue, his sister an emerald green.

"Perhaps we should start with how we met. That might allow us to move to the other timeline easier." Heather touched the small purple disc and watched as their first meeting unfolded. "We can be observers here. I want you to keep this screen in front of us."

"Alright." He kept his focus on the scene in front of him as well as the screen that held his memories. "What is that gray one?"

"That should be the memories from the other timeline." Heather tapped it but it refused to open. "I'm hoping as this scene unfolds, you'll be able to access it."

"Like this?" The file still remained gray but opened to show a few of the discs that held his memories. "Why so few?"

"I'm assuming your childhood didn't change just the last few years. From the point where we should have met."

"So you assume you're the top one?"

"No. If you look at your other files the latest people you have met are on top. Me, Sam and Skye." She touched the file, and it vibrated. "Since you only have a few and you met Skye and Sam after me I should be the third one."

Storm focused on the file Heather had touched. It vibrated for him as well, but still didn't open. "Perhaps if we touched it at the same time?"

"And maybe I should tell you about how we met. Maybe that will help unlock the memory." She turned to face him. "I worked for Admiral Barrister. He was in charge of protecting our president. Any functions he was supposed to attend Bear had to oversee. You and he had become friends because of it."

Storm frowned. "The first time I noticed you was when you were trying to get something from under your desk."

"Noticed?"

"We had met before, but you were always in the background." He grabbed her by the arms. "I remember!"

The scene unfolded around them.

"Your eyes were the first thing I noticed about you. So beautiful. You did your job well, never speaking unless spoken to. Making sure your admiral and president were cared for and protected." Storm touched her face. "Then one day I came into the admiral's office."

FIVE

The doors opened for Storm, and he stepped into the room to find the admiral's assistant on all fours, trying to reach something just beyond her grasp. He tilted his head and watched as her derriere moved while she tried to reach whatever was eluding her. He had to admit he loved the view. The admiral's assistant was a beautiful woman, and he bet she'd be a passionate lover.

"Come here, you stupid stylus." As she reached a little further her uniform tightened around her buttocks. Well-rounded and firm, a part of him wanted to see what it looked like without the uniform hiding it from him.

He shook his head. He wasn't intimate with humans anymore. He had put one too many in the hospital in his desire to have sex with humans.

The doors were silent so she couldn't know he was there, yet something alerted her. In her haste to stand up, she bumped her head on the underside of her desk. Rubbing the injured spot, she stood and faced him. "So, how long were you there?"

"Long enough." He smiled. Even upset at being caught

that way there was a grace and beauty about her. "I know how troublesome those styluses can be."

She laughed and he thought it was a beautiful sound.

"The Admiral is out of the office for the moment, Ambassador. Did you want to come back? I can make you aware when he returns."

"He already made me aware that I might arrive before him and since my schedule is clear for the moment I shall wait for him." He moved over to an oversized chair. Storm knew he was early, but he didn't want to spend too much time in the embassy. If he did, he might have to spend time with Susan and he found her boring. "If I was on Vespia I'd have plenty to do, but on your planet, I end up with a lot of time on my hands."

"The Admiral isn't due back for a half hour." She picked up her pad. "Perhaps you would like to go get some coffee?"

"Yes. Your admiral has introduced me to the liquid, and I found I like it." He wasn't sure if being amongst humans was a good idea. His pheromones could wreak havoc with some, but the thought of being with this woman had him agreeing anyway.

She led the way. They entered a quiet cafe within the security building. After she ordered two coffees she gestured to a table. Someone brought their coffee over a few minutes after they sat down.

A quiet stretched between them, giving him time to study her. His steady gaze must have made her uncomfortable.

"So how is married life?" Her mannerisms showed she wished she hadn't asked that. She hunched her shoulders and looked down.

"You wish to know if we have sex."

"What? No!" A beautiful soft shade of pink filled her

cheeks. "I was just wondering how Susan was adjusting to Vespian life."

"She isn't allowed to interact with our people." At her questioning look he held up his hand. "I know your people would probably not be happy to learn that, but within a few days she upset the entire council, our religious leader, and a handful of our leading citizens. It was decided if we want this treaty to go through, we must isolate her so she doesn't cause any more harm."

"I'm so sorry. Susan wasn't one of my favorites either, but I thought she would have been trained better." Heather looked behind him before she focused on him once more.

"You know her then."

"We went to school together." Heather straightened in her seat and looked off into the distance. Then she started talking to herself.

"Yes, sir." Then there was a pause. "Yes, sir." She pressed a small disc on her collar and looked at Storm. "The admiral would like to talk to you."

She must have been talking to him through some sort of insert.

"Admiral?" He wasn't sure what to expect until he heard the admiral speaking.

"Storm, I'm sorry, but the president asked for my impute to get ready for the function this evening. It has taken longer than I anticipated, and I can't make our appointment. My assistant has all the details on what you need to know about the event tonight. She'll be the one to escort you as well."

Storm smiled. He found the captain fascinating so spending more time with her made him happy. "That is fine, Admiral. I will see you this evening, then."

Several women were inching closer to the table they sat at. Storm knew his pheromones were starting to affect the people in the small cafe. "Perhaps we should go back to your office to discuss this?"

Heather nodded. As they walked back to her office, she explained how the evening would go so he could relate the information to the rest of his party. He nodded at the right times as he watched her. Why was he so fascinated by her? What he needed to do was focus on the conversation, not her.

His mother and sister had been through several of these Earth functions before, so he knew all he had to do was remind them of some of the expectations. Susan lived here and he hoped she would know how to behave, but he would have to talk to her to be sure.

———

Heather arrived in a large private transport. Storm was happy she brought such a large ship to fit everyone. If she hadn't, he would be the one to pilot the other ship. This way would give him more time with this alluring woman. Personally, he would have been happier if it had just been the two of them, but it was safer this way. Having his family with him kept him from doing something he might regret.

She wasn't wearing her uniform this evening, but a beautiful black gown that hugged her frame. The dress covered one shoulder but left the other bare and the slit in the skirt had him wanting to explore to see how high it went.

She greeted his mother and sister with the proper bow. She stood by the door as they entered the ship.

"Why is she here?" hissed Susan.

Storm gripped her arm. He kept his voice low as he spoke to her. "She is our escort so behave."

She gave him a hurt look but remained quiet after that.

They arrived early to give the Vespian party time to meet with the president before the function started. He didn't care about any of that. All he wanted to do was talk to Heather again, but after bringing them to the president's suite she went to work, protecting her president and the admiral.

He didn't see much of her that evening, but he found whenever he did spot her, she had his undivided attention. Heather had a beautiful comb in her hair, and it caught the light, allowing him to find her in the crowd. Susan also noticed where his attention kept going because she complained that he never gave her that kind of attention. He didn't have the heart to tell her she didn't fascinate him the way the captain did.

Storm spent most of the evening wishing he was alone with the captain instead of being trapped at Susan's side. The only good thing was when she demanded she sat next to him which made her spend most of the evening with her back to the crowd. He got a perverse joy from that.

Storm knew she always wanted to be the center of attention and pushed to give her the right seat to so she could have that, even when it went against protocol. Vespian mates sat opposite of each other instead of side-by-side. He always gave her the seat he should occupy so she could look out at the crowd, but Susan didn't understand the Vespian way and tonight proved she didn't care.

A flash caught his eye once again, and he thought it was Heather, but he didn't see her. Instead, he saw a man running at him with a blade in his hand. Storm stood just as the man landed on the ground and Heather dropped a knee into his back. She pulled the weapon from his hands as she stretched out the leg next to the slit and pulled out restraints from a small circle high on that thigh.

The man struggled with her, but she jammed her knee harder into his back. "I don't think so."

Storm headed toward her to offer assistance.

Guards came to her aid and took the man into custody.

Heather stood, grumbling.

"Problem?" He was close enough now to touch her. The desire to pull her into his arms and make sure she was okay was powerful, but he was able to maintain their distance.

"Sorry, ambassador. It's not easy to apprehend a man in this dress." She looked up at him with a smile. "It seems that the air system isn't doing its job anymore. Unless you want more of that I suggest you say your goodbyes to the president. The admiral has arranged for someone from our security to take you back to the embassy."

"I cannot leave until my mother makes the decision. She is the head of the council." He touched her hair. "You seemed to have lost your comb."

Heather's hand went to the spot where it had rested. "Well, crap. That was given to me by my guardian."

She looked around but didn't see it. A signal from the admiral had her touching his arm. "I'll check with security tomorrow. Hopefully, they will locate it. Thank you for trying to help me find it."

Such a simple thing and he felt it deep inside. Her president was leaving. He made his way around to say goodbye to all the dignitaries then headed to his own people. Once Heather was gone, he caught a bit of sparkle out of the corner of his eye. He crouched down and found her comb. Even though he knew he should just turn it in to Earth's security, he slipped it into a pocket then strode to his mother's side. Hopefully, she would be ready to leave now.

Storm sat in his office, playing with the comb. The design reminded him of a few Ancient pieces they had found over the years. Perhaps they had been to Earth as well. He couldn't stop thinking about Heather. His body wasn't helping either. The erection he had wouldn't go away. A sigh escaped him as he stood. He pressed a button in his collar. "I'm going out for a while."

No one would dare argue with him. Before he left the embassy, he knew this wasn't a good idea, but he couldn't help himself. He was a little bit obsessed. He knew where her quarters were. Something he had researched earlier today. Storm found himself standing outside her room, debating with himself. Not quite sure how it happened, he heard the buzzer then her voice permitting him to enter.

The doors opened for him, and he stepped in.

"Ambassador?" She stood when she saw him.

She looked beautiful. A simple white shift rested against her skin, the silky material not leaving a whole lot to his imagination.

"Were you expecting someone else?"

"I normally get the report from the functions that happened the previous night about now." The door sounded again. Heather looked at him before she opened it. Instead of allowing whoever was there to enter she stayed by the door, took a small crystal and thanked whoever was on the other side. After they left, Heather closed the door and sat the crystal on the glass coffee table, turning her attention back to him.

"I found your comb." He held it out to her.

She gingerly took it from him. "Oh, thank you so much." Instinct had her hugging him before she remembered who he was. Heather dropped her arms and stepped back. "I'm sorry, sir. That was a bit forward of me."

She looked down, which he found endearing. She must

have studied because she knew the Vespian way. He hooked a finger under her chin and lifted her head so she would look at him. "I rather liked that."

The smile she gave him melted any reserve he had. All he wanted to do was touch her again, feel her body beneath his, and watch her face as her release overpowered her. He stepped up to her, wrapped his arms around her, and claimed her mouth with his. Her lips were soft, pliable, and fit his perfectly. They opened for him, allowing him to deepen the kiss the way he wanted.

The gown she wore hid her from him. Hooking his fingers in the thin straps, he eased it off her shoulders before he broke the kiss then blazed a trail down her throat. She might be tall for a human woman, but she was petite by Vespian standards. Storm wanted to level the playing field. He also didn't want to take her by force.

He broke the kiss and gently ran a finger against her jaw. "You are so beautiful, and I wish to be intimate with you, but if this isn't something you want, I will leave. Whichever way you decide will not affect the way we will work together."

"What about Susan?"

"Vespians don't pick their mates by signing a piece of paper and end that same choice with another piece of paper. Susan is in charge of the treaty. That is all she means to me. I live in my own apartment on Vespia." He traced the edge of her collarbone. "I don't really like her that much."

Heather didn't say anything but took his hand and guided him to her bedroom. "This might not be the smartest thing I've ever done, but I want you, too."

Her nightgown now rested on her hips. He slipped his fingers inside to help it over her hips and watched as it pooled at her feet. Storm broke the seals of his shirt while Heather worked on his trousers. Soon he was devoid of clothing, like her. Wrapping his arms around her again, he captured her lips with his and moved them toward the bed. He didn't want to give her a chance to back out now that she said yes.

Easing her onto the mattress, he joined her and continued his assault. He pressed kisses to her throat and collarbone then worked his way down to one breast. He paid homage to it before he moved to the other one.

She started to move beneath him, reaching for him, wanting more.

"Ambassador."

He lifted his head to look at her. "Please, would you want me to call you captain right now? You can use my name."

"Sorry. Habit, I guess, Storm." She looked at him. "But I'm a little nervous."

He liked the way she said his name. "Why?"

She laughed. "You know how much trouble I'd get into if anyone found out about this? It better be worth it."

"Oh, I promise it will be worth it. I never leave a woman until they are fully satisfied." He centered himself and drove in deep. She felt so good. Her muscles rippled against him, surrounding him with her incredible heat. He gave her a few moments to adjust to him before he started to move. Slowly at first, but he picked up the pace because each time he entered her felt so right.

She met him thrust for thrust, her breath started coming out in little pants as she got closer to her release. He changed the pace, making them longer and deeper. Heather kept up with him, angling her hips more so he could get the best penetration. His body wanted its release and pushed him to pick up the pace, but he made a promise. One he planned on keeping.

He could see she was getting lost in the sensations

racking her body. She was very quiet, so he watched her for the physical signs showing she was close. Those beautiful violet eyes opened just as her breath hitched.

He started to move faster. Heather picked up the tempo as well. They raced together for the elusive prize they both wanted. Heather hit hers and he was only seconds behind hitting his.

———

Storm touched her face. "That moment was when I knew you were the one I wanted to mate with. No woman had ever brought me to such heights before."

"That is because we belong together." She smiled as she gripped his hands. "Be prepared, my heart."

"For what?" He looked at her curiously.

"For the rest of the memories. They should start flooding your mind now."

Another memory dropped into his mind, then another and another. Soon they were coming too fast for him to keep up. He heard Heather's voice from a long distance. "Don't let go of me, Storm. We have to stay connected here in your mind or you won't get your original memories back."

The speed at which they raced through his mind continued to pick up, driving him to his knees but he didn't let go. Finally, they started to slow down, decreasing the pain in his head. It wasn't too much later when he could see Heather again.

"How are you feeling?"

"I'm fine, my heart." He didn't want to stop. "My head is still settling, but I can keep going."

She touched the second grayed circle. "This one could be a lot worse. You'll have the memories from our life twice and there was a lot more than what you just went through."

"Twice?"

"You lost your memory once so I'm assuming to gain back all your memories, you'll have to go through that again." Once again, the file wouldn't open. She looked at him. "It's not working for me."

Storm touched the grey circle, and the file opened, but all the attachments were the same gray color. "Which one?"

"I don't know. Focus on something powerful that happened, like the birth of the twins."

"Or the first time I met you?" He touched her face as the scenery around them started to solidify.

She laughed. "It wasn't the best beginning. When I was assigned to protect you my first impression of you was of a playboy. Then you compromised my security position by coming right up to me and mimicking me."

"Why did you put up with me?" He brushed a few hairs behind her ears.

"At first it was because of my job, but we shared a kiss that started thawing out the ice princess."

"Ice princess?"

"My nickname."

"That's right." He smiled. "You hadn't found me yet to thaw you out."

"Do you remember?"

"I'm not sure. Were we in a closet or something?"

"Yes." She pressed her hand against his heart. "There were intruders in the embassy, and I think we had the same idea, hide until they passed then attack from behind. But we never made it out of the closet."

"Were we intimate?"

"Not then."

He captured the hand she had rested on his chest. "But I do remember this. Our gesture of affection."

Heather nodded. "Something you started."

"In the first timeline, you have your mark, long hair, and a nice strong body. You are too thin in the timeline we're in now."

"Not something I could have helped. The rations were meager, and I wanted to be sure everyone had enough food."

"Everyone but you. My heart, you can't put yourself last all the time."

"You would have done the same thing. My people came first. I can survive on what I gave myself. I did survive."

"Do you know what happened to the twins?"

"No. I have no connection with them, but I don't feel a void either." She rested her head against his chest as they continued to talk. Unlike the last time, the memories seem to come to him at a nice slow pace. They talked about things and the memory would be there. They didn't come out of their room until they reached Vespia.

Sam looked frightened until Storm smiled at her and held his arms out to her. She ran to her father and hugged him. "I'm so glad to have you back."

"I am glad to be back."

They were flagged by Vespian security once more when they entered Vespian space, but the image of Storm on the bridge gave them the clearance they needed. Skye landed the ship, and they disembarked. Storm headed to the council chambers with everyone in tow.

His mother showed surprise for a moment when he entered the hall. He bowed then waited for them to allow him to approach.

"I wish to know where Susan is."

"We have not seen her. She is probably in her apartment." His mother looked at the rest of them. "You have strangers with you?"

Always straight to the point. Heather wanted to smile but knew any reaction she gave would raise more questions.

"I do, and I shall explain it all, but first I wish to speak to Susan."

"I believe you need to introduce these people before we allow them to wander around Vespia."

"Mother, they won't be wandering, but with me the whole time."

She kept waiting.

"This is going to sound a bit fantastic." Storm turned to Heather and offered her his hand. "This is my mate, Heather. We were mated in another timeline, and someone has been trying to change that. This is Samantha, my daughter, and her bond mate, Skye." He turned to Sam and offered his other hand so she would step up with him.

Toki came from behind the chairs the elders sat in. She didn't speak as she walked around them. She stopped in front of Heather. "You know me?"

"Yes, Toki, I do. You are Storm's sister and my brother's mate."

"Mate?"

"In my timeline, yes. Just before you became religious leader you met him, and you were granted permission to mate with him before you took over for Storm's uncle. We are also very close. Your position forces you to keep a lot more secrets, but our friendship is strong." She smiled at her friend. "We don't have a lot of time. We think Susan is behind this and we need to stop her before she changes the timeline again."

"Storm could have told you enough about our way of life so you could create this story."

"Anseri, you tested me before, perhaps you should again."

"My heart." Storm's voice made her turn to look at him.

"Their trust is as important as catching Susan." She turned back to the council. Ancient language flowed out of her. She knew her father would understand her. Her mother would ask the questions, and Toki would test her ability to read it. "I was genetically engineered and am Ancient. I can speak, read and understand the language. I am the child that was sent away for my protection."

Her mother gasped.

"How is that possible?" asked her father.

"I was created by an Ancient named Ialog." She waited for her father to translate.

"Why don't we know about him?" asked Anseri.

"Because the information was blocked from your memory. I was the one to unlock those memories in the original timeline." Heather knew they were getting into dangerous territory. It could take hours for her to explain everything if they continued down this path. "He was on this planet and even helped you become pregnant with Storm and Toki, Anseri."

"We need to fix the timeline, Mother. The longer you hold us, the greater the chance Susan will change it again."

"How?"

"We don't know."

Anseri looked at one of the guards. "Go and get her."

He nodded before he left the chambers.

"Now," she faced them. "You have no proof of this other timeline. The fact that this woman can speak Ancient doesn't prove anything."

Skye had gone to the screen the hall had. Heather had watched him out of the corner of her eye when he first moved. He had synced his handheld with the Vespian system. "I can."

"How?"

"Sam and I were protected when the timeline changed.

This device has a temporal block so all the data from where we came from is in here. I can show you the Vespian news feeds about your son and his mate." He brought up images and feeds that showed the life Heather and Storm had shared.

Susan could be heard arguing with the guard escorting her long before she entered the room. Skye turned off the screen and disconnected his handheld so Susan couldn't see the data he had shown the council.

The moment she saw Heather, Susan stopped arguing and focused on her. "You! How do you keep turning up?"

"What are you talking about Susan? The ambassador just rescued me." Heather knew not to give Susan any information.

Susan shifted her gaze to Storm. "That was the mission you were on? To help her?"

"And her people." Storm crossed his arms over his chest. "Who is this woman to you?"

"We went to school together." Susan shook her head, trying to get her hair to fall the way she wanted. She ended up having to push it behind her ears. The Vespian air was different than Earth and made it difficult for her to do what she wanted with her hair.

"I wish you to go back to Earth," said Storm.

"Why?" Susan narrowed her eyes at Heather.

"You have taken too long to get this treaty signed. I have spoken to your planet, and they have picked a replacement for you."

"It's Heather, isn't it?" Susan demanded. "Somehow she weaseled her way in anyway."

"Anyway, Susan? What do you mean?" asked Heather.

"Never mind."

"I have no control over who our government chooses," responded Heather, she wasn't going to push Susan. It could give them away before they could stop her. "They just knew you weren't doing your job."

"Why not?"

"Because we need the Vespians, not the other way around. You dragging your heels didn't help the situation. They are tired of it and want this treaty signed."

"And why didn't they say this to me?"

"Because they have tried, but you chose to ignore them." Storm stepped forward. "You are no longer wanted on Vespia. You are to pack your bags and go back to Earth. A replacement will be chosen later."

"Right. You have already chosen my replacement and it's her." The venom in her voice made Heather want to step back a little. "There is something about her that you can't stay away from."

"Why does this woman bother you so much? You haven't complained about any of my partners, yet she shows up and you are acting like you can lay claim to me when we know that isn't true. You're here to get the treaty signed. That is all, and since you can't get that job done properly, you're going to be replaced."

Heather watched Susan as Storm spoke to her. He portrayed the man she met at the outpost perfectly and didn't give Susan anything to latch onto. The woman started to rub a bracelet she wore on her wrist. It was a very unique design. Not one she recognized. A stone that dominated the design started to glow and just as she realized what was happening everything went black.

SIX

Time stopped as Susan touched her bracelet. "Damn it! How do they keep finding each other?" She circled Heather. "What is it going to take?"

This should have been so easy. Even though she altered the time when Heather and Storm would have met, she had only been able to be the wife of an ambassador for a few weeks. Not enough time to enjoy her new position and Storm didn't treat her the way he treated Heather when she did get time with him. Somehow, she needed to make him love her and forget about Heather.

She needed to get to the machine and try again. Thank goodness she had found this bracelet when she found the machine so she could stop time. No one could possibly know what she was up to, so it was time to try again.

———

Heather watched in amazement as her reality faded away. The hall came apart in front of her, giving way to stars whizzing by her and she moved from Vespia to Earth. A building started to go up around her.

At first, the walls surrounding her were nondescript but then she noticed a light pink hue to them, then furniture started to appear and personal effects. She found herself lying down when the new reality kicked in and time started moving again. When she went to sit up to take in her surroundings better, she found she couldn't move. Fear sliced through her. Was she restrained?

Lifting her hands, she found nothing to stop her from moving then she looked toward her feet.

"Well, crap." She was pregnant, very pregnant. It looked like she was in her third trimester by the size of her stomach. Oh, if she had to go through childbirth again, she was going to beat Susan to a pulp.

The door to the room opened and her brother popped his head in. "Sweetheart, I thought you were resting?"

"Kuarto?" The words just blurted out of her mouth. He called her sweetheart. He wasn't responsible for this was he? She touched her stomach. *Eeww.*

"Can't sleep?"

"Can't get comfortable." She shifted on the bed but couldn't find a way to a seated position. "I also feel like a turtle trapped on its back right now."

Kuarto chuckled as he helped her up. "It won't be much longer before you can sleep on your stomach again."

Not something she wanted to hear. Her brother just confirmed what she feared. She was going to have this baby, and soon.

"Look, I know this frightens you." He sat down next to her. "To make it all this way without knowing if the babies can make it through childbirth is nerve-wracking, but we've done everything we can do. They will be as healthy as they can be for the birth."

Babies? As in more than one? Was she carrying the twins? Why couldn't she feel the connection she had felt before? Could it be because in this timeline she hadn't developed her mental abilities? So many questions with no answers. She needed to focus on what she could learn right now.

Her brother didn't say their child. That was a good sign. If it wasn't him, who was the father? She didn't notice any pictures of her with a man. Maybe a casual encounter caused this. She nodded, grateful he misread her concerned look. "What if the father wants them?"

"You know the sperm I used came from a Vespian male. There is no way he'd find out."

She stood, bracing her hand against her back. Vespian male? Could it be Storm's? She had a thousand more questions but knew her brother would become suspicious if she asked any of them and trying to explain that she was from another timeline would just make him think she was going crazy. "Perhaps if I worked on my journal a little, that normally calms me."

"Good idea." He helped her to a large, overstuffed chair in her room. After settling her, he went and retrieved her journal as well as something cold to drink. "Dian will be here in an hour. I'll come and get you when she arrives."

Dian? Was she her guardian in this timeline as well?

Heather spent the next hour going through her journal. The other her knew Kuarto was her brother. Dian had found him several years before and introduced them, but they never told anyone about their relationship. It worked in their favor, too. She and Kuarto had pretended to be a couple and married to keep people from questioning her pregnancy.

He had been one of the many doctors trying to find a cure for the almost zero population and had been lucky enough to be part of the team to go through the files of the Vespian doctors trying to find the same cure. He found notes that he wanted to follow up and at first the government went along. He was able to get a hold of several vials of Vespian semen. When none of the eggs he had used had taken the government decided to shut down his research.

Kuarto tried to make them see how close he was, but they refused to listen. That was when he turned to her. He had snuck one set of Vespian semen home, and he thought he could make it work. He had run his computations and felt if he used it on her she would become pregnant. She had been excited about the idea. Even gave up her commission when the time came, and she couldn't hide her pregnancy anymore.

"Heather? Dian is here."

She looked up from her journal. Turning off the screen she sat her small pad on the table then pushed herself to her feet. This ought to prove interesting.

"Look at you!" The shocked look on her face hinted she hadn't seen the other Heather in a while. They hugged then moved to the couch. "How are you?"

"As well as can be expected." She wasn't sure what to say to Dian. One wrong thing could give her away. A smile filled her lips as she rubbed her stomach when she felt a kick.

"You look radiant."

"That's what everyone says to a pregnant woman."

"True, but for you my dear it is accurate." She studied Heather. "You're different. More confident. I think this pregnancy has given you something you were missing."

"You think?" Heather knew where the confidence came from. Her mate.

"I have a present for you." Dian handed her a small box.

"You didn't have to."

"I wanted to give this to you when I first learned of your pregnancy, but I decided to wait." She touched Heather's cheek. "I've been called away and I fear I might miss the birth of my newest niece so wanted to go ahead and give it to you now."

Heather sat the package on her knee. She looked at Dian then opened it. Pushing the tissue paper aside, she lifted a beautiful comb out. It was the same comb that brought her and Storm together two timelines ago. Was this something she needed to keep? "It's beautiful, Dian."

"I had it designed with you in mind."

"How so?" Heather tucked a piece of stray hair behind her ear before slipping the comb into her hair. "I've always had short hair before this and always seemed to be in uniform. A comb this pretty would have sat in a drawer most of the time."

"I know, but you're no longer in the military."

Kuarto came into the room, and he looked worried.

"Is there a problem?" Heather welcomed the intrusion.

"I'm not sure. I'm wondering, though, if we should move."

"Move? Where?"

"Off planet?" He sat in a chair near the couch she and Dian sat on. "I think the Vespians have gotten wind of what we're trying to do, and as much as I want to share this information with them, I want to be sure it works, and we won't know until you give birth."

"What makes you think they have gotten wind?" Heather looked at Dian. Storm was probably looking for her and somehow her brother found out about it.

"Because they have been asking about you."

Heather wanted to tell him about Storm but wasn't sure if her brother would believe her. "And you want to run because they're asking about me? This close to my due date?"

"I know, I'm probably just being paranoid, but I'd rather be safe than sorry."

"And how do you plan on hiding this?" She rubbed her stomach. She needed to think fast. "Look, I've heard of this guy who can check into why the Vespians are looking for me without drawing attention. He'd be able to find out if they learned about my pregnancy. His name is Skye Latimer and he's very good at his job."

"You think that's smart?"

"I have heard of him," said Dian. "He's one of the best."

"He can find out why my name is being bandied about. If you're right, he'd know, and then we can decide if we need to leave and find some backwater little planet to have these babies or can stay put."

Kuarto didn't seem happy about her idea, but she needed to connect with Storm, Skye and Sam. If her brother wanted to hide them, her friends needed to know where to find her.

"Please? The thought of running right now frightens me. I don't want to hurt the twins."

"Can you get an appointment with him today?"

"I'm sure I can." She smiled as she relaxed. Skye wouldn't turn her away. All she had to do was find him.

———

They sat in the waiting room of Skye's office. In this timeline, he had given up his commission and started a private security business. Earth security used him from time to time to go after things they couldn't. It was one of the reasons he had such a nice office.

Heather was wrapped up in a dove-gray cloak to hide

her pregnancy as they waited to speak to him. Dian didn't come with them. She had to head out on the mission she had hinted about earlier.

Kuarto made her wear the hood as well to hide her face, even while they sat in the lobby waiting. He didn't want anyone to recognize her in her condition which made her wonder if he had kept the other her secluded in her last trimester. She found the damn thing suffocating and wanted to take it off, but when she had opened her cape earlier, he blocked her from view as he readjusted everything. She didn't want that to happen again because the last time she wanted to slap his hands away and if he tried it again, she might not be able to stop herself.

Her brother was pacing back and forth. It was obvious he was worried they'd be caught before they could get away. "What is taking so long?"

"Kuarto, sit down, please. Mr. Latimer said he could squeeze us in. I'm sure he'll be with us as soon as he can."

The young woman in the reception area called their name after Skye's previous appointment left the office.

"He'll see you now."

Kuarto was the first up and helped her to her feet. They entered his office and took two chairs opposite him. Skye didn't even look up when they came into the room. Heather smiled. What would his reaction be when he saw her? She lowered the hood of her cape to her shoulders but left the cape on to hide her pregnancy.

"We need your help." Her brother started right in. "There is a Vespian searching for my wife, and I want to know why."

The word wife caught his attention. Skye looked at her then her cloaked figure before focusing in on Kuarto. "And you want me to find out why?"

A voice loud enough to break through the walls was demanding to see Skye.

Heather smiled again. It seemed her mate had found them.

"I don't care if he is with a client. He will see me." The door burst open and in came Storm.

"Sir! You have to wait until he is finished with his clients." The receptionist was right behind him, trying to stop him, but her mate was hard to stop once he was on a mission like this.

"It's alright, Lee. I'll handle this," said Skye. He gave Storm a bored look. "You want to close the door?"

The moment Storm entered the room Kuarto was up and moving. He pulled her to her feet and was trying very hard to get her to move with him. Now why was he afraid of Storm? Was it because he was Vespian? Or because he was *the* Vespian? The father of her child?

"It's okay, Kuarto." Heather put a hand on his arm to reassure him. "He means no harm."

He just pulled her behind him as he worked his way to the door.

Storm ignored her brother. He wrapped a hand around Heather's wrist and dragged her toward him. When she was close enough, he pulled her into his arms. She wanted to laugh at the confused look on his face when he realized her condition. He held her at arm's length and tried to see through her cloak. "Do you have something to tell me?"

"I don't need to say a thing." She opened the cloak. She loved the little outfit she had on. It was soft and very comfortable. The pants hugged her legs and the tunic she wore hung nice and low and covered everything she needed it to. Plus, the turquoise color looked good against her fair skin.

Storm ran his hand over her protruding stomach. "My heart?"

"Surprise." She felt the baby move at his touch.

A frown creased his forehead. "Who's the father?"

"I don't know." Although she had suspicions, she didn't want to voice them until she was sure. Heather turned to ask her brother who the father was, but he looked about three shades paler than he should and she knew she needed to calm him down before he could answer any questions. "Kuarto, you alright?"

"What do you mean you don't know." Storm's frustration brought her attention back to him.

"I don't know who the donor was. Look, it was done through artificial insemination. Something my brother is working on. He's the one to ask. Which reminds me." She turned to Skye and handed him her journal. "Make a copy. It has all the details he'll need when we get home."

"Heather!" Kuarto tried to take the handheld from her, but she moved it out of his way as she gave it to Skye.

"It has all my formulas in it."

"I know and you're going to want them once everything is fixed."

"Fixed?" squeaked Kuarto. "You're not making any sense."

"I know, but I need to deal with Storm first. Then I'll explain everything."

He didn't look convinced.

She knew no matter what she said he wouldn't understand. Lowering her voice a few octaves she used her voice to calm him. "Storm means us no harm, Kuarto. I will answer his questions while you wait then I will speak to you."

He gave her a quick nod as he stared at her mate. She turned her attention back to the man in question.

"Pregnant? With some stranger's baby?" Storm growled at her.

"Hey, this was here when I got here." She gestured to her stomach as she stood her ground. Storm might be upset that she was pregnant without him, but she had no control over this, and it wasn't like she had sex with anyone to get this way.

"How many women were you with since Susan changed the timeline?"

He didn't answer her just demanded, "Who is the father?"

"I said I don't know."

"Excuse me," said Kuarto.

"You know nothing?" Storm's voice dropped several octaves in anger.

"It was a Vespian sperm donor. That's all I know." She jammed her hands on her hips. He was being too pigheaded for her to mention her theories.

"Excuse me." Kaurto spoke a little louder.

Heather was getting mad. She fell into this timeline just like he did, and he had to understand that she had no control over what happened before she arrived in this time-line's body.

"I know who the father is." Kuarto didn't raise his voice, but he got everyone's attention. "But first you need to answer some questions for me. What did you mean when you said you landed here, Heather? And do you two know each other because you talk to each other like well, you're married."

"Then tell us who the father is." Storm focused his glare at Kuarto.

Most of the time she loved Storm's one-track mind, but not right at this moment.

"Storm."

"I should be the one fathering your children. You are my mate." He drew her to him and wrapped his arms behind her. The twins thumped at the contact. He gave her his heart-stopping smile. She knew he couldn't stay mad at her because of this. Children were rare and always wanted. "You do have a beautiful glow about you. I'm just not happy this has happened. We have enough to deal with. You being pregnant complicates things."

"I know, but it can't be helped." The baby kicked again. "Oh!"

"Perhaps you should sit down." Storm switched his hold on her and helped her retake her seat.

"Heather." Kuarto got her attention again. "You going to explain this?"

She nodded. "How much do you know about alternate timelines?"

"I studied it in school just like you did, why?"

"Because you are living in one." Heather shifted in the chair so she could get comfortable and patted the empty one next to it. "Don't make me look up at you as I try to explain all of this. It will make me get a crick in my neck. I promise Storm won't hurt you. He's just very protective of me."

Kuarto looked at Storm, who stood behind her and probably had his arms crossed over his chest, before he sat beside her. "So you do know him."

"He's my mate." Heather held up her hand when he went to open his mouth. "I have a story to tell you."

———

Storm listened as Heather explained what happened and how the timeline kept changing. Kuarto didn't look like he believed what she said.

The man still hadn't told them what he wanted to know. "Who's the father?"

Kuarto gave him a cross look. One he had seen many times before. "You are."

That filled Storm with relief.

"He was one of the donors?" asked Heather.

"Yes. As I started testing the sperm his turned out to be the most likely match." Kuarto looked from Heather to Storm before he looked at Skye, who still looked bored with the whole thing. He turned back to Heather. "And how is he your mate? Did you bump your head or something?"

"No." Movement out of the corner of her eye caught her attention. Skye had picked up his handheld. "I know this is a little hard to believe."

"And we really don't have time to explain this," interrupted Storm. "We need to find Susan and that machine."

"All of this is a little far-fetched." Kuarto glared at Storm before he took Heather's hands, drawing her attention back to him. "Do you have any proof?"

"Yes." Skye's voice drew everyone's attention. He loaded data onto his screen so Kuarto could see some of the news feeds from their timeline. It showed a progression of images of Heather and Storm together. They showed her pregnant then the first time they presented the twins to Vespia.

"Wait, who is that?" Kuarto saw an image of him and Toki together.

"That is your mate. Storm's sister."

"My mate?"

"Yes." She smiled. "In our timeline, you've been hiding from the medical world. Your talent had them wanting you to do things you didn't want to. You live on Vespia now, where no one can bother you or try to get you to work for them. You also have access to the most advanced technology there."

"And how is that possible?"

"We have access to Ancient technology. The same people who made this." She pinched the chain around her neck and drew out the temporal device located there.

"This is made out of the same material as your insert."

"Then I did have it."

"You do have it," Kuarto corrected. "It's still in you."

"But I've tried to pinch it out to see it and couldn't."

"Pinch it out? You've never been able to do that. Dian sealed it years ago so it wouldn't be detected by any scan."

"Not in my timeline. Dian wasn't there."

"My heart. We don't have time for this," said Storm.

Heather agreed. She took her brother's hands. "Do you trust me?"

"You're my sister."

"Who is spouting nonsense about coming from a different timeline." She cleared her mind. "I'm going to show you proof that we're from another timeline. Things you will understand as you see them."

She shared her and Storm's life together, how they met him, and how he became Toki's mate. Heather made sure he saw some of the problems they have had along the way.

"Do you remember Susan Harris?"

"Yeah, you two were in classes together. She pitted herself against you when you kept excelling."

"We think she is responsible for this and need to find out if she has an apartment on Earth," Storm told him.

"Susan? How? She never did that well in the sciences."

"She either found something and figured out how to use it, or she's had help."

"I'd go with the second one," commented Kuarto. "Her apartment isn't far from here."

"What makes you say that?"

"You were assigned to seal it while she was on Vespia.

You took me there once." Kuarto stood after Heather did. "You don't think she has this thing stored in her apartment, do you?"

"No, but we need to see if there are any clues to what we're looking for are there. I want to know where she's hiding it."

"And how," added Skye. "The woman had lost her job over what she tried to do to you in our timeline so didn't have the easy access to exotic worlds where something like this might turn up."

They traveled to the building that held Susan's apartment. Heather wasn't sure how they would get in, but the guard at the main entrance recognized her. He stood as she approached.

"Captain? I heard you had resigned your commission."

"I did." She smiled, pulling her cloak about her so he wouldn't see why she had stepped down. "Needed a little time to myself but promised the admiral I would still check on the apartment from time to time."

"I don't have any record of that."

"Really? Well, damn. It must have not come down the pipes yet." She sighed. "He's away right now so I can't contact him to give you a verbal, guess I'll see you once he gets back."

Storm put an arm around her as she turned to go back out of the building. They'd have to find another way in.

"Captain, why did you bring these three?"

Heather smiled up at her mate before she turned back around. "Well, I didn't want to come today because I had company, but I promised. You should know Skye Latimer, and my brother has come with me before. I know it's a little unorthodox, but it wasn't a problem before, so I thought I'd try." Heather wrapped her arm around Storm. "I also brought someone very special to me, my fiancé. He's the reason I resigned. I couldn't see getting married and being sent off planet all the time."

"You're engaged? Congratulations!" He studied Storm. "Look, I know you came out of your way to stop by, and I might get into trouble for doing this, but you are one of the most honest people I've met. Go on up and do what you need."

"Thanks. Do you mind if they come with me? I promise they won't touch anything, just keep me company."

"I guess." He hesitated for a moment before waving them on. "Just be quick about it."

"Of course. You know me, always busy." She flashed him a bright smile as she took the chip he handed her and headed to the elevators. Kuarto let them know what floor they needed then pointed out the apartment. Heather inserted the chip and the doors opened.

"Any idea what we're looking for?" asked Skye.

"Nope." Heather scanned the room. "I'm hoping it will jump out at us as we look around."

They all headed in different directions. Heather went into Susan's bedroom while Storm covered her living room. Skye went to the computer.

Opening drawers then cabinets, Heather didn't see anything out of the ordinary. She searched the closet next, banging against panels. The thought of getting on her hands and knees in this condition didn't appeal to her. A sigh escaped her as she brought a chair over.

"Problem, my heart?"

"Oh good. The floorboard needs to be checked." She tapped it with her foot.

Storm wrapped his arms around her. "And you wish me to do it?"

"Or help me up and down." She rubbed her stomach. "This sort of makes it hard to do that."

He laughed as he crouched down in front of the opening. "There is a small panel in the back, but it needs a key to open it."

"Try the one we used to open the door." She handed him the chip.

"Sorry. Doesn't work."

"I wonder if that bracelet is the key."

"The one she wore in the last timeline?"

Heather nodded. "Just before everything changed it started to glow."

"That wrist band did stop time, but it didn't have anything to do with the time change. Not sure what the crystal on top of the bracelet does. That was what you saw glowing." Skye said from the doorway. He held up his handheld. "Have it all recorded if you'd like to see it."

"Really?" Heather nodded. "Of course we want to see it."

Storm stood as Skye pulled the monitor up from his screen. "This is the last thirty seconds."

Heather checked Susan's neck and ears for any jewelry that could conceal the key to the panel but didn't see anything out of the ordinary. Susan wore a necklace, but she had that as long as Heather knew her. Same thing with the second bracelet she had on. The new bracelet was intricately wired metal with one bead that reminded her of a sphere-shaped sapphire stone. The way it caught the light was amazing. The stone did start to glow moments before the screen went blank.

Next the data on the bracelet loaded on the screen.

After Heather read the data, she sighed. "If that isn't what we're looking for where the hell is it? Behind that little door?"

"I've scanned the apartment so anything hidden behind the walls will show up when we view it." Skye put his handheld into a pocket. "But I'd rather not use any of the basic computers to look at this."

"Then we need to find Bert," said Heather.

"Who's Bert?" asked Kuarto, who had come in from the bathroom when Skye had come in.

"A friend of ours." Heather found a chair and sat.

"Off planet?"

"Yes." She rubbed her stomach.

"Then I'm going, too."

"You can't," said Storm.

"Then my sister is going to have to pass as well," Kuarto said.

"We'll be back in a few days."

"Heather, you're due in a few days. I can't let you leave without me until after you give birth."

"Oh, hell no." She struggled to her feet.

"My heart. We can go see Bert then come back and tell you what we found out."

"I'm not talking about that. I'm talking about this." She touched her stomach. "I'm not going through labor."

"What?" Kuarto stepped toward her.

"It's not what you think, Kuarto. I've already been through this once before with the twins. Giving birth then having a timeline change? I can't do that." She shook her head. "You can't ask me to do that."

Storm nodded. "I'll need to go back to my ship so I can contact the council."

"Hurry."

"See you in the next timeline." Storm gathered her in his arms and covered her lips with his. The kiss started out sweet, but then he deepened it, swirling his tongue in her mouth, and drawing a sigh from her. When he broke it, he touched her face with his fingers.

Heather pressed her hand against his heart then stepped

back and linked arms with Kuarto. "Skye, I'm not sure what happened to Sam, but I fear she ended up with Ialog. You need to go find her."

"My thoughts, too."

Heather opened the door and escorted everyone out of the apartment and back down to the guard. Heather signed out of the building then turned to Storm and Skye. "I hope you are successful."

"We will be, my heart. Storm took a moment to give her a quick but heated kiss before he contacted his ship and disappeared from sight.

"I'm not going to be able to do that. My ship is at the spaceport." Skye smiled. "I'll let you know the moment I find her, no matter what timeline we're in."

Heather nodded. She watched him go and hoped her daughter was safe.

She turned to Kuarto and linked arms with him once again. "So, my brother. Let's get back to our place."

He patted her hand, and he led the way.

"What will happen now?" He unlocked the door to their apartment and let her enter.

"Hopefully Storm will be able to frighten Susan into using the machine again." She rubbed her stomach as she crossed the threshold.

"But what about me?"

"You won't remember any of this." She gave him a sad smile. "When she changes the timeline, you will only know that new world, but I promise to tell you all about this when we get everything fixed."

"You have my files to prove this timeline happened."

"I do, and that information will help you fix the birth problem for all the planets." She gave him a hug. "Even though Susan messed up our lives, something good is going to come out of this."

Storm contacted the council to learn they were in session. Perfect. The look on his mother's face showed she was surprised to hear from him. "What is so important you chose to interrupt the session?"

"Is Susan with you?"

"Yes. We were working on the treaty." His mother looked frustrated. "Again."

"And can she hear me?"

"Yes. Why?"

Just what he wanted. "I'm not sure if she should hear what I have to say."

"If it deals with Earth I deserve to hear." He heard her squeaky little voice raise an octave with his comment.

"Fine. I am sorry to interrupt, Anseri, but I have learned the humans have been keeping something important from us."

"What?" his mother wore a smile, but he could tell by her tone that she wasn't happy with this news.

"They have been successful in using our data on Vespian pregnancy to create an offspring between Vespians and Humans."

"A child?" Hope filled her voice. "They were successful?"

"They will be in a day or two. That is when the child is due, and Anseri, it is my child."

"Yours?" He saw the soft smile spread across her face before she hid her emotions. "Why didn't they tell us about it?"

"When I confronted the doctor about it he explained he hasn't even told Earth. He wanted to be sure the child would survive the birth."

"We are on our way. Have you seen the mother?"

"Yes, very pregnant. I confirmed everything before I contacted you." He smiled, knowing his mother's next question.

"And the mother? Will she be willing to come to Vespia and raise her child?"

"Her name is Heather Drexel, and yes, she has agreed." He heard a faint squawk out of Susan.

"We will speak more of this when you arrive," she said.

"Of course, Anseri."

Bert had the ability to record the timelines as they switched. The last time Susan froze time because she knew she couldn't escape. Hopefully this time she wouldn't have to do that. It would give them a point in time to see how fast everything changed after Susan knew she needed to make adjustments again and allow them to pinpoint where she was hiding the machine.

SEVEN

Storm found himself on his Vespian ship. He looked around, hoping he could pretend to know what was happening before anyone realized he had no idea what was going on. Susan had changed the timeline again.

"We have her, sir."

Storm looked at the guard speaking. They had who? "Good."

"Where do you wish us to put her?"

"Is she aboard ship yet?"

"No, sir."

"Then first let's get her on the ship." That should give him enough time to see if he left enough information to slip into the timeline without anyone being the wiser.

He went to his room and pulled up his private logs to see what they could reveal. His government wasn't happy with the way the treaty was going. Susan was in a security cell on Vespia. She couldn't be happy about that. The council had sent him on a mission to capture a key member of Earth's security. The problem was he couldn't find the name of this woman they had anywhere in his comments.

He hadn't seen Fridon yet but had read he was part of the team who was extracting the female. Copying Skye's amulet had worked so Fridon remembered and helped cover for him in the last timeline.

Storm hoped they would return quickly so he could go and look for his mate. Storm received the notice that the scout ship had docked and headed to the bay. When he entered, his men had the woman surrounded so he couldn't get a good look at her. She had been pushed to her knees and he bet she was in restraints that had her arms behind her back. They only did that when the captive was a fighter.

"You were bested by a human female?"

"She knew our moves, sir."

He saw the woman straighten when she heard his voice. A smile spread across his face as he stepped close enough to see short white, blonde hair. "Well, Captain Drexel. You have been a bit of a handful, I hear."

She looked up at him, not happy with her situation. "You are enjoying this a little too much."

He flashed her a bright smile.

"Put her in my room, Fridon. Make sure she showers first then restrain her." He looked at the rest of the men. "In the meantime, you can explain to me how one woman bested you for so long."

———

Heather wanted to throw something. Storm had the upper hand again and no one except him knew who she was. It was just wrong.

Fridon ushered her to Storm's room. He pointed to the sonic shower where she could clean herself.

"You going to stand there and watch?" she asked.

"I'm sorry, but I must."

Now that was an odd comment from Fridon. He shouldn't know about her shyness. She looked at him and noticed he had his small device in his hand. In their timeline all the members of the elite team had one. And he had been working with it when Skye had brought them the medallions Burt had created to keep them from being affected when the timeline changed. He must remember the last two timelines and knew she was Storm's mate, not some prisoner. "You know."

"I remember."

Heather had forgotten he had pressed it up against one of their medallions, copying the program that kept them from being assimilated into any new timeline when they were on the outpost.

"What happened to you during the last timeline?"

"I was ordered to stay on the ship when Storm went to look for you."

"Does he know?"

Fridon nodded his head.

Now they had one more to help them, even if it was from the sidelines. Heather knew it didn't matter if she showered before Storm showed up because he would join her if she didn't. But they had to keep up appearances. She stripped off her uniform and stepped into the shower. Once she had gotten all the grime off her body she stepped out and approached Fridon. "Am I allowed to wear anything while I wait for Storm?"

"I'm sorry, but you are a prisoner." Fridon had her turn around and put the restraints Storm requested on her. He then helped her to her knees. "In case he isn't alone you have to be that prisoner."

The moment her hands dropped to the floor she found

she couldn't lift them. The cuffs had anchored themselves to the floor.

"I'm going to kill him."

———

Storm found Fridon outside his room.

"How is she?"

"Very mad, sir."

"You're dismissed, Fridon. I'll contact you if I need you."

"Yes, sir."

The doors opened for him, and he smiled when he saw Heather, naked, restrained and on her knees next to his bed. He stepped in and let the doors close. "I hear you aren't happy with your situation."

"Would you be if our roles were reversed?" Anger snapped in her eyes. She tried to lift her hands, but the cuffs wouldn't budge.

"I'd be excited if I had such a beautiful woman as my captor." He ran his knuckles along her jawline. "I'd be thinking about how I would arouse her to get those elusive screams I love to hear."

"You, my heart, have a one-track mind." She shifted her weight. "Why am I here anyway?"

"According to my journals, the council isn't happy with the way the treaty is being handled and have decided they need a little leverage."

"And I'm the leverage? Why?" She watched him, wondering why he hadn't released her yet.

"I never put that information in my journals but considering what your position was in the other timelines I'm not surprised. After all, you worked for the admiral, the highest-ranking man in your military." Storm opened the seals of his uniform, slipping it off his shoulders then down over his hips until it dropped off him.

"You going to release me?"

He knelt in front of her. "I have thought about it, but you know how much I love to arouse you and having your hands locked behind your back would let me do what I want without any interference."

"You want to take advantage of this." She pulled against the cuffs locked to the floor.

"You know me well, my heart." He leaned over her for a moment to break the hold the restraints had on the floor before he picked her up and deposited her on his bed. "What I like the most about these cuffs is that they can be magnetized to any surface."

"Which is why I couldn't move."

"Fridon was just following protocol." He climbed on the bed with her. Bringing her hands around front, he lifted them so they could connect to the wall. Once again, her hands were immobile.

"Storm."

"When I walked in the door and you were there, naked, beautiful and waiting for me. Your breasts were thrust forward, begging for my kiss." He bent his head and circled one of her nipples with his tongue before drawing the sweet tip into his mouth. Once he was done with one, he pressed a kiss in the valley between her breasts. "Crying out for my attention."

She shifted as he paid homage to her other breast.

"Then I remembered when I had you restrained on our ship. How I was able to arouse you the way I wanted to." He pressed a kiss against her stomach. "Two screams was my prize. They were beautiful. Music to my ears."

She remembered that moment too. He brought her to

heights she didn't know she could reach. Excitement bubbled up inside of her at the thought of experiencing that again.

His mouth closed over her other nipple. Need filled her. His fingers caressed her hip, glided across her stomach, inching ever closer to her core. Heather wanted to drag his hand where she wanted it, but the cuff wouldn't let her hands move.

He broke his hold on her breast and rested his head against the soft skin. "Having a problem, my heart?"

"I need..."

"I don't need my sensitive nose to know what you want, but I also know what I want, and those precious screams are something I desire." He pressed another kiss against her flesh.

"I can't take much more." Her words came out breathless.

Storm placed a hand on her thigh and felt her quiver in anticipation. Using slow deliberate caresses, he worked his way up to her core. Each stroke made her desire spike.

"Storm, please." Her legs started to move, trying to get him to enter her.

"Sorry my heart, but I can't let you take control right now."

Heather couldn't stop the whimper that escaped her.

"Not yet." He placed a kiss next to her navel then nipped at her hip. He continued working his way down her stomach until he reached his goal. First, he used his tongue and brushed it against the sensitive tissue. He started alternating between licking her then sucking on her until he elicited a moan.

"Storm."

"Soon, my heart."

He inserted two fingers inside her, sliding them against

his favorite sensitive spot. He knew this one normally brought the screams out of her. He also knew he wouldn't be able to wait much longer. The desire to enter her was all encompassing, focusing his thoughts on how wonderful it would feel like to have her muscles tighten against him the way they tightened against his fingers.

"Please."

He couldn't deny that plea. Storm climbed up her body and released her hands as he slid in. She sucked in her breath as he filled her. Heather arched her back and he used that to slip his arms under her to bring her into a sitting position. They moved together, each time she slid down his erection her muscles created a wonderful vice that had him shaking.

"You feel so good."

His mate didn't respond, she was lost in the sensations. Her release only moments away. He leaned her back so he could brush against one of her sensitive spots as he filled her again and again. He was close now, the tight grip her sheath had on him had his orgasm racing toward him.

A moan escaped her as her grip tightened and he soared through his orgasm with her. They clung to each other afterwards. Their hearts beating wildly. Storm eased his boneless mate to the bed then withdrew so they could curl up together. No scream, but there was always the next time.

He brushed his hand along her spine. Their time alone wouldn't last long, and he wanted to make the best of it.

————

They were wrapped around each other, enjoying the few moments they had.

"You really enjoy tying me up, don't you?"

"I enjoy arousing you and there are times when you

won't let me. Those restraints allow me to get my way." The door sounded. A sigh escaped her. He touched her face. "I had hoped for a little more time." Storm got up and opened the door.

Fridon stood there. "Sir, our religious leader wishes to speak to you and your captive."

He turned to look at his mate who had sat up and was getting to her feet.

"I'm not walking around this ship naked." Heather gestured at her state of undress.

"I don't have a full replicator in my room. This one only does food and drinks."

"Toki took that into consideration." Fridon held out a gown.

"You mean she is here?" Storm took the gown from Fridon.

"Yes. She's waiting in the briefing room."

Heather took the dress from him and pulled it over her head. "Then let's get this over with."

———

Heather wore the restraints around her wrists as they headed to the briefing room. "I wonder what sort of vision she had for her to come here."

"With all the different timelines?" Storm looked at her. "The one thing that would bring me here is the birth of the twins."

"This is going to be hard to explain."

"As religious leader she has probably seen things none of us would believe and we have been through a lot. Just be yourself. She'll see right through you if you're not." He pressed his hand against the small of her back and ushered her into the room. "You wished to speak to us?"

Toki sat in her royal robes, looking regal and mysterious. Heather knew she was doing it to cut their confidence, but this Toki didn't know how close they were and how Heather knew exactly what she was trying to do. Heather couldn't help but smile. She sat opposite of Toki and returned her gaze.

"This is her?"

"What were you expecting, Toki?" Heather was going to be herself. Storm was right. If she tried to pretend she didn't know her, Heather knew Toki would see right through it.

She tilted her head as she studied Heather. "I thought your hair would be longer."

"If I was in the right timeline, it would be." Heather ran her hand over her hair. She hadn't had short hair since she mated Storm. Bouncing through these different timelines reminded her of how short she had kept it. "But still being in the military keeps it short."

"Excuse me?"

"What was your vision?" Storm asked, knowing Toki would push until Heather told her everything which they didn't have time for. They needed to keep her on track.

"You are different, too. Something has changed in you." She continued to look at Heather, not answering Storm. When she did speak it was off-topic. "Are you going to keep her in those restraints the whole time we talk?"

"You know the rules, I am a prisoner." Heather rested her bonded hands on the table.

"One who my brother has been intimate with." She watched as Storm slipped an arm on the chair behind Heather as he released the cuffs. He didn't remove that arm once he was done.

"Is there a rule that says I can't be intimate with a prisoner if I so chose?"

"No, but it's not something you've done before."

Storm leaned back in his chair. "What have you told mother?"

Toki just smiled. "So, you want me to believe this woman is your mate?"

"Yes." Storm knew better than to pretend otherwise. Whatever she had seen had showed that to his sister.

"Where is her mark?"

"I haven't given it to her yet." He rubbed his knuckles against his mate's arm.

"But hopefully he'll do it soon. It's strange not having it." Heather brushed her fingers against the spot where her mark should be.

"You know where your mark will be?" Toki seemed surprised by the way they were responding to her.

"Yes. I also know what it looks like."

Toki slid a pad at Heather. "Draw it."

Heather looked at the blank screen on the pad. She shrugged as she pulled it to her. Using a stylus, she drew the intricate pattern on the screen.

Storm looked at it and frowned. "That's not quite right, my heart." He drew one very close to the one she drew. They sat side by side. On the screen.

"Is that what you see?" asked Heather.

"Yes."

"Hmm." She looked up at him. "My mark is not at the perfect angle for me to see it clearly. This is actually the one you have, my heart. I just assumed they looked alike."

"I thought they were identical, too."

"Each mark, even shared by a couple is slightly different." Toki pulled the pad back. She took the two images and laid one on top the other. "To everyone else they will look alike."

Heather could see how close the designs were.

"Mated. Interesting." Toki looked at her brother, then

Heather. "I'm curious to know what you need to do to fix what has happened."

"First, we need to catch up with our daughter and her mate."

"Daughter?"

"It's a long story, Toki."

She nodded. "And it falls to me to explain to the council why you aren't bringing back your prisoner?"

"Yes, and you must keep Susan locked up. Somehow, she is instigating these timeline changes."

"That winey little human? You were the one who put her there in the first place."

The doors opened up and Fridon stepped in. "Sir, we have more visitors."

"Who?"

"The ship isn't in any of our databases."

Storm stood. If they didn't recognize the ship, it could be Skye and Sam. "I'll be back in a few minutes. I'll leave Fridon outside the doors, so you won't be interrupted."

Skye hailed the Vespian ship as he approached it. His goal was to get a message to Storm somehow. He couldn't help but smile when the man in question filled his screen.

"Took long enough." Storm crossed his arms over his chest. "You are Latimer, correct?"

"Yes." Skye had read the communiqués from Earth and knew he needed to rendezvous with them to get back an Earth diplomat. No name was given, but he had an idea of who it could be. Each time the timeline got them together. No matter what Susan tried.

"We have Captain Drexel. She is in good health, but she

will not be returned until your government makes some concessions toward the treaty."

"I need proof she is okay." He was right. Once again Heather was the focal point.

"Fine." Storm shifted so he could hit a few keys. They were playing their roles well.

"In person. If I speak to her personally, my people will be more apt to try to work this out." Skye waited while Storm pretended to deliberate.

"Fine. No more than two of you." Storm turned from the screen and looked at his head navigator. "You are in control of escorting them to the room. I need to get back to our prisoner. Leaving her alone with our religious leader concerns me."

Skye broke off communication. The man cleared them to transport aboard. Sam remained quiet as they followed the guard who was leading them to Heather. He was worried about her. Skye had transported her onto his ship just before the timeline had changed again and every time he asked her what happened to her during the last timeline she brushed him off with either she was fine or she would talk about it later. He knew not to push her, but until she told him what happened his focus would be split.

Right now, he needed to find out what was going on in this timeline. So Heather was a prisoner this time? Skye wanted to know why. Did Susan have something to do with this? If so she must be pissed to know Storm was the one in charge of her.

The doors opened and they stepped in. Heather sat at the large table dominating the room. The gown she wore was familiar and he realized he had seen pictures of her in it when she first moved to Vespia. Opposite her was Toki. What was Vespia's religious leader doing here?

Her abilities to realize what was going on every time had him a little bit in awe of her.

"Mom?"

"I'm fine, Sam, and I'd hug you, but I'm a prisoner." Heather looked at her and smiled. "I don't want to be tackled because I showed affection to my daughter."

"You may approach your daughter, Heather," said Toki.

"Then you know who I am?" asked Sam.

Toki only smiled.

"I did mention you to her earlier and we do look alike. Even though we know she has this uncanny ability to know what will happen, I think this time she is just assuming." Heather stood and wrapped her daughter in a loving embrace.

"I heard about your unfortunate incarceration." Sam returned her hug then took the chair beside Heather. Once they sat, she took her mother's hand. "My question is why?"

"It seems that Vespia isn't happy with the way Earth has been handling the treaty and decided to use me as leverage." She squeezed her daughter's hand.

"But in the original timeline Vespia only offered the treaty because uncle, who was religious leader at the time, told them to do so." Sam looked at her aunt, wondering how she was taking in all they were saying. "If he hadn't, I don't think they would have built the embassy on Earth since they didn't need anything from Earth. They only asked for Earth's help with the lack of births as an afterthought."

"I know, but Susan made the changes after the embassy was on Earth. Their search for me had already started. Somehow, she was able to take my place, and keep the treaty going, hoping it would allow her to stay on Vespia."

"I hate the fact that she kept you and Dad apart. Where is he by the way?"

"He was delayed on the bridge," said Toki.

"We need to get to Bert." Skye said it softly, but everyone heard him.

"You're right." Heather looked at Toki. "And we need your help to do that."

———

"I have done as you asked, Heather." Toki clasped her hands in front of her and rested them on the table.

Heather leaned against Storm. "Thank you."

"I know you see things that we don't always understand, sister, but what did you see to help us?"

"Two beautiful children. A boy and a girl."

"The twins." Heather smiled. She missed them terribly.

"Then there was another image. Heather surrounded by hundreds of Vespian children."

"The image Bert talked about." She looked up at her mate. "That one we haven't lived yet."

"This Bert you keep speaking about, he will help you put things the way it should be?"

All four nodded.

"Then you better get going."

———

Skye wanted to punch Storm. He was annoying the crap out of him. He kept asking questions, second guessing him at every turn. At one point Heather laughed, reminding him that they could be doing better things than him annoying Skye to death.

He breathed a sigh of relief when they went back to their

room, but they came back before he could reach Bert's compound and now Storm was hanging around behind him again.

"You're sure that is where Bert lives." Storm leaned over his chair.

"Yes."

"Dad, this is Bert's compound." Sam spoke to her father. "I've been here with Skye. Now relax."

"Relax?" He turned to his daughter. "Susan could change the timeline at anytime. I'll relax when we're back in our proper time."

Heather finally pulled Storm back and wrapped her arms around him. He seemed mollified by that since he stayed with her as they got closer to the compound.

Skye contacted Bert. He gave them clearance so they could land.

"You're back."

"You remember," commented Sam.

"I made sure I could." He smiled as he pulled a medallion out of his skin. "Introduce me."

"You don't know us?" asked Storm.

"I know who you are," he said to Heather. "I've seen your face many times in my dreams, but I was caught by the first timeline switch. Whatever we shared before I don't remember."

"I'm Heather and this is my mate, Storm."

"Bert, time is of the essence. We need to know what you learned from the different shifts. Did you figure out where they originated?" asked Skye.

"All my data is inside." He gestured for them to follow him. His main room was a lot like his command center on his ship orbiting Vespia. "After Skye and Sam were here three timelines ago, I made sure I wouldn't be affected by the changes and worked on pinpointing where they were originating. Unfortunately, my system is pointing to a planet that doesn't make sense."

Bert pulled the data up on a screen. "This planet has been abandoned for thousands of years. Earth has done some excavation there, trying to learn what happened to the race, but besides a few guards there are only archeologists there."

"How was Susan involved then?" asked Heather.

Skye knew Heather's question was rhetorical, but he must have the data in his handheld. He found the information quickly. "She was on site, doing an interview with the historians working there. She could have been poking around and found something."

"Wait. I thought she was fired after my run-in with her."

"According to the data she found another job." Skye continued to read. "Still in news, but nothing like she had before. This one was dealing with scientific studies. Her job was to interview top scientists out on the field, then create updates for other scientists to view. Not very exciting, and it kept her out of the limelight she was used to, but it also kept her from becoming a ward of the UCE."

"And it gave her access to this planet."

Skye nodded.

"In the last timeline, I told the council, who happened to be speaking to Susan at the time, about Heather's pregnancy. I did it so she would change the timeline, but I was also hoping it would give us a point to see how long it took her to make that change."

"Doesn't she freeze the time before shifting it?" asked Skye.

"That's what I'm hoping we can find out," said Storm. "Maybe she doesn't do it every time."

"Susan must. It's the only way she can get to her equipment without being caught," said Bert.

"How? Unless she has access to a ship like Skye's how would she be able to get to this planet and alter the timeline so quickly?"

"My ship goes dead when she makes the change."

"That is when she changes the timeline." Burt moved to another computer. "But she must have a way to move through space without time running."

"How are we going to be able to stop her then?" Heather leaned against Storm. "Do you have this type of technology?"

"I've been working on a prototype for years but don't have a power source. The ones I have created had a limited range. Its power wouldn't make it much past the orbit of a planet."

"Bert, this doesn't make any sense. Susan doesn't have the background to do any of this, but we haven't found any leads to show she has been working with someone else. Do you honestly think she just found all of this?"

"I wish I could answer your questions, but you'll have to go to the planet to learn how she's doing this."

"You think she is going to that planet each time she wants to change the timeline?" asked Storm.

"It is possible. I'll be sure once I pinpoint the location."

They all looked at him.

"You just said it came from that planet."

"I sound like I'm contradicting myself, don't I? Time has a ripple effect. My technology can see the change as it moves out through space." He moved to another screen and pulled up the data from the last timeline. "I had to set up my machines to see what happened when the time changed, unfortunately, I hadn't calibrated everything until the last timeline. That last shift shows that planet in the center, but until Susan changes the timeline again, or you go there to find the equipment she is using I won't know for sure."

"The only change I want to happen will be to make our real timeline appear again," grumbled Storm.

Heather wrapped an arm around his waist and gave him a squeeze.

"After Skye alerted me to the changes, I shielded my compound so I could track them. Susan might have frozen time, but once I shielded everything, the time changes no longer affect this place. I can see how long it took for time to restart once Susan learned the truth and knowing where she had to travel from, I should be able to prove she traveled to this planet to make the changes. All I need is your data, Storm."

He gave him the exact moment when he told the council about Heather's pregnancy which Bert entered in his computer. "Hmm. It took her three Earth days to make the change.'

"Three? She had no access to any ship how did she travel here?"

"That I can't explain. I have monitored the area and would have noted any ship that arrived. I saw nothing that left a mark the way the ship would during the space between timeline changes. I'll check for spikes in energy to see if she might have traveled some other way, but this does prove that I believe what we're looking for is on this planet where the archeologists have been working. Earth calls it Rolam."

"What sort of technology have they found there?" Storm wrapped his arms around his mate.

"Earth has made it top secret," said Heather.

"The technology there equals what the Ancients have achieved," said Skye. He pressed his handheld against the screen and the information on the dig downloaded. Each change had him adding whatever data he was cleared for to it so he would know what was expected of him. When he and Heather worked for the admiral, they had full clearance to the files. "We've found this technology before and have used it to our advantage. That's where our latest weapons and faster engines came from."

"They must have found something else to reverse engineer. But how did Susan end up with it?" Heather looked at him.

"They aren't working on reverse engineering a time altering machine," said Skye. "They found a cache of weapons they are analyzing. Just like before."

"Is there anyone on the planet?" asked Heather.

"The usual, a small security contingency, and a half dozen scientists working on the find."

"Are they due to be inspected?" asked Heather.

"Yes." Skye knew what she was getting at.

"Then you and I need to make a visit."

"My heart?"

"Storm, you need to stay here. We don't normally bring guests when we do inspections."

"You forget your government thinks you're my prisoner."

"Crap. You're right." She looked at him. "How do I explain how I got away?"

"Why do you need to?" Storm smiled. "I can be your explanation. We go there under the pretense that Vespia plans on taking control of the planet. We can gain access to whatever I want to see under that guise."

"It would make sense," commented Skye.

"Now how frightened do you want them?" asked Storm.

"Why?"

"You could wear the suit."

"The one where you have total control of my body? It is in this timeline?" Her eyes widened when he nodded. "I don't know about that."

"It will make a statement."

She looked at him. "And you're going to put Sam and Skye in security uniforms with their helmets on, aren't you."

"Wouldn't you?"

She nodded. Heather wasn't happy, but she did agree with him.

"I promise to make it up to you."

"Oh, I know you will." She placed her hands on her hips. "I'll make sure of it."

EIGHT

torm made sure the true weight of the suit wasn't felt by his mate, but he knew he had to make this look serious or no one would believe them. The gangplank descended and he touched her face. "Understand this is all for show."

"I know my heart, so will my reaction."

"Time to go," reminded Skye.

Heather shook her head, getting into character. Storm stepped up and locked her hands behind her. She headed out first. He watched as she staggered as if someone had pushed her.

"Don't shoot." Heather spoke to the guards' pointing weapons at them.

Storm snapped on his helmet. Out of all of them only his mate was vulnerable, and he hated it.

"Captain Drexel?" One of the guards spoke as they all lowered their weapons. "We heard you were captured."

She nodded. "But it took twenty of them."

Storm stepped out with Skye and Sam flanking him. They stopped just a few feet behind Heather. Storm turned on the weight at the knees, making Heather drop to the ground hard.

The security force there started to lift their weapons again.

"Don't." Heather shook her head. "Our weapons can't penetrate their uniforms. All you're going to do is get yourself killed. They heard about the find here and plan on claiming this planet as their own."

"But Earth has given us permission to study these artifacts," said one of the scientists. By the tone of his voice, he didn't care who was in control as long as he could do his research.

"And we won't stop you." Storm's voice broke through the conversation. "For now." He turned to Skye. "Secure the guards."

Skye and Sam stepped forward and restrained the guards, locking their hands behind them and pushing them down into a sitting position. Once he locked the restraints and magnetized them Storm signaled for Sam and Skye to go and explore.

"This planet has a strong metal content," said Storm. He turned up the cuffs so they couldn't move. "It should keep you out of trouble while my team investigates."

Heather watched him wearily. Even though he knew it was all an act, he didn't like to see her look at him that way.

"And you, Captain, shall accompany me. I wouldn't want you and these men to try to come up with some foolhardy escape plan." He pulled her to her feet and pushed her in front of him. He didn't change the weight, and it hurt him to see her struggle.

Once they were out of hearing distance, she snapped at him. "This damn thing is heavy."

"I know, but while you were in front of those people, I couldn't have it too light or they could question us."

"And now?"

He turned down the weight in the outfit. "Better?"

"Yes." She moved her shoulders a little as she adjusted to the lighter load. "Has Skye found anything?"

"No." He opened the seals of his helmet then removed it. "He and Sam are following the path Susan left while she was here but haven't found anything yet."

"Hmm, Earth requires everyone to have a marker embedded when we go off planet so they can follow our trail months or even years later if it is needed. I don't know if Susan is smart enough to do it, but it can be overwritten." She thought for a moment. "We need to search for her DNA. Since there are limited amounts of new DNA in the area hers should be easy to track."

"I'll need to put my helmet back on." He snapped it into place. "I see several trails. She must have wandered a bit before she found what she wanted."

"That might be from the first time. You should be able to see date codes to let you track her last visit."

"My heart I know what to look for."

"Sorry." Heather gave him an apologetic smile. They were all under the stress of stopping Susan and she couldn't help herself.

He wanted to wrap his arms around her and show her he wasn't mad, but that suit she was in wouldn't allow him to do what he wished.

"Susan wandered on her last visit just like she seems to have done the other times. I'm assuming she did it to keep someone like us from finding what she was looking for." Storm turned his head and followed the marks he wanted to track. "But ultimately, we know what she was going after. She might have been able to hide this from Earth sensors, but not ours. Susan went into that cave over there quite a few times." Storm pointed to their left.

"What cave?"

"You can't see it?" It was obvious to him, but he had his helmet on. He moved toward it.

"No."

"Interesting." He stopped in front of it and studied the information filling his screen. "It starts here."

Heather watched in amazement as Storm stuck his arm into the opening and it disappeared from sight. She stepped up to the spot and suddenly noticed the opening. "Wow, that's camouflaged well."

Storm took her hand and pulled her in behind him.

They entered the cave to find more technology. All kinds of machines lined the walls. The floors once were polished marble and Heather noticed that parts of the cave walls were still smooth, and some had pieces of murals on them. "Wow, Susan found all of this and didn't tell anyone? How did she know what was here?"

"Didn't she study with you? Learn the sciences like you did?" Storm removed his helmet once again.

"Susan wasn't very good at them." Heather walked up to one of the computers and ran her hand over it. "The only reason she was in the academy with me was because she flunked out of all the private schools. Her dad wanted her to have a degree and had donated to the government to help the less fortunate. His daughter fit the bill. She wasn't allowed to fail any of the classes though. She either had special tutors or teachers who let her slide by."

"Two more visitors, how wonderful!"

Heather turned at the sound of the new voice. The image of a woman flickered in front of her before it solidified. It must be some sort of holographic greeter. "You have had other guests?"

"Yes." The hologram smiled. "That nice woman was here not too long ago and now I have you!"

"So you met Susan." Storm's voice held a hard edge.

"Oh, yes. It is so nice to have guests. The hologram looked at him. "You are Vespian, correct?"

"Yes."

The hologram turned to Heather and studied her. "But I don't recognize your race. You're not human, although you could pass for one."

"I'm from a race we call the Ancients." Heather didn't care for her scrutiny. She stepped close to Storm. "How do you know about Vespians?"

"Their ships have passed by our planet from time to time." She clasped her hands in front of her. "I don't know about a race called the Ancients, but I will search my data base to see if we have ever encountered them, but in the meantime, welcome. I haven't had guests in such a long time. It is a great thrill to have someone to talk to."

"You are a very strange computer." Storm put his arm around Heather's waist.

"I don't think that is a computer, Storm." She studied the hologram in front of them. "This one acts like a real person, like someone's consciousness has been uploaded into the system."

"Very good." She gave Heather a bright smile. "The other young lady never figured that out about me."

"Not surprising. Did you volunteer for this?" asked Heather.

"Oh, yes. Being able to exist forever? Everyone wanted this position. I was lucky enough to get it." The hologram sighed. "This planet was designed for scholars. The people who came here were students as well as our best in the field. We had something for everyone. Then the war started. In the beginning, people still came, but as the war went on their visits were less frequent. I monitored the transmissions, wanting to hear what was happening. They too started to be less frequent. Then they disappeared alto-gether. I'm all that is left, and I sat dormant for years. When the human scientists showed up, I realized I had people around again, but my system is in need of repair. I couldn't appear to them like I could years before. I can only appear here."

"That's why they don't know of your existence."

She nodded. "I thought I would be trapped here, never to be found again, but Susan found me and now so did you. Perhaps you could help me so I can help the scientists. Those weapons they found aren't our most powerful. They are more like children's toys."

"We'll see what we can do," said Heather. She had no plans of telling anyone about this hologram. "You told Susan about a machine, a time altering device."

"Not really." The hologram shifted so she was facing Heather. "She found one of the devices we used to teach visitors of our history. It was designed to put you into the scene as it explains our life. There have been children who figured out how to do what you are suggesting, but they were stopped pretty quickly, and the timeline righted itself."

"Which is our problem. Susan has manipulated the time-line several times now and each one gets worse. We need to know what machine she might be using and stop her."

"She shouldn't have been able to do that. The device I believe you are talking about isn't designed to maintain a timeline change for long." The hologram frowned.

"Can you tell us where this machine is, maybe we can figure out how she used it."

"Of course. It is in an old building about two clicks from here."

"There are no old buildings, just a bunch of caves." Storm informed her.

"Of course, over the years the buildings fell into ruin,

the caves, as you call them, were the buildings I speak of at one time, but they were eroded down to what you now see."

Heather thought for a moment. "Can we see a map? It would help us know the layout so we can find what we're looking for."

"This was the layout when it was in its prime." A map of a large city appeared on the wall near them.

"And which one are we looking for?" asked Storm. The building glowed on the screen. "What was that building?"

"An orientation building. All new guests went there to find out what we had to offer. Our history was rich and very diverse so depending on what someone wanted to study, they would learn the history of that subject there."

"Is there any research into altering the timeline?"

"Oh, yes. That was a popular study. Of course, we learned that changing the timeline normally made matters worse so we banned the practical use, but the studies always had great training purposes."

Heather looked at Storm. "That explains a lot."

They headed to the ruin that the hologram marked.

"These must have been beautiful when they were created." Heather pointed to another mural.

"And if Susan had been paying attention to that one, she would have figured out playing with the timeline wasn't a smart thing to do," said Storm. The images that still remained showed the issues one person had with it.

"Let's look for the machine. Or a spot where one should be if she took it out of here."

"If it is here, we need to figure out how she is controlling it."

Heather nodded. They each chose a corner and worked their way to the center of the room. She didn't notice anything out of the ordinary, so she went to another room and moved to the center once again. She found one devoid of the dust that caked the rest. "How about this one?"

Storm came to her side. "It doesn't look like much."

"Not real sure what it should look like." Heather studied it. "But it's the only one that doesn't have the pound of dust the rest have."

"Looks like there is a piece missing too." Storm pointed to a spot that showed no dust. "It is circular in design."

"Like the bracelet Susan wore."

"We need to speak to Skye. He has the image of it."

Storm nodded then snapped on his helmet.

———

Sam and Skye joined Heather and Storm in one of the five caves nearby. Still wearing their helmets, data streamed in front of them as they looked at the different pieces of equipment. They focused on the machine Heather pointed to.

"That's the machine that stops time," said Skye.

"Then where is the time altering one?" asked Heather, placing her hands on her hips and looking around once more. "We were told it was in this place."

"By who?" asked Sam.

"There is a hologram still running in another cave. The data she had was very helpful. She said there was a machine here that might be what we're looking for."

Skye continued to scan, making sure he didn't miss anything. "Behind that wall." He pointed to where another machine was hidden.

Storm walked up to the spot. Several items were in his way, and he shoved them with his boot, clearing the path. The moment he got them out of the way, everyone saw the hole in the wall. It was big enough for them to enter one at a time.

"Do you think Susan put the debris there to hide the opening?" asked Storm as he stepped through to the next room.

"I'm sure there was some there before she found it, but she could have added to it to keep it hidden from the scientists here." Heather followed her mate into the next room. They fanned out and continued to search.

"Now that is more like what I expected." Heather looked at the complicated machinery that dominated the room. There were several screens as well as lots of flashing dials and buttons. She knew by a look that this was advanced technology. How did Susan figure any of this out?

"There is something missing." Storm pointed to a circular hole in one of the machines. There were small circular crystals across the front of it, all different colors.

"And it's the only thing missing here," said Heather. As she watched the crystals changed color. "That was interesting."

"They all match our eye colors now," commented Sam. She went to touch it and found her father had grabbed her arm.

"We need to talk to that hologram again. See what she knows."

"Hologram?" Skye pulled his helmet off. "You mentioned that before."

"Yes." Heather turned to face him. "The planet's main computer system still works in another section of the city. It's not too far from here. The interface was a hologram, and she was the one who told us where this machine was at."

"Could it have an access port here?" asked Skye.

"It's possible." Heather paused. "I don't know how Susan learned how to use this. It's beyond her training."

"She did end up with a gem," commented Storm.

"Could she have received her instructions when she removed it?"

Skye scanned the machine. "There's nothing dangerous about it that I can detect. The only way to see if there is something to what Storm is suggesting is to try it."

Heather stepped forward. A strong arm wrapped around her waist. "Where do you think you're going?"

"I make the most logical choice."

"Why?" He turned her so he she was facing him.

"Because I'm your prisoner?" She looked up at him.

"Heather, those men aren't going anywhere. The cuffs can't be broken."

"The UCE aren't morons. The moment your ship showed up in orbit they probably sent one of their own here to protect their find. If something does go wrong, and they search for us, they will question why you didn't use me."

"I don't care about what Earth might do. We'll probably be gone before they get here." Storm brushed his fingers along her jaw. "You can't take the risk."

"So who? Sam?" She gestured toward Sam. "She's our daughter. Skye and I would fight against it. Skye? He's the one who has been the anchor on this mission. Helped us figure out what was going on. And Sam and I will fight against it. You? No. As your mate I can't allow it. What would happen if something were to happen to you? Vespia would declare war on Earth. And the first place they would destroy is this planet and any way to change the timeline back." She touched his face as well. "I'm the one with the ability to keep in touch with you mentally so you'll know if I get into any sort of trouble."

Before he could react, she stepped away, grabbed the small circular stone and placed it in the palm of her hand. Closing her eyes, Heather focused on it.

"Open your eyes, my heart." It was Storm's voice. She

was sure of it, but their connection told her it wasn't him. Her eyes fluttered open, and she found herself back on Vespia with Storm beside her, walking through the gardens she loved so much. "Is this the reality you want?"

"Yes." The words came out of her automatically. She looked at him, wondering if she had slipped into a dream.

"Then you can have it whenever you hold that crystal."

He smiled at her, and she felt her insides melt. Her reaction to him was instinctual, but his words told her this wasn't a dream. Was this how she would interact with the computer?

"What if I wanted it all the time?"

"Then you would have to find a way to wear it all the time, but that wouldn't be healthy." He brought her to a shaded bench. "Perhaps I should explain the rules to you."

"Please." She sat on the bench and inhaled the beautiful aroma of the flowers nearby. "This seems so real."

"We strive to make it that way." He took one of her hands in his, making her turn toward him. "Now, as long as you hold the sphere you can visit this world, but like any fantasy this isn't living."

"But what if I wanted to make this reality the real one, how do I do it?"

"I have been asked that before." His fingers softly caressed Heather's hands.

"I thought so. That is why we're here." She looked at him. "We know Susan came to this planet and figured out how to activate you. I've also spoken to the hologram that greets everyone and learned that your function is to teach and entertain, but somehow Susan figured out how to take the reality she found with you and made it real by using technology here."

"Our people know better than to compromise the timeline."

"Susan isn't from your people. She is human and has no idea how much damage she is causing. We need to stop her."

"We?"

"There are four of us trying to fix the timeline, myself, my mate, my daughter and her mate."

"Your mate? He is the one I am fashioned after?" He brushed a few strains of hair from her face.

"Yes."

"Interesting. I wore the same persona for Susan."

"You did?" She didn't like the sound of that.

"I always take on the image of something the person accessing my system will trust. Sometimes it is a relative or friend. Other times it is something the person desires."

"And Susan desires my mate?" Heather paused for a moment. "Did you touch her the way you touch me?"

"It was her desire, like it is yours."

"But she wanted more, didn't she?"

"I'm not sure I understand your question."

"Did you have sex with her?" Heather knew he wasn't Storm, but she knew anger would take over if he said yes.

"I don't know that word."

"Were you two intimate?"

He just looked at her, which frustrated her. Somehow, she needed to get this machine to understand what she was asking about.

"How do your people procreate?"

"They are genetically engineered."

"Then how do your people show affection toward each other?"

"Ah, you speak of physically satisfying each other." He smiled. "I am programmed to fulfill any fantasy. Is that what you desire as well?"

"No! I have the real thing." Heather could feel the anger

boiling up inside her. "Susan's desire for my mate is something I will have to fix."

"This makes you angry?"

"Yes." She pulled her hand away and stood. "She had no right to pretend you were something she could have. Storm is my mate, not hers and no matter how many times she tries to change the timeline she will never take him from me."

"You said Susan has changed the timeline. Do you know how?"

"No." Heather shook her head. "She was wearing the orb on a bracelet. Our data said the metal came from a machine that we found in another building. That one stops time, but we can't figure out how they tie together."

"Hmm, to alter the timeline she would need a catalyst. That piece might do it, but I'll need to run calculations to know for sure."

Heather felt Storm pushing to get into her mind. "Excuse me for a moment."

My heart, is everything okay? I felt frustration then anger from you.

I'm fine. I just learned something not to my liking.

Is there someone in there with you?

The computer took on a persona for me to communicate with. Heather could feel his desire to join her, protect her from whatever was upsetting her. She opened her mind then waited.

"Why are you watching the horizon?"

"Because we're about to have company." She saw Storm heading straight for them.

"How is this possible? We're in your mind."

"My mate and I have a mental bond that allows him to enter my mind." Heather watched as her mate grew closer. He came right at her, wrapped his arms around her and claimed her mouth. Their tongues danced and when he broke the kiss he drew a sigh out of her.

"My heart." He brushed his fingers along her jaw.

She smiled up at him. "Storm, I'd like you to meet Storm."

He shifted his hold to her waist so he could study the man in question. It was possessive, yet gentle and Heather knew he was marking his territory again. "And this made you angry?"

"I found out that Susan took advantage of the situation. She was intimate with your image. All this time I was under the impression she just wanted what I had because she thought I had a cushy job. She has always tried to take anything she thought she deserved more than I did. Her having sex with your image tells me she wants you, not just my position. It changes things. I should have wiped her mind when I had the chance."

"That is the anger making you think that." He gave her waist a gentle squeeze. "You have too kind a heart to harm another. Susan is a nuisance, but that is all. I have proven she doesn't attract me in any of the timelines. You did in every one of them."

"I will have to do something. We can't have her constantly trying to interfere with our lives. We have enough of that from our enemies."

"And we will, but first we need to know how she was able to make these changes and take that power away from her." Storm turned his attention to his image. "Computer, how did she learn to do this?"

"I don't know."

Storm growled. "I wish Skye could join us, I bet he could find what we're looking for."

"You know he hates it when I enter his mind."

"This Skye, he is with you?" asked the image of Storm.

"Yes."

"Then he needs to pick up his crystal. You all do."

Storm touched her face. "I'll be right back."

She nodded and watched him walk back the way he came. It took only seconds before all three were standing in front of her.

"Good. Now that you have your orb it has bonded to you. No one else can use it. You may take it with you as well and it will work wherever you are." The computer explained. "Consider it a gift to help you when you need it."

"Now we need to show you how to use the orb." Storm's image looked at Heather. "Think of something that happened in your past. Something no one else would know."

"Like what?"

"How about something from your childhood?" suggested Storm. "Something you feel comfortable sharing."

Her childhood was spent in classrooms. The garden on Vespia faded away to be replaced by the classroom she had spent most of her time in.

"Very good. You have a knack for this." The image smiled. "Now share a memory with us."

"What?" Heather hadn't planned on doing that. Her childhood was something she never spoke about. She looked at her mate, then her daughter and Skye. They were her family. People she knew she could trust.

"You don't have to do this if you don't want to," said Sam.

"I know." She smiled at her daughter. "I've kept my childhood to myself. Not because it was bad, but because I don't have the great funny stories about friends or family. My life was pretty simple, I went to school and when I wasn't in school, I studied."

The classroom filled with children. There were about a dozen, including Heather. They all worked on their computers. What were they doing? She couldn't remember. Stepping up to her image she looked at the detail on the screen.

"What are you doing, my heart?" Storm's voice sounded in her ear.

She jumped.

"You don't have to worry about disrupting this. It is your memory, so you won't be able to interact with it," Storm's image explained.

"I'm taking a test." Heather had to think. They took a lot of them. Why did her mind bring this one up? She would never reveal something that would embarrass her. And why was her younger self just staring at the screen? There was no way she didn't know the answers. She rarely got one wrong. Then it dawned on her. This was a challenge given to her. One that involved a prize if she beat it. A soft smile spread across her mouth.

"What is it, my heart?" Storm wrapped an arm around her waist.

"This is when I got my necklace."

"Necklace? I don't remember you ever wearing jewelry." He linked fingers with her. "Except for your wedding rings."

"Once I started to go on missions, I asked Bear to keep it safe and never thought to ask for it back when we moved to Vespia." The scene started moving then. Young Heather sat there, watching the clock on her computer count down to the moment when she could start answering questions. The moment she was able, she worked her way through the questions, marking the answers and showing her work when needed. When she was finished, she submitted it to her teacher.

The teacher looked up at her once as the score loaded.

Heather wouldn't know if she won the challenge until after their class was over. That was set up after another win that caused a lot of trouble between the students. The winner would be allowed to use the replicator to create whatever they wanted.

Heather stopped the scene and allowed it to drop away.

"Now your file is part of everyone who saw it. It's also in my main system to be accessed by all who come here.

"And if I don't want it shared?"

"Then you set the commands with your orb." He showed them how to use the settings. "Think of it as an access port."

"Then this is an extension of you," said Skye. "Does it have all your data?"

"Yes," the image of Storm smiled. "This will allow you to access my system anywhere."

"You think this is how Susan was able to access the system?" asked Heather.

"There was a three-day lag when she made the last change so I'm assuming she had to physically come here." Skye worked with his handheld. "Could she have accessed one of your ships?"

"There are no ships on this planet, but we do have a transporter in another building that is still functional."

"And how far does it reach?" asked Heather.

"It was designed to reach our home planet."

"Where is your planet?" asked Skye as he pulled up a map of the galaxy. He made sure it showed most of the populated planets, including Earth and Vespia.

"Here." The planet glowed.

Skye took the information calculated the distance from planet to planet the checked the distance to Vespia then Earth. "This transporter does cover Vespia, but not Earth."

"So now we know how she gets back and forth, but that

means she should have switched it almost instantaneously and she didn't."

"It would take time for her to make the proper calculations," said Storm's image.

"We took the calibrator from her during the first timeline change. It would make sense that she had to figure out how to do it each time. The question is how."

"Does Susan's orb store the data, or will it download into your system as she uses it?"

"It stores it until you return here to download. You do have control of the download. You don't have to put anything you don't want in my system."

"Do you have all of Susan's files?" asked Heather. "Maybe what we need is in them."

"She did do a download each time she was here, and temporal change doesn't affect my system."

"Then that is where we need to start."

———

"So how did Susan use this to trigger a time change?" asked Storm. Skye had been going through the data and Storm stood behind him.

"She shouldn't have. There are safety protocols in place plus people to watch and guide against that," said the computer.

"Your people are gone. This planet is nothing more than a ruin now. Could those safety protocols been disabled?" asked Storm.

"Or maybe dismantled?" offered Heather. Everyone looked at her. "The other system told us the planet's people, by the way, what were your people called?"

"Xendarians."

"Thanks. Anyway, it told us the Xendarians were at war.

What if they were losing and thought if they could change the timeline, they would be able to get the outcome they wanted?"

"Yeah, but if they did that why aren't they here?" asked Sam.

"The timeline will always correct itself. If they did do something like that and they were destined to die out something else would have caused their extinction," the computer commented.

"Then why hasn't the timeline tried to fix this mess Susan has started?" asked Storm.

"It could be because she keeps changing it. No matter what she does, you two seem to find each other and that is what she keeps trying to stop." Skye pulled up the data he had been working through. "The data points to one thing. She must have another piece, something that is allowing her to make this real. It also allows her to make some of the calibrations we know she isn't capable of and change the timeline when she's not happy with the last one."

"What could she have that has that type of technology? And how did she figure out how to use it?" asked Storm.

"Susan did find the files on how to manipulate timelines from this planet's science system," said Skye. "They were designed for children to access it which is why she was able to use them. A lot of what she has been able to do was spelled out for her. The rest was just pure dumb luck."

"So there is no one helping her?" asked Heather.

"Not that I can tell."

Heather crossed her arms over her chest. She didn't care for what Skye said. Even though she was relieved there was no one lurking behind Susan's jealousy, what he said just reinforced that Susan's desire for her mate was something she was going to have to address. She didn't need one more person trying to come between her and Storm. "We need to figure out a way to stop her."

"And we will my heart."

———

Susan banged against the bars of her cell. She must have been out for hours, if not days. All she knew was someone put her here on purpose. "I want to speak to Storm."

One of the guards came to the cell. "Storm isn't here and we have been told to hold you until he gets back." With that he turned on his heel and left.

Something wasn't right. Each time she changed the time-line she hoped it would work, but it never seemed to. She sure wasn't going to sit in this cell and wait for him. Time to fix this problem right now. Lifting her wrist, she touched the bracelet then turned the orb.

NINE

Heather noticed as the color dropped out of the world around her just before everything fell away. Susan did it again. When she landed, she found herself standing at attention while Bear yelled. Oh no, what did she do now?

"Do you understand me, young lady?"

Young lady? Since when did he use that phrase when dressing down a soldier? She wanted to look around and take in her surroundings, but she knew better so kept her eyes straight ahead.

"I'm waiting for your answer, Miss Harris." The admiral's voice had a hard edge to it.

"I'm not in your military."

Heather heard her voice come from her right. Susan was standing beside her? Heather wouldn't dare move her head while standing at attention, but at least she knew she wasn't the one in trouble.

"Oh, I know that, Miss Harris, but you decided to interfere with my orders and that I won't tolerate." He stepped up so only a few inches separated their faces. "Captain

Drexel has been assigned, by me, to protect the ambassador. Nothing you can do will change that."

"What did she do, run to you the moment she found she couldn't be near Storm?"

Heather had come to the same conclusion. She must have been caught away from her post and she told the truth.

"Captain Drexel is an officer. When I found her away from her post, I demanded to know why she was AWOL. She told me she had been reassigned." He leaned in. "No one can countermand my orders. Especially by someone not in the military. Do you understand?"

Heather heard her gulp. Good. At least Bear could scare her a little.

"Now, Captain Drexel has been assigned to protect the ambassador. If you think you can do it better than by all means I'll take you down to headquarters and test you to see how capable you are. The captain is the best in security and if she hadn't turned down the commission two times, she would be an admiral." He looked at Heather for a moment. "Something she won't be able to turn down the next time it is offered."

———

Storm found himself in the ballroom of the embassy on Earth, not sure what was going on. Not too far away, he spotted Heather in a beautiful black gown, standing at attention. Bear was standing in front of her, yelling. It took a few seconds for him to realize he wasn't yelling at Heather, but at Susan. His long stride took him to them quickly.

"Admiral, is there a problem?"

"Ah, ambassador." Bear turned toward him with a big smile. "No, I was just instructing your wife on how over-riding my orders could land her in the brig."

"And what order was that?" He watched his mate as she continued to stand at attention.

"That Captain Drexel is your bodyguard. There have been too many attempts on your life for us to ignore it."

"I am quite capable of defending myself."

"I'm aware of that but being a visitor on our planet complicates things if you are forced to defend yourself. The captain is our best and no one will question her if she is forced to use brute strength to keep you safe."

"Brute strength?" He walked around Heather. "But she's so small."

"Maybe by Vespian standards, but not human, and she can take down anyone who threatens her, including you, ambassador."

"I'd like to see that." He smiled at her, knowing she couldn't react.

"All right. Who do you have in mind?"

"How about me? Right now?" Storm looked at Heather who remained at attention. "I am head of Vespian Security. I have trained the best on Vespia."

"I don't think that is wise," replied Bear. "Your guards would probably attack Heather the moment she dropped you. How would it look if one human took out your entire security force?"

"You think that highly of her?" Storm walked around her, studying her.

"I do."

"Does she speak?" He knew Heather would be angry with him for such a question, but he had to play the role of a Storm who didn't know her, and that is exactly what he would ask. The fact that Bear hadn't released her hadn't gone unnoticed. There had to be a reason he kept her that way and Storm wanted to know why.

"She does, but when she is standing at attention she only

speaks when spoken to." Bear addressed Heather. "At ease, Captain."

His mate relaxed her stance and exposed a luscious leg when the slit she had in the lower half of her dress opened up. She still kept her gaze forward instead of looking at him.

"Captain Drexel understands what discipline is. Ms. Harris does not." Bear kept his voice even, but anyone close could hear the anger in his words.

"And you thought Susan would see what you were trying to prove?" Storm knew better. "Perhaps another lesson is needed. I'd still like to see how good your captain is. How about a small demonstration on one of your people? Someone close, like Susan."

Bear gave him the slightest smile. He liked the idea. "Captain, why don't you show the ambassador just what you can do."

"No!" Susan didn't get a chance to say another word or even move before Heather had her on her knees in front of her. Her arm had been twisted up behind her back. It was the same arm the bracelet was on, and his mate had maneuvered it in such a way that the small crystal popped off, banged against the floor and started to roll.

Storm stooped down to pick it up, but it bounced against a pair of polished shoes and was scooped up before he could touch it. He looked up and saw Skye smiling at him. He placed the crystal in his pocket before addressing the admiral.

"Admiral Barrister." Skye saluted him.

"Captain Latimer." He saluted back before offering his hand for a handshake. "Good to see you."

"Same here, sir."

"I thought you were away." Bear studied him. Storm found it hard to acclimate himself in the beginning and wondered how Skye would handle this.

"I finished my mission early and was told to report here."

"Good. I'd like you to escort Ms. Harris to the Vespian security center."

"What?" whined Susan. "Wait! I let Heather bully me, why are you still punishing me?"

"Because I'm not done talking to you and am tired of making a scene. My soldiers never question me and anyone else who knows me knows when I'm serious and when to back down, but not you." Bear nodded to Skye, who took the arm Heather still had bent up behind Susan's back and pulled her to her feet. "You will understand that I mean business by the end of that conversation."

———

Skye had to half drag Susan out of the hall. She struggled to get away as he manhandled her to get her to security.

"Will you let go of me?" she snapped as she tried to pull out of his grasp.

"Nope." He continued to pull her along. "I've been given an order."

"These stupid orders! I don't care about your orders! I have to keep them apart."

"Who?" He gave her a bored look.

She hesitated. "Never mind."

He gave her a little shove as they entered the security center. She stumbled a bit before she turned toward him and glared. Skye smiled at her and shrugged before turning to head out.

"Wait! You have something of mine."

Skye turned back to look at her again.

"The crystal from my bracelet."

He knew not to react. So, she knew what happened to it.

If he refused to give it to her, she might figure out they were onto her, but if he gave it back, she'd continue to wreak havoc. When he stuck his hand into his pocket, his hand hit his crystal, and he knew what to do.

———

Heather stood on the side of the dance floor as Storm danced with yet another partner. The women were swooning all over him because in this timeline they hadn't mated so his pheromones were searching for her again.

The desire to charge out there and chase them off was strong, but she knew she had to pretend she barely knew him. He was playing his role as ambassador, but in their timeline the people they danced with knew they were mated, plus Storm didn't emit the level of pheromones he was doing now. Their dancing partners knew better than to step over the line. No one knew she was his mate, and it was driving her a little mad.

"Captain." Skye stepped up to her side.

"Captain." Heather looked at him for a moment before continuing her surveillance of the area. "Did you have fun with Susan?"

"Of course." He stood beside her and helped her keep an eye on the crowd.

"Did she ask for her crystal back?"

"She did."

"What did you do?" Heather glanced at him again.

"Gave her mine."

Heather grinned. At least she couldn't cause trouble right now. "You still had yours?"

"Just like you do."

"How?" She looked down at her dress for a moment. "There is no place to hide the thing."

"In your hair. You have a beautiful hair piece keeping that bun in place."

She reached up and brushed his fingers against the comb. There was the crystal. How interesting. "Skye, two o'clock. Brown hair, mustache."

"I see him."

They moved together, heading toward the man who had been staring at Storm a little too long. He pulled out a weapon and they started to run. Skye got to the assailant first, but not before he was able to discharge the weapon. Heather knew she had seconds, so she grabbed a tray away from one of the waiters. Glasses crashed to the floor when she angled it so the blast would bounce off it and up into the ceiling. Although the brunt of it went where she aimed, she could feel some of the energy from the blast fill the tray then flow into her arms. When she dropped her arms, the tray snapped in two.

Skye had the man on the floor and was keeping him restrained until other guards could come over to take him.

Heather felt her world start to dim, but she knew she had to stay conscious. Any scan would show the difference in her brain information. It would put her under a microscope, and she didn't need that. Warm arms slipped around her waist before she heard her mate's deep voice.

"Are you alright?"

She turned her head so she could look at him as her world went black.

———

Storm was glad he was standing behind Heather when she fell unconscious. He held her up, just has he got ready to scoop her up in his arms Skye came to his side.

"I wouldn't do that." He spoke softly so no one would

pay attention to them. He also wrapped his arm around her waist and placed one of her arms over his shoulder. "We need to move her before a doctor realizes what has happened. She can't be examined yet."

Storm looked at Skye with a frown. How could he understand what was going on with his mate? Did Heather tell him about her ability to heal fast?

"We have the same DNA." Skye had to know what he was thinking to say that.

"And she had a mind link with you."

"Let's just get her outside." Skye's words were clipped. Storm had struck a nerve.

He kept his thoughts to himself as he helped Skye make it look like Heather was moving on her own. They got her out the double doors that led to the garden and followed a path they knew wasn't used that often. They eased her onto a bench.

"Why isn't she coming around?" growled Storm.

Skye eased the two sections of the tray from her fingers and put them behind the bench where it wouldn't be easily seen. He took her hands and searched for a pulse then sighed when he found one. "Because that blast should have either killed her or burnt her so badly, she would die within a few hours. Look at her hands."

Ugly burn marks on her fingertips and palms marred the skin and had turned them black. The damaged tissue on her wrist looked just as bad and it went halfway up her arms. The angry welts started to disappear along her palm and wrists. Just as her eyes fluttered open all of her skin had healed to a point where she could face the medics.

"What did I do this time to have you two staring at me like I've grown a third eye?"

"Took the brunt of a blast as you bounced it off of that tray," said Storm.

"Something that should have burnt the crap out of you, if not killed you," added Skye.

"Yet your burns don't look that bad." Storm crouched down in front of her. "And your eyes, they have no color right now."

"I feel fine." She held out her hands and turned them over then back. Storm heard her whistle when she saw the damage. "Have the medics tried to check me out?"

"No, we got you out here before they could." Skye looked over his shoulder for a moment. "But it sounds like they're looking for you."

"I'm ready." She stood. "My eyes back to normal?"

"Yes." Storm touched her face.

She touched his as well for a moment. The contact hurt. Habit had her brushing her hands against her gown to get back into character. She winced at the pain the movement caused. That wasn't a smart move. She squared her shoulders and walked to where the medic could find her. Storm and Skye stayed back where they wouldn't be spotted easily.

"Captain? How much damage did you take?"

"Enough." She held out her hands.

He ran his scanner over her wrists. Opening his kit, he gave her a shot then sprayed her palms, fingers then the backs. "That should do it, Captain. Try not to touch anything for a few minutes or I'll have to respray your hands."

She nodded.

Storm and Skye came up to her once the medic had treated her and moved back into the ballroom.

"The admiral will be looking for us." Skye gestured for her to go first, but before they could reenter the ballroom Bear was out the door, looking for them.

"Something strange is going on with the three of you and I'd like to know what it is."

Heather smiled. Bear's sixth sense was kicking in. "Strange how?"

"Let's find a safe place to talk," suggested Storm. He gestured for the Admiral to go back into the ballroom. "Security is the safest place we can go."

No one spoke while they walked. Once everyone entered one of the interrogation rooms, Storm sealed the room off so no one would hear them. A press of a button stopped any recording of their conversation. He sat next to Heather, taking her hand under the table.

"I know you two have been lovers for a while and until now I have turned the other way. But something has changed. There is a relationship between the two of you that wasn't there this afternoon." Bear was very straight forward.

"That's about right." Storm spoke. He knew anything Heather or Skye would say could be grounds for a demotion or incarceration so they remained silent. "We have a story to tell you, Admiral. You might not believe it, but it is true."

———

"So you're from another timeline?" Bear didn't know what to think. They sure were acting different.

"Yes, sir," said Heather.

"You have any proof?"

"How does anyone prove something like this?" asked Storm, a frown on his face.

Heather's eyes widened. She turned toward the ambassador. "Sam."

"At the front doors?" asked Storm.

Heather nodded.

Storm stepped out of the room for a moment then Bear watched as someone transported into the room.

He stood as he studied her. She had Heather's violet eyes and Storm's smile. Skye took a protective stance next to the woman.

"Admiral, I'd like you to meet our daughter," said Storm. He smiled. "How is this for proof?"

———

"Are you okay?" Heather brushed her fingers through her daughter's hair.

"Yes, but I want to stay on the ship from now on." She looked at Bear. "Have you explained things to him?"

"We have, but I'm not sure if he believes us," said Storm. He searched her eyes. "Is everything okay?"

"I'm okay but, when the timeline changes and I'm not on the ship I keep ending up with Ialog." Sam placed her hands on the table. "This time I must have escaped before the last change because I found myself in some hell hole I never would have gone to in my right mind."

"Oh, honey, I'm so sorry." Heather placed her hand on top of Sam's.

"Let's just avoid it if there is a next time." Sam squeezed her mother's hand before letting go.

Heather nodded. She turned to face Bear. "We need clearance to go to Rolam."

"How do you know about that planet?"

"Because Susan went there and found a machine that alters time. Bear, we need your help to fix what she has caused."

Bear crossed his arms over his chest.

"Let me ask you a question." Heather knew she had to

appeal to the one thing she knew drove him. "Who would you have sent to get the treaty signed with Vespia?"

"You."

"Exactly. How was Susan picked? She's a newscaster not an ambassador."

"I didn't have control over who was picked."

"But when it comes to protecting our planet and their guests you always make the decisions."

He didn't say a word, but Heather knew what she had said was true in this timeline too. It took him a moment or two before speaking. "What do you need?"

"Thank you, Bear."

———

"Susan is locked in a cargo hold. I made sure there were no access panels for her to find. She's there until we release her." Storm told Skye as he entered the bridge. "How far to the planet?"

"It will take most of the day." Skye set the ship on auto pilot before looking at Storm then Heather. "I can't allow this ship to go as fast as it normally can until we're out of Earth's space. That will slow us down by several hours."

"Then I have time to talk to her."

"Yes."

Heather knew what her mate wanted to do, and she could never tell him no, but she needed to talk to Susan before she became boneless. She couldn't let this go anymore. Susan needed to know just how many lives she ruined in her selfishness.

"My heart." His voice flowed over her as he took a hold of her arm and stopped her.

"I know, but I need to talk to her before I lose my

resolve. She has caused a lot of pain and still didn't achieve what she wanted."

He touched her face. "Are you sure talking to her with your anger simmering close to the surface is the right thing to do?"

"No, but we've tried to reason with her before and that didn't work. I think the soldier in me needs to confront her."

"We just saw Bear try that. He wasn't successful."

"Yes, but he didn't have you to back him up. He also didn't mean anything to her. He was the man who championed me, and she's ignored him all her life. She wants you and hates me. I think we will make a bigger impact on her."

"You're going to push until you get your way, won't you?" He frowned at her.

"Yes." She gave him her best smile.

"Which means your focus will be on what you want to say to her if I try to distract you."

She nodded.

"Let's go." He let her walk in front of him. The heat of his hand against the small of her back relaxed her. Handling Susan was going to be tricky. She lived in her own little world and when someone tried to shatter that world it didn't always work.

The moment they stepped into the room Susan started in on them.

"Why have you locked me up? I have done nothing!"

"Really? I think messing with the timeline is a little more than nothing," Heather crossed her arms over her chest.

"What makes you think that?" She wasn't quite as angry after she heard Heather's comment.

"Why are you trying to deny it?" Heather stepped up to her and grabbed her arm. With a quick move she snatched the bracelet off her wrist. "You won't be needing this."

"That's mine!"

"Actually, this little bauble belongs to Skye." Heather pulled three others out of her pocket. "One of these is yours."

"My heart, what are you thinking?" asked Storm.

"She wants to be me. I think she should see what my life is like. Maybe she'll see my life wasn't as easy as she thinks." She glared at Susan. "And if you get some crazy idea to try to grab this bracelet back." Heather put it in a small slot, and it disappeared from sight. "It's gone."

"No!"

"You won't be using that again, Susan. We're going to put the timeline right and I'm going to make sure you never get a chance to do anything like this again."

"What are you going to do, kill me?" Susan showed no fear though. Venom dripped from her voice.

"What makes you think I would do something like that? Throw you into a Vespian cell for a couple of decades? Or the Vespian penal colony so the Vespians there can make you understand what it means to be a Vespian? That has crossed my mind." Heather smiled. "But I have something better in mind."

"I don't care what you have in mind. You can't harm me."

"I wouldn't be so snug. I could kill you and change the timeline back so no one would know you were ever on Vespia. They might investigate what happened, but I couldn't be touched as the mate of the Vespian ambassador." She sighed at the look of pure hatred Susan gave her. Murder wasn't her style but causing a little pain might be a step in the right direction. "I don't plan on harming you, Susan. If I wanted to it would have already happened. Be glad you aren't worth my time."

"Then what are you going to do?"

"You need to take my hand." She held out her empty

hand to Susan. The one that held their three crystals she offered to Storm.

"Why?"

"Because you're going to see what my life is like."

Susan looked at Heather's outstretched hand.

"Oh, come, on, Susan. Are you afraid to see? You think it's perfect. Here's your chance to live vicariously through me. The offer will only be on the table for a few minutes. If you miss this opportunity, you won't get a second one." Storm laced his fingers with hers, helping her hold the crystals in the palm of her hand.

Susan stared at her hand for a few more seconds before she took it.

They now stood in the same classroom Heather had seen when they used the crystals the first time. Susan sucked in her breath when she realized where she was.

"Recognize this, Susan?"

"I do." She looked around.

The scene started when an adult came into the room, looking for Heather. "Can Heather be excused?"

Her teacher gave permission and Heather stood.

"Why does she get special treatment?" The younger Susan mumbled. "No one ever takes me out of class."

"You could hear that?" asked Susan.

"Every snide comment." Heather didn't look at Susan. She knew if she did the anger simmering just below the surface would take control and she would lose the scene she had brought up from her memories.

They followed Heather to the medlab where four doctors waited for her.

"Heather, how are you doing today?"

"Fine." She slowed her steps when she saw how many doctors were there. "Are you going to exam that thing in my back again?"

"Yes." One approached her with a smile she knew was fake. "We're going to try to remove it."

Heather took a step back. "You can't."

"Why not?" The doctor speaking looked at his peers for a moment before looking back at her. She could tell by his fake smile he felt she didn't know what she was talking about. "It would give us a chance to study it better."

"Your scans give you all the detail you need." She placed her hand on her back. "You can't take it out."

Fear radiated off her and transmitted to Susan and Storm. They felt what she felt.

"It won't hurt."

But she knew better. She wasn't sure how but knew what they wanted to do was something that could cause her great harm. She pressed her hand against her back to keep them from taking it from her and she found the device in question in her hand. She held it out for the doctors to see.

"How did you do that?" The doctor picked up the small cylinder and moved over to his workstation. A faint beep filled the air. "Interesting."

One of the other doctors placed a hand on her shoulder. "Go on back to class and we'll call for you when we're done."

She nodded but didn't want to leave. Something told her to stay near the device.

"Go on back to class, Heather."

She nodded again. This time one of the other doctors ushered her to the door. The further she got from the device the stranger she felt. She stumbled then felt her body sway before she crumbled to the floor. The doctor walking with her picked her up and took her to another area of the medlab. Her device emitted a louder sound and continued to grow in volume until the doctor and his assistants working on it crumpled like Heather did.

"Is this what you went through when they took you away from class?" asked Susan.

"Yes." Heather switched the image, getting the reaction she hoped to get from Susan. Then she showed how she felt from the snide comments Susan made throughout their years together. The moments flew by, snippets to make Susan understand her life hadn't been easy. She had things she had to deal with that no one else did.

One particular scene caught Heather's attention, and she brought that to the forefront so she could share her version of it.

Susan and her friends sat at a lunch table, talking quietly. Heather sat by herself, doing her best to ignore them. She played with her necklace while she ate her meal. She knew they were talking about her. They would look at her and whisper to each other than laugh at some comment one of them made.

She was ready for any cruel comments they would make so she wouldn't react but knew it would still hurt. So far, they had left her alone. Maybe this time they would allow her to leave without saying anything. Finishing her meal, she stood to leave.

"Did you hear that one of the new transfer students tried to ask Heather out on a date?" one of Susan's friends said loud enough for everyone there to hear.

She forced herself not to cringe. Instead, she picked up her tray and carried it to the recycling machine. The boy in question had talked to her and seemed very nice until he learned her name.

"Yeah, I heard the Ice Princess struck again. The moment he figured out she was our resident freak he turned and ran," answered Susan.

The thought of taking a fork and stabbing Susan in the throat did cross her mind, but she was so close to getting away from these people she didn't dare ruin her chances. Then Susan started to laugh, and that laughter made Heather see red.

Susan had her hands flat on the table as she continued to reticule Heather. She jumped when something slammed into the table, just pricking one of her fingers. Looking down, she found a fork buried deep into the table, surrounded by a small pool of her blood. She looked up to find Heather towering over her.

"You dropped this." Heather turned on her heel and walked out of the room. As soon as she cleared the area, she placed her hand on her hammering heart. That felt so good. The fear in Susan's eyes was worth it. She had good intentions until Susan started laughing. That was all it took to make her take action.

She had gotten in trouble for it of course, but instead of keeping her at the school, Bear put her on a remote planet. He thought the boring assignment would teach her better than any punishment. What he didn't plan on was the station being attacked because it was protecting a rare mineral that everyone wanted. One way or another.

She didn't fit in on the outpost any better than she had at school, but at least they treated her as an equal. Someone had called her wet behind the ears, but this was her first mission, so it wasn't an insult, just a fact. Heather found it hard to carry on a normal conversation. All she knew was what she studied in school. She had no battle stories or family antics to speak about. When the stories were told, though, she always listened.

She had just gotten off duty and decided to go for a walk around the perimeter. There wasn't much to look at, but it was so different from Earth she found the area fascinating. A large rock outcropping covered the area. Their outpost was built against it.

A flash caught her gaze, and she looked in the direction of the light. Barreling at their group of buildings was a ball of fire. Acting instinctively, she pressed her com and yelled. "We're under attack."

She ran back to the main building and was greeted with someone thrusting a gun in her hands.

"Welcome to the real world, wet behind the ears. Don't get killed."

The blast was met with one from their security grid, encompassing it and extinguishing it. Someone shouted that enemy ground troops were coming at them.

Her heart beat hard in her chest. She turned and followed the other security members as they poured out of the building. Heather stuck to the man who kept calling her wet behind the ears. Orders were shouted and people were moving.

Following those orders, she kept low and inched forward, waiting for their enemy. The moment they came into view, Heather's team started firing. She noticed several of the enemy had broken off and were moving around them. Everyone was so busy fighting the group coming at them they didn't seem to notice some heading off without engaging them. Creeping up to one of the other soldiers, she signaled she was going to go to the back to make sure no one was going to try to attack from behind. The man nodded, but she didn't think he really paid attention to her.

Inching her way toward the rear, Heather spotted the half dozen people trying to box them in. She found some foliage to camouflage her approach, and as soon as she was close enough, she started picking them off. The first two fell easily. No one had caught on she was there, but the next two fought back. Several blasts whizzed by her head, and she wasted a few shots before she took them down as well.

Pain slammed into her as her shoulder heated up. Damn

it. She had been hit. All it did was make her so angry she became hyper focused. Watching for movement, she noticed shadows dancing against a wall. The rhythm she saw was too irregular to be foliage moving with the breeze. It was easy to judge how far away her quarry was based off the size of the shadows. It also let her know where they were hiding. Heather knew she couldn't hit them from where she was. She needed a new vantage point.

She found one closer, but it wouldn't shield her as well. Heather only saw one of the two left. Her six-sense told her the other one had climbed up on the roof for a better vantage point. She knew the moment she took a shot at the one on the ground the other would look for her and find her. She had to do this right. That first shot had to strike her target then she had to roll on her back and take that last assailant out before he or she could shoot her.

Heather held her breath as she waited for number five to shift. The moment he did she took her shot, rolled over and took aim. Number six leaned over to take her out, but she got her shot off first. A yelp filled the air then the two bodies dropped to the ground.

She heard the pounding of feet and readied her weapon once again. Fear filled her when she realized she didn't have time to move before whoever was coming would be on top of her.

"Drexel!" The man who had been calling her wet behind the ears burst around a corner.

"Here." The desire to get sick filled her. That was the first time she killed anyone, and it made her nauseous. The look on his face had her wondering how bad her wound looked. "I'm fine."

"Rookie, that was brave and stupid. Never go off on your own."

"I saw them break off and told Jenkins."

He turned to look at the man in question. Jenkins had a frown on his face as he tried to remember. The officer talking to her turned his focus back to her. "Did he acknowledge you?"

"No, sir." She shook her head, knowing she was at fault. The slight acknowledgement wasn't enough for her to call the man out. "But I knew I couldn't let them get behind us."

"Where's your mike?"

She tapped her collar.

"And you didn't think to use it?"

"No, sir." Another mistake, one that could have cost her dearly.

Several soldiers helped her to her feet.

"Take her to the medic then the captain's office. Contact me when she is on her way."

———

Storm felt the pain as the shot seared through her flesh. He heard Susan whimper. She felt it too. Heather was sharing as if they were her. Anyone else would have begged her to stop, but Susan didn't. He wasn't sure if anything his mate showed would convince Susan to leave them alone. The woman had hated Heather for a long time.

His mate continued to show them different parts of her life. The missions she shouldn't have come back from. The demotions for taking such crazy chances. Personally, he found her amazing. She cared more about being successful than her own life. A true Vespian. That was what she didn't understand. What she did all those years was follow her heart. Her Vespian heart.

Watching the part of her life she never spoke about humbled him. She felt she was wrong in so many of these instances because of rules and protocols that she never wanted to share this with him, afraid he'd look down on her.

He so badly wanted to stop her and tell her how proud he was of her, that all the things she went through made her the woman she was now, but the images kept coming. They finally made it to the point where she met him for the first time.

He wanted to laugh as she showed her feelings about him and the whole situation. He annoyed her. Being around him twisted her emotions into knots and she didn't like it. Each time she tried to get away from him the noose just got tighter. She was hired to protect him, but he didn't need protecting. Instead, he invaded her space and each time she tried to put space between them either he or her assignment brought them closer and closer to each other.

She skipped their first kiss and the first time they were intimate. Too bad. He would have enjoyed reliving that first time with her, especially through her viewpoint. He inwardly cringed when she came to when Ialog had kidnapped her and tried to alter her mind to believe a fake world he had created was real.

They felt her pain when she faced the fake Storm and realized he didn't know her, that everything they had shared was nothing but a dream. She was in love with him, and he didn't know her beyond her name. The fear she felt when she woke up on that table after she figured out how to break free of Ialog's hold, knowing no one knew where she was. The relief she felt when Storm rescued her.

Then she went into her pregnancy. Her frustration with the weird side effects she had to deal with. The glow she had when angry. The problem her brother had keeping everything balanced inside her. Her overprotective mate who watched her like a hawk and wouldn't let her move without his permission.

He had to grin at that. He knew how miserable she was, but he didn't want anything to happen to her or their unborn children. Then she showed what she went through while kidnapped by Ialog again. How she put her life and the lives of the twins in jeopardy because of her fear of the man. She knew what he was capable of and couldn't trust him. Her fear for her children, the pain of missing her family, him especially, washed over him.

Susan eye's glistened with unshed tears. "I didn't know."

"You didn't care." His mate's voice came out harsh.

The images moved to when they were on Akura, and she was being whipped by Lewmard. When it happened to her, she refused to share the pain she felt, but now he felt each time the whip bit into her skin. It was excruciating. He didn't know how she kept her feet or why she didn't cry out.

Susan was screaming and on the floor.

"Oh, come on, Susan. You wanted my life. You need to see what it has been like to live it." Anger dripped from her words as Heather tried to pull her back up to her feet. She had made sure Susan didn't lose contact with her.

The next thing he saw was Reasta's ship. He watched out the large bay of windows as a Vespian ship maneuvered around in space. She squeezed his hand then cut him off from the emotions. This one she didn't want him to feel.

"My heart."

"This one is for Susan only."

"But you haven't shown her the joy you've had in your life."

"She would probably latch onto that and block out everything else."

He looked at Susan who hadn't gotten over the pain of the whipping. "I think you have made your point."

"Have I?" She broke the link with them and crossed her arms over her chest. "This woman has gone out of her way to torture me every chance she got."

"Heather, please, no more," Susan whimpered. "I'll fix the timeline."

"No you won't. You will tell us how you did it and we will."

"The bracelet focuses my wants and sends it through the crystal."

"How?" Heather looked at Storm. "The crystal isn't designed to change the timeline."

"I know, but this does." She pulled an amulet out of her top. "I've had this for years and have always worn it. My mother gave it to me on my thirteenth birthday."

"This? How did your mother get it?"

"I'm not sure. Mom was on the board of some dig and gave it to me for my birthday. It was the last thing she gave me before she died."

Heather wished she had access to the computer she had found on Vespia at that moment. It could probably tell her what race created it. Not giving Susan a chance to slip the necklace back in her shirt, Heather wrapped her hand around it and pulled it off her. "And how did this change the timeline?"

"I don't know. I just wished for a different timeline, and I got it."

Heather looked at Storm. "I need Skye. He has a way with computers. Maybe he can figure this out."

Storm nodded. He headed out the door and came back with the man.

"What do you need me for?"

Heather held out the medallion. "Susan said this was what changed the timeline."

"And what do you want me to do?" He looked at her

wearily.

Storm grabbed Susan's elbow and moved her out of the way.

"Work your magic."

"Excuse me?"

"You know what I'm talking about. You have a way with electronic devices." Heather held out the necklace. "I want to know if you can 'see' how this works."

He took it from her. "Isn't this Susan's necklace?"

"Yes." Heather glanced at the woman standing next to her mate. "She says it focuses her desires and makes the world the crystal creates real."

"Really?" He looked at the amulet. "I'll need to take it apart."

"No, please. It's all I have left from my mother." Susan took a step toward them, but Storm's grip didn't allow her to take another one.

Heather closed her eyes for a moment. Her hatred for the woman was at war with her compassion for people. "Do what you have to do."

"Heather!" Susan cried.

"Why should I show you the compassion you never showed me?" Heather turned to her. "You never had a kind word. I never knew what sort of mean thing you would do to me. You had it all. A family, friends, love."

"My parents never loved me. They loved you."

"What?" Heather dismissed Skye before focusing on Susan. "Your parents didn't even know me."

"Yes, they did. Father paid for me to go to the academy after I flunked out of every other school they paid for. If I didn't graduate from the government school, they threatened to disown me." Susan wiped tears away from her eyes. The hatred Heather had always seen in her eyes reappeared. "But you they wanted. Father had donated so much he was on the school board. He saw your scores, noticed how you behaved in class. He would threaten me every time I brought a bad grade or got caught causing trouble. 'Susan, you are such a disappointment, perhaps I should make you live at the school like Heather. She seems to thrive in that environment.' He also threatened to put me in the barracks at the school and bring you into our home."

"That's why you hated me?" Heather watched Storm push Susan into the chair and retrain her. "Because your parents tried to use a scare tactic to make you a better person? Your father never spoke to me. Not even in passing."

"That didn't matter to him. If he wanted to move you it would have happened." The hatred she felt for him dripped off her words. "My father was a bastard."

Storm stepped to Heather's side and wrapped his arm around her shoulders. "Perhaps we should rest for a bit? Let her think about what you have shown her?"

Heather looked at him. She didn't want to leave. Storm had stopped her before she shared how she felt when she thought he had been killed. Susan's last comment told her the woman hadn't learned a thing.

"Come, my heart." The hand he pressed against her back urged her to walk and she knew he would be angry if she fought him.

She gave him a slight nod and allowed him to lead her out. Her silence bothered him because he started to rub his hand up and down her back. "I'm fine, Storm."

"You're angry."

"She'll never learn. Wouldn't you be angry, too?" She turned her head to look at him.

"We could bring her back to Vespia. Our people will make her understand." He steered her toward their room.

"And Earth will hound us to release her." She paused as

they waited for the door to their room to open. "I have a better plan."

"What?" The doors opened and they stepped in.

"I'm going to wipe her mind."

"You hate doing that."

"I know, but I have to. I have to give her the life she thinks she should have had so she'll leave us alone." She didn't want to look at him. The thought of entering Susan's mind and seeing how she viewed Heather wasn't something she wanted to face.

"We have survived her interference so far. What more could she do?"

"I don't want to find out." Her shoulders drooped. "I'm tired of our relationship being tested time and again. Why can't we just live our lives? Why is there always something trying to tear us apart?"

"My heart, we are stronger than any force set against us." He took her into his arms. "Each time she changed the timeline Skye said we kept finding each other."

She sighed as she rested her head against his chest. "I know. It's just frustrating. Susan doesn't understand all the work that had to be done to make that treaty happen. How active I've been since that has been done. She thinks I sit around all day, doing nothing."

"Then show her. You showed her what your life was like why not show her all the tediousness you've dealt with as my mate on Vespia."

"Do you think it will work? Nothing else has."

"I think you touched her more than you realized. Some of the things you showed her brought her to tears."

"I'm willing to try anything."

"Later, first I think you need to relax."

She looked up at him. It was weird not to see his eyes glow when he was aroused, but in this timeline, they hadn't

mated, she hadn't gotten pregnant and those were the cata-
lysts that led to his shifting ability.

"What?"

She could see the concern in his eyes. "Nothing, I can't
help but notice your eyes don't glow."

"Ah, the way you could always tell when my desire for
you was strong in a crowded room." He dipped his head to
where her mark should be for a quick caress. "Just like the
way you would react when I brushed my lips against your
neck. This isn't our timeline, but it doesn't mean we're not
affected. What I feel for you has been in every timeline."

"Yeah, but I freed your mind when Sam freed mine. You
remembered our relationship then."

"Yet we had been intimate before she did that." He
brushed a piece of hair from her face. "We were still drawn
to each other. Your mind reached out to mine and shared a
memory and the times before that we still found each
other."

"I know."

"This truly bothers you." He stepped back and took his
jacket off. Then he worked on the seals of his shirt. "Do you
question we belong together?"

"Of course not."

"Good." He peeled his shirt off then worked on his
pants.

"What are you doing?"

"Getting comfortable. How about you? Are you comfortable in that gown?" He smiled as he stepped up to her and
brushed his hand against her bare shoulder.

"I am a bit overdressed." She smiled back at him. Before
she could reach for the seals Storm's hands touched her face
gently before he opened the seal on the one shoulder. Her
dress dropped to her hips, then with a soft urging from her
mate, fell to the floor.

"Much better." He took her hand and led her to the bed. "You know me, and I always want you, but I know you're trying to work through this."

"You want to snuggle?" She sat on the bed.

"I want you to be happy." He climbed in beside her.

"I am. I have you as a mate."

He grinned as he took her into his arms. "So what are you going to do about Susan?"

She snuggled against him. "I still think wiping her mind of her hatred of me is the right move. She has lived with it for too long."

"I'm glad to hear that."

"But you were against it a few minutes ago."

"Because it was your anger that fueled it. You wanted to hurt Susan. Now you sound more like my mate in wanting to remove her anger."

Heather rested her head against his chest and listened to his heartbeat. She felt the soft sweep of his hand against her hip. Calm entered her mind and body. Even after showing Susan all the trouble they have had as a couple, she wouldn't change a moment of her life. Lifting her head, she looked at him.

No words needed to pass between them. Storm pulled her toward him and touched her lips with his. The kiss was gentle, sweet. He was going to let her make the first move. All she had to do was open her mouth for him and he swept right in. Their tongues danced with each other. Passion flared. Need filled them.

Storm wrapped his arms around her and rolled them over. He braced his weight on his elbows so he could look into her eyes. His fingers brushed along her jaw. Heather wrapped her legs around his waist, and he answered her unspoken request by driving into her. Her breath caught.

He set a slow pace, wanting to make his mate know how

precious she was to him. Her muscles rippled against him. Watching her face, he shifted his weight and changed the pace, depending on her expressions. Each time her muscles tightened on him he felt it to his toes. Keeping the slow pace was taking all his control.

Heather wrapped her arms around him and flipped them over. She started moving up and down his shaft faster. Her eyes closed and her head dropped back, she got lost in the sensations. Storm slipped his fingers between them and caressed her core, causing her to shudder. He knew she was going to lose control soon, so he flipped them back over.

The smile she gave him when he started moving made him want to please her. He knew how to get a scream out of her and made sure he hit the spot that caused them every time he drove into her. She moved with him. Her muscles clamping down on him as she reached for her elusive goal. He was having trouble keeping his release under control. A beautiful flush filled her cheeks. He picked up the pace and got a moan from her.

She was close, but so was he. He filled her again and again. His need driving him to push them over the edge. Her body tensed and he knew she hit her climax. So beautiful. The aftermath glow that flushed her skin. The half-hooded look she gave him before she smiled. He followed her into the euphoria they found in each other's arms.

He drew her into his arms and waited for her to be able to speak again.

"Wow."

"Are you back with me, my heart?"

She snuggled against him and nodded. "You know how to relax me."

"And you needed to be relaxed. I never saw you that angry before. This is something you have harbored for a long time."

"I know." She lifted her head to look at him. "Susan found a way to pick on me the whole time we were in school. I didn't know about her father threatening to replace her with me, but at least she had parents. Her jealousy doesn't make sense to me."

"You are getting agitated again." He rolled them over so she was beneath him. "Do I need to make you boneless again?"

"You can make me boneless anytime you want, my heart."

"Really?" he gave her a bone melting smile. "Anytime?"

The heat of a blush filled her cheeks. "You going to take that as a challenge?"

He laughed. "I know my mate and know although she has relaxed a lot of her inhibitions there are still a few that she can't shake."

TEN

Heather stood outside the door to the hold they had Susan in and wiped her hands on her outfit.

"There is no reason to be nervous, my heart. She can't hurt you."

She looked at Storm. "I know but just seeing her makes me angry."

"I can make you boneless whenever you wish. That normally melts any anger you have."

She grinned and triggered the door. Time to get this over.

"How long are you going to keep me chained like an animal?"

"You just don't know when to be quiet do you?" Heather wanted to pinch her. "I could pop you out of an airlock and no one would know."

"Yes, they would."

"Nope." Heather shook her head. "We're changing the timeline back to where it should be. If I do it before the change happens no one would know what happened to you."

"My heart."

"I'm sure she has tried to write me out of a timeline at least once."

Susan wouldn't look her in the eye.

"Thought so." Heather let her words hang for a few seconds. "My mate thought I should show you my life after I arrived on Vespia. Let you see that I don't just sit around waiting for Storm to come home."

"What could you possibly do that is that hard?"

Heather looked at Storm. "I knew this wasn't a good idea."

"Show her, my heart. Let her see what is like to work two jobs a day."

"Two?" Susan looked from Heather to Storm.

"Yes. In the mornings I work with a security team. One of Vespia's best. In the afternoons I am helping the Vespian council." Heather wasn't going to give more detail than that. Susan didn't need to know she was from the planet even though she wouldn't remember it when the timeline changed. She didn't trust Susan.

"What?"

"I'm assigned to work as a security guard during the morning because of my training. In the afternoon I listen to people's grievances because of my marriage to Storm."

"You have to work?"

"Yes." Heather wanted to strangle her. Susan just didn't understand. "Do you think they would let me stay on their planet if I had no value to them? I went through a series of tests to prove my worth to them. Then I went through more so they would know where I could be of most value."

"They tried to get me to take tests, too, but never assigned me any work."

"That means you never passed any of the tests. No matter how many times you changed the timeline, eventually you would have found yourself banned from Vespia. Your plan never would have worked," said Storm. "We don't take people in unless they would be an asset. Heather had the security training. The doctor who mated with my sister had medical training."

"What could you contribute to Vespia, Susan?" asked Heather. She knew showing Susan her life on Vespia wouldn't do any good. "Newscasting background? The Vespians who are in charge of that must have security training. They deal with sensitive material all the time and need to know what should be broadcast and what shouldn't. One mistake could mean the penal colony."

Heather heard Skye's voice in her head. They had just gone into orbit. Good, she didn't have to show Susan anything. Soon she'd have her life back and Susan would have no memory of what transpired anyway. She looked at Storm before turning her attention to Susan. "We're going to the planet now. You are going with us, and we are changing the timeline back."

"I don't want to go back to my life." Susan pulled on her restraints.

"I really don't care. You're playing with people's lives, Susan, and that is going to stop." Heather turned her back to her and crossed to the panel that restricted her nemesis movements. She hit the button to release her. "Don't think about trying to escape or I *will* pop you out an airlock."

———

The five of them arrived on the planet undetected. Skye used some of Bert's technology by erecting a shield to keep them hidden from the local security scans that way they wouldn't be disturbed. They entered the building that held the machine where their crystals came from, which everyone had. Sam had a hold of Susan and her crystal so she could see the computer's hologram interactive when it appeared in seconds.

"You came back! I truly enjoyed the scenes from your life, Heather."

"Thanks." She looked at Storm. He hadn't said anything about what she had shared. Perhaps he was waiting for the right moment, like when she got into trouble again. "We came back to fix the timeline."

"But I don't know how Susan changed the timeline with our equipment."

"I do." Heather pulled the necklace out of her uniform. "She used this with the items from your system to make the changes."

"Interesting." He moved to one of the many systems in the room. "This records each of the timelines."

Heather smiled. She had hoped the data they needed to put the timeline right was here so she wouldn't have to expose Bert to Susan. The fewer people who knew how advanced his technology was the better, even if Susan's mind would be wiped by the next timeline change. "Then all we need to do is go back to the original one and reset it."

"It is a little more complicated than that, but yes. There are constant changes to the timeline, but they occur naturally. I need the exact moment when the first change was made."

Heather turned to Susan. "Well?"

"I don't know."

"It's recorded on the ship's computer." Skye reminded her as he handed over his handheld. "My system went blank for a moment while we approached Vespian space. Facing guards who didn't know who we were let us know something had changed."

"Thank goodness you two were in that ship or we would have never known about the change," said Storm.

Heather pulled up the data and read off what the computer needed to pinpoint the first moment when the timeline changed for them.

"Will we go back to the point where the changes happened?" asked Susan.

"Time has already flowed to this point so when the adjustments are made you will go to wherever you should be at that time. Understand that it still might not be the timeline you came from since smaller time changes happen all the time, but it should be close."

Heather reached for Storm's hand. As long as it was close, she would be happy, and once they got close, she hoped Bert would be able to make the proper changes to get it back where it should be. She would have gone to him first but didn't want Susan to know about their special friend.

"I've made the necessary adjustments. Will I see you again?"

Heather smiled. "Time will tell."

The hologram gave her a sad smile.

"Wait, before you make the changes I need to speak to my friends."

He gave her a slight nod.

Heather turned to Skye and Sam. "We need to make plans to keep the timeline safe once the change is done. Skye, you and Sam need to come back and remove the equipment. I know Bert can help you do it right."

Skye nodded.

"What about Susan?" asked Sam.

"I'll deal with her," said Heather. Sam handed her Susan's crystal.

Once they had talked, she turned to the hologram. "We're ready."

The system reset the timeline.

The world dropped away. Heather watched in awe as she flew across the galaxy. Not knowing where Storm was in all of this worried her. What if they still weren't mated? Two suns came into view and her heart started to beat a little faster. Vespia had two suns. As walls started to go up, she found herself lying on her back again. Euphoria filled her. Good Lord, she was having an orgasm.

She kept her eyes closed. Fear of who might be in bed with her made her too afraid to open her eyes. Warm fingers brushed along her jaw.

"Open your eyes, my heart."

Her mate's voice washed over her, melting her fear. She opened one eye and saw his face inches from hers then opened the other.

"What were you afraid of?" His voice held a growl of disapproval. "That someone else could be in bed with you?"

"Well, in the timeline when I was pregnant, I feared my brother was my husband at first." She wanted to handle this right so he wouldn't get too angry.

"That the child you were carrying was his?"

She knew his jealousy over other men showing her attention. How would he handle her honesty? Heather nodded.

"But he wasn't. It was mine and he was trying to hide it by marrying you. No matter what timeline we're in, we belong to each other and no one else."

"And I want to keep it that way. We need to get to Susan before she causes more trouble."

"But I have you right where I want you." He brushed his knuckles against her mark. "Soft, pliant, and beneath me."

He continued to fill her, and she felt each caress deep inside. They needed to get to Susan. He knew it too. But she would never deny him. The joy she felt in his arms was something she wanted to experience again and again. His mouth found hers, his tongue eased the seam of her lips open, dipping in and searching for its mate. Desire filled her. All she could think about was her need.

She slid one leg against his. He started to rock into her a little quicker and she moaned into his mouth.

He broke the kiss and lifted his head. The smile she gave him had him smiling back. "You are smiling."

"I see that beautiful glow in your eyes."

"And that makes you happy."

"Very." Her muscles tightened against him when he hit that sensitive spot.

"My heart." He picked up the pace again.

Every stroke brought her closer. Intense feelings gripped her. Her breath caught in her throat. "So close."

Storm switched his pace, using quick deep strokes and she felt everything tighten, heat unfurled inside her, bubbling up and out through her body. Euphoria filled her as everything inside melted. She floated, the only sensation she felt was the warmth of her mate.

He touched her face gently. "Are you back with me, my heart?"

She nodded, not quite able to speak.

He pressed his lips to her mark. "I am so happy to see this again."

She sighed. "We seem to be back to normal."

"And as you said we need to keep it that way."

———

Skye and Sam watched as the world faded away. They lost contact with each other as they flew across the galaxy. Sam knew she wouldn't end up with Ialog this time, but there was still a part of her that feared it could happen. As everything started to build up around her, she found herself in a restaurant. Her meal was just about done. So where was she?

As discretely as she could, she looked around at the other guests. There was a myriad of different races. Maybe she was at a spaceport. There were two other places set at the table, but she was alone at the moment. Who was she eating with? And why had she started without them?

Where was Skye? Then she saw him heading straight for her. She stood and he wrapped his arms around her then pulled her close. "You okay?"

"Better now that you are here." She relaxed against him. "How did you know where I was?"

"I didn't, but my handheld led me here. I had a luncheon date on my calendar." He looked down at the two empty plates. "Who's supposed to join us?"

"I don't know, but I didn't know you were joining me. I seem to be without any devices." She looked over Skye's shoulder and found Bert coming at them. "Bert?"

"I am glad to see you. Have you fixed the timeline? This is the first time I haven't been at my old compound."

"Mom did her best." Sam gestured to the table. They had to act normal, so they sat and waited for the waiter. "We were sent to look for you. See if everything is back the way it should be."

"Have you heard from Heather? Is my ship back around Vespia?"

"No." Sam shook her head. "I'm sure we will hear as soon as they can contact us."

———

Susan found herself back in her apartment. "Damn it!"

She had hoped she'd be on the planet with the machine. Maybe she'd be able to access the timeline again before they caught up with her but being here killed that idea. One thing was for sure, she had to get out of there before Heather and her friends came for her. As quickly as she could, she threw some clothes together and loaded a bag. The next thing she went for was her money. Most of it was in credits, which she could convert at the first spaceport she landed at. Her journal could be accessed from any Earth system. She checked everything and realized she had forgotten her jewelry. Going into her bedroom she brought out the small box that held the few pieces her mother had given her.

Time to go. She picked up her bag and opened the door. Two security guards stood there.

"Susan Harris, we've been told to escort you to headquarters."

"Why?" She needed to get away. If she thought she could escape she would have scooted around them, but they blocked any space she could have used to run away.

"Admiral Barrister gave the order."

Damn it, Heather must have gotten to him before she could leave.

Heather held the necklace she took from Susan in her hand. With a sigh she stood and went to the small replicator. She sat the necklace on the smooth surface and programmed it to make a copy.

"This cannot be duplicated perfectly," the computer told her. "There is technology inside that is more advanced than anything I can recreate."

"That's fine. Recreate the jewelry aspect only. Once it is

completed, please transfer the original to the ship's vault." She returned to her seat.

"You're making a copy for Susan?"

"She got it from her mother." Heather shrugged.

"Soft heart."

"If our roles were reversed, I'd want mine back."

"And we both know Susan wouldn't think about what you would want."

Heather didn't comment.

Storm decided to move on. "You haven't spoken about what you plan on doing to her once we get to Earth."

"I'm going to alter her memories." She looked out at the black expanse littered with diamond points of light in a myriad of colors. Was she too soft?

"Thought so." Storm was quiet after that.

Heather sat, her thoughts rolling around in her head. She really didn't have a lot of choices. Susan could either be locked up for the rest of her life, which would make her Heather's responsibility in a way. Heather could kill her, but that didn't sit well either. The only people she had ever killed were people threatening her life. The threat she gave Susan was a hollow one. Her last choice was to wipe the hatred she had for Heather away, then let Susan live her life the way she should have lived. That was the right way, wasn't it? "What would you do?"

"If I had your ability, I would do the same thing. She's caused us trouble, but I don't consider it life-threatening."

"I heard back from Bear." Heather changed the subject, feeling better knowing he agreed with her. "Susan was on her way out when his men caught up with her. Bags packed and everything."

"She was running from us."

"That's what I was thinking." She looked at him. "And if I were her, I would keep trying."

"Then we need to get there quickly, before she gets herself into trouble."

———

Bert looked at the readings from the timeline they were now in. His ship around Vespia was one of the things that had changed. It wasn't there, but still on the planet and there was no sign of Dian, Ed, any of the people they rescued from Reasta or the twins. Skye had uploaded the data from his handheld so they could see what needed to be fixed.

His silence as he worked annoyed Skye. "What do we need to do?"

"Well, the major damage was done by that machine. If we could take that out of the equation, then the timeline should straighten itself out. I will probably still have to tweak the timeline a bit, but we would be very close to where we want to be if we take care of the machine."

"You want us to go back in time and remove it before Susan can find it?"

"That is the best solution."

"Can we use the ship? Or do you have another way to get the machines out of there?"

"Your ship has a time travel component on it." Bert smiled. "All I have to do is activate it."

———

Heather and Storm got the clearance they needed to land their ship near Earth security. Heather wore her Earth security dress uniform. She didn't want anyone to question her presence, even though Storm wasn't happy with what she wore.

"They continue to pay me. I might as well take advantage of it."

"And if you continue to use them like this, they might not let you go." Storm frowned. "You are my mate and part of our society now. They need to understand that."

"They are going to pretend that hasn't happened so I'm going to make them understand I will take advantage of their stupidity. I ask to resign every time I'm allowed. They just refuse to sign off on it."

"Do they think you're going to come back some day?"

"I think the people love the happily ever after we have. We're like royalty to them. Role models. You are the next leader of a planet, I'm a security agent, yet we fell in love. Bear sends me the feeds and we're always in them. As crazy as it sounds, they don't want to lose me because I represent hope to the masses."

"At least that makes sense." Storm took her hand.

"We're coming up on the security check." She squeezed her hand against his.

He squeezed back then let go. They stepped up to the guard.

"Commander Drexel to see Admiral Barrister."

"Yes, ma'am." The soldier saluted her. "He's expecting you and the ambassador."

She walked into his office with Storm right behind her.

"Before the yelling starts, I want to say I'm sorry."

"What happened?" Heather took a seat he gestured to.

"There was a lapse in our security and Susan was able to escape. We've been tracking her and know where she's heading."

"Fine, please give me the coordinates and I'll go get her myself."

"I can't do that." He sat back in his chair.

"Sir, if you don't allow me to pursue Susan I will resign."

"How many times have you tried?"

She smiled. He knew the answer to that. "I have the clearance to apprehend her, sir."

"I'm sorry. Susan is heading to a top-secret dig."

"The planet Rolam."

"How the hell do you know about that?" Bear glared at her.

"I do have clearance and do receive missives from earth."

"Not on this. All communiqués have been one way. To Earth only."

Heather leaned forward. "You're not going to believe me."

"Try me."

"Somehow Susan altered the timeline. Before she changed it, she had gone out there to interview the scientists stationed there, wandered around and found some artifact to change the timeline." Heather touched Storm's hand. "We want to find out what she used and stop her."

"You need to let Earth's security take care of this."

"Bear, everything she did was aimed right at me. You keep me as part of this security, and I have the right to go there and stop her."

"You might, but Storm doesn't, and our government won't go along with him accompanying you."

"Fine." She crossed her arms over her chest. "I'll go with your team."

"You know I can't allow that. Security officer or not it would cause too much trouble if the rest of the planet were to find out."

"So you're going to keep me away?"

"I am only following orders, Commander."

"Admiral Barrister if you try to demote me for disobeying orders, I will resign. If you lock me up to keep me from pursuing that woman, I will resign and make the biggest stink you've ever seen on any video. No matter what you do, if I can't go after Susan, you will lose me and your treaty with Vespia."

"You can't mean that."

"She does," Storm confirmed.

————

Skye, Sam, and Bert stood on the bridge of Skye's ship. Bert had made the changes needed to activate the time travel device.

"Are you coming with us?" asked Sam.

"To keep the timeline right I think it should just be the two of you. You're the ones who had been kept out of the timeline change in the beginning."

Skye didn't question and started the power-up sequence for them to leave. Sam just stood there, like she wanted to convince Bert to go with them. He knew she was afraid that this wouldn't work. "Strap in, Sam. We need to get going."

"I'll see you after this last change." And Bert transported out.

He finished the final sequence, and the ship took off. Skye set the coordinates for Rolam. "It won't take us too long."

"The sooner we get this done the happier I'll be."

"A little tense?"

"Anxious."

"I know how to relieve that." He turned in his chair and smiled at her.

She smiled back. "You complain about my father, but he would use the same excuse to be intimate with my mom."

"Don't remind me." He braced his hands on his knees. "I

want you happy and if that means relaxing you by orgasm, I'm more than willing to do that."

She laughed. "And you're very good at it."

Sam always embraced their love life. Having been rapidly aged she didn't have the inhibitions other women did. He could make a suggestion, and she would be eager to try it.

He took her hand and led her to their bed. This time it would be for comfort. Just the two of them enjoying each other.

Sam was quiet. Her fear of the time change was etched on her face.

"It will be okay, Sam."

"I hope so." She sat on the bed, looking so lost.

He touched her face, making her focus on him. "Look at all we've done to get everything fixed. Your parents now remember. There is nothing to worry about."

"I want them back just the way they were." She took his hand and pulled him down beside her.

"And they will be." He brushed a few strands of hair from her face. Skye opened the seals of her uniform, using gentle fingers he caressed her, drawing a sigh from her.

She helped him out of his clothes, smiling when she could touch his skin.

He eased her back onto the bed, knowing he needed to take control. Skye pressed soft kisses along her collar bone, across her cheeks then captured her mouth with his, brushing his tongue against the seam of her lips, slipping in when she opened her mouth for him. Their tongues danced as their desire for each other rose.

Skye centered himself and drove into her. She moaned her pleasure. He loved the fact she didn't hide anything from him. Not growing up the way everyone else had, she never faced the pain of rejection. Each time was new and wonderful. He couldn't ask for more.

Her legs moved against his hips while he set a nice quick pace, filling her as deep as he could with each thrust, but he knew she wanted more.

He continued to pound into her, bringing them closer to their releases. Skye felt Sam's hand skim up his body and he knew what she was trying to do. Brushing his fingers along her hips, he slid up her waist and her arms to lace his fingers with hers.

"Skye?" She looked at him.

"You want to take control and normally I let you, but this time I want to be in control. You need to just lay there and enjoy."

She grinned up at him. "I think I can do that."

"I hope so. You always like to be in control, like your father."

She blinked. "I do not."

"Oh sweetheart, you know better." He pressed a kiss to one cheek then the other. "That's why I love you."

"You said my dad was obnoxious and overbearing."

"And he is, but you're also like your mother with that giving heart."

"I'm not sure that is a compliment."

He laughed. "You're my mate. Loving, sweet, and a little pig headed when you don't get your way."

"You mean like now." She relaxed a little beneath him.

"And I wouldn't change a thing about you." He started moving inside her again. "You are everything I've ever wanted."

"That you didn't even know you wanted." She arched against him when he hit a sensitive spot.

They moved together, racing toward that elusive release they wanted to reach. Each time he entered her, her muscles tightened against him. The exquisite pressure had him shaking.

Skye held his release as he waited for those two precious words. He kept up the pace, drawing a moan from Sam. One stroke had her shuddering in his arms, and he heard the barely whispered words from Sam's lips.

"Oh my."

———

They arrive at the planet to find a security ship orbiting it.

"What are they doing here?" asked Sam. She sat beside Skye in her chair, staring at the screen.

"It's a normal routine." Skye looked at her. "According to the chatter I'm getting, they're bringing supplies and some fresh guards. They transfer them out every six months."

"Can we do what we need to while they're here without raising suspicion?"

"I don't expect them to stay around that long. By the time you change into your uniform and power it up they should have already broken orbit and be heading back to the nearest star base." Skye checked his readings then sat back and looked at her again. "Thanks for agreeing to go to the planet and tagging the ones we need. I know I could bring them up from here, but with the age of those machines I want to make sure there is no damage done in the transport."

"I now have three sets of uniforms to use." Sam stood. "Which one would you recommend?"

"The one that we always use." Skye got up out of his chair and wrapped his arms around her. "Sam, we're going to be successful. Don't let this get to you."

"I'm trying not to, but it's hard."

"You are a very strong woman, just like your mother. We are so close to fixing all of this."

She nodded. "I'll go get changed."

"I'll have what you'll need ready when you come back." Skye knew she needed to be professional right now. Later, when they fixed everything, she would cry on his shoulder.

———

Sam went to their room and changed. The uniform she ended up choosing had a few more options that she might need while off the ship. She turned on her screen to see if the other ship had left while she was climbing into it. The ship powered up as she watched and headed back the way it came. Good. Now they could get their mission done. She wanted her parents back. The good, the bad, and the annoying parts. She wanted everything to go back to the way it was. Sam walked back into the bridge.

"You need to hurry," Skye said. "There is another ship on its way."

"This is sure a popular planet for being top secret."

"The ship coming is an Earth science ship. It has to be Susan. We need to remove these things before she can find them so she can't change the timeline."

"I'm ready." Sam felt the weird sensations everyone felt was they were digitized to be transported. Skye put her by the opening of the buildings. She darted in and marked the first machine her mom had found then went into the other room and marked four more. That should remove everything Susan would need to make the changes she did.

She smiled as the equipment she tagged disappeared. Then she found herself back on the ship.

"Now let's go home."

Sam nodded. She hoped what they did worked.

———

Bert watched as the timeline adjusted again. Skye and Sam must have been successful. He watched the timelines shift and merge, but he still found a few items out of whack. He pinpointed the time, and it was when Heather was sent to Earth. He compared the data Skye had downloaded into his computer. Heather had been a ward of the state in their original timeline, but somehow Dian ended up being her guardian. Did Susan go back in time and keep Ialog from kidnapping Dian or did something else happen that coincided with the time change?

He knew he had to go and find out.

He used his fastest ship to get to Earth. He programmed it to maintain orbit and set the time computer to bring him back to when Heather first arrived. He had to see what could cause Ialog to leave Dian alone.

He watched the settings as the time machine sent him back. Space around him settled as he emerged back when Heather first came to this planet. He saw the Vespian ship swing by Earth. A short burst of a beam came out of the belly of the ship before it took off.

He transported himself down to the site where Heather was left. She wasn't there. Pulling out his scanner, he searched until he found her nearby. Bert kept himself hidden from view as he watched the scene unfold. Dian was the next to arrive. She crouched down in front of Heather, who seemed to be sleeping.

A few minutes later he saw Ed materialize. Ed? He was in hiding. Then he remembered. Ed said he had spoken to him and told him to go into hiding. Was this the moment when he did it? To keep him from helping Dian? He knew he had to make the timeline right and Heather never knew Dian until she was already mated with Storm.

Ed walked by where he was hiding as he approached Dian. Bert grabbed him by the arm and pulled him into his hiding place.

"You have to go into hiding."

"Bert? What are you doing here?"

"Ed, listen to me. We are being hunted. Reasta is after us. You must be saved. Go into hiding. Stay away from any Ancient until I come for you."

"But that child—"

"I know how important that child is, and she will be protected, but you need to go. She needs to grow up to help us and that might not happen if we interfere with her life."

"What about Dian?"

"I will warn her, too. Now go." Bert had to get him to leave before Ialog showed up.

Ed looked at him. "You will explain this one day?"

"I promise."

Ed faded from sight and Bert let out a sigh of relief. Now he had to deal with Dian.

Bert stepped out of his hiding place. "Dian."

She whirled at his voice. "Bert!"

"I have a horrible request to ask of you." He touched her face. She meant everything to him and now he was going to ask her to do the unthinkable.

"What?"

"Ialog is coming. He wants the child, but he can't have her. She must grow up on this planet, raised by their government."

"Then she is the one."

"Yes." Bert looked down at the sleeping child. "I hate what I must ask of you, but I know if anything changes, she won't be the woman we need her to be. You must force Ialog to send you back in time. He will trap you there in the Washington State area in the early twenty-first century. You will need to hide in your wolf form so he can't find you until you see this child all grown up and searching for her mate. They will bring you back to me."

"What do you know, Bert?"

"I can't say, but I will be in the same timeline. You must stay away from me, too. I never knew you were in that time." He looked at her sadly. "If you are successful in getting him distracted the humans will find her first and everything will be as it should be."

"And she will be safe with the humans?"

"Yes. We'll give her this insert." He held out his hand. "This will let her read as human. People will question what it is, but it will keep her protected."

They worked together to insert the small device in her back. "When I see you again you can't mention my presence here. Not until I tell you I was here with you."

"Bert."

He pulled her into his arms and gave her a quick kiss. "I will see you again and I promise to explain everything."

They heard someone approaching. Dian touched his face. "You need to go."

"I know, but I will be watching to make sure you're successful."

"Just keep her safe and I'll keep Ialog away from her."

Bert ran back to his hiding place just as Ialog came into view.

"Dian! What are you doing here?" asked Ialog.

"I'm here for her." Dian put her body between Heather and Ialog.

"I created her. She belongs to me."

"She's not a program you created. That is flesh and blood." Dian banged her chest. "I'm going to take care of her, raise her to be the woman she is supposed to be."

"I can't let you do that." Ialog advanced on her. "That child isn't going anywhere, but you are."

She backed up. "You can't harm me, Ialog."

"I would never try, but I need to get you out of the way." He looked at the sleeping child. "She's not going anywhere for now." Ialog jumped at Dian and wrapped his arms around her. They faded from site.

Bert came out of his hiding spot and scooped little Heather up in his arms. He had to move her where Ialog couldn't find her right away and call the Earth government to make them aware of her presence. He carried her quite a distance before he noticed a large field filled with heather. That was what she was found among in the original time-line, so he sat her down then contacted the proper authorities.

He went and found another hiding place then waited. It only took a few minutes for several of Earth's security to show up. Once they felt Heather wasn't a risk, they took her away. Bert hoped he set the timeline right as he transported back up to his ship.

ELEVEN

Heather wasn't getting anywhere with Bear, and it frustrated her. Her threats fell on deaf ears. He knew she needed to clear everything with the Vespian council. Even though she could, it would take time, which would defeat the purpose of the threat. He was still pushing to let Earth's security take care of Susan, but she needed to be the one to speak to the woman. Somehow Heather needed to convince him to let her do it.

A ripple started near her. The slight movement caught her attention. She watched in awe as the ripple created small changes. Bear was no longer behind his desk but leaning against it in front of her. Her Earth uniform changed into one of her Vespian gowns.

"You have to understand that no one can talk to her until after we've questioned her. If it wasn't for that I'd let you go after her."

More than her clothes changed. Why were they questioning Susan? "Why?"

"It was her special. You haven't seen it, have you? She released it without allowing security to see it. That was part of the contract when we gave her permission to go there. She showed things that she wasn't supposed to." Bear stood. "We have a ship arriving on the outpost she is hiding on in an hour or two and they will apprehend her. Once we are done with her you can have her."

Heather didn't want her, but she had to make the changes to keep her from trying to interfere with their lives again. "Thank you, Bear."

"Oh, and the next time you might want to come here in your uniform."

Heather wanted to laugh. She had been in uniform before the last time change. "I thought about that but knew the uniform would draw attention. Everyone is used to seeing me in outfits like this when Storm is with me."

"But he's not."

Heather never thought to look at her mate when the change happened. Bear was so close to her she was focused on that, but one glance showed his seat empty. She had to think fast. "He had something to do but will be joining me in a moment or two."

My heart? Where are you? Heather sent her thoughts out to her mate.

I ended up in Susan's apartment but am on my way now. Are you still with Bear?

Yes, and he wanted to know why I wasn't in uniform.

But you were.

Then the timeline altered itself once more and suddenly I sat here with my Vespian clothes on. I hope that was Skye and Sam being successful.

I am at the security check. I should be there in a few minutes.

Bear pressed his collar. "Yes, let him in." He looked at Heather with a smile. "Looks like your mate is now here."

Heather stood as the doors opened. Storm walked in and wrapped his arms around her. He captured her lips with his for a quick, but heated kiss. When he broke the kiss he whispered against her lips.

"Are you okay?"

She gave him a slight nod.

After a quick squeeze, he changed his hold on her so he could greet Bear.

"Good to see you, my friend."

"Same here."

"Have you been able to achieve your goal, my heart?" He turned his attention back to her.

"Not yet, but Bear has promised to allow me to speak to Susan the moment they are done with her."

"But we need to get back to Vespia."

"Storm, I know you have a war to get back to. I was very surprised to hear you two were here so I know talking to Susan must be very important, but she's running and part of my responsibility." Bear reached behind him to do something before he turned around to talk to them again. "The ship won't be here for four days because of the path they have to take."

Heather wondered what he was up to when he flipped her a chip. She caught it and slipped it inside her dress. "You will contact me when I can speak to her?"

"I will."

"Thank you for seeing us, Bear," said Storm. "But we do need to be going."

"I understand." He offered his hand which Storm shook.

They headed out of his office. Storm leaned down to whisper near her ear. "That was not the same man we were talking to before."

"No, but I suddenly didn't feel the anger toward Bear I felt before either." She leaned into him. "I saw the changes happen. Did you?"

"No, I was just suddenly in Susan's apartment. My

uniform changed as well. It was subtle but it's different." He ushered her past the security checkpoint and out of the building. "I assume our ship is at the embassy."

"I'm hoping too because I don't want to ask."

A young guard approached them. "Your ship is ready, Commander."

"Thank you," said Heather. "Has it been moved?"

"Oh, no Commander. It's still right where you left it." The guard handed her the pad, showing repairs done as well as the fuel being replenished. It also showed where the ship was. She signed it and handed it back.

"Ready?" she asked Storm.

He smiled at her as he slipped an arm around her. "Lead the way."

She walked toward the main tarmac then guided them to the left, where the president's ship was kept. Theirs was at a safe distance, but still in what was considered the VIP area. Very few were allowed anywhere near where the president might show up.

The moment they stepped one foot on the VIP tarmac they were greeted by a guard. "Ambassador, Commander, your ship is standing by."

Heather found it funny that they didn't know what to call her now that she was mated. Vespians didn't have last names, so no one assumed the other's name. One time someone called Storm Mr. Drexel and found himself lifted off the ground by his throat. Then Storm politely told him to just call him Storm. No one tried that again.

"Thank you." She didn't miss the four guards walking behind them to make sure they went where they were supposed to. She also noticed the media area filled with reporters. Somehow, they must have heard she and Storm had landed, and many came to catch a glimpse of them.

The gangplank started to descend when they drew close.

Storm shifted his hold so he could scoop her up in his arms then he headed up into the ship.

"My heart," Heather squealed as he lifted her.

"Isn't this what all human males do with their wives?" He gave her his heart-melting smile as he carried her like she weighed nothing.

"There is a tradition of the husband carrying his bride over the threshold, but that is normally the first night after the wedding. He doesn't do it all the time."

"Ah, but I didn't get the chance to do that and with the media people training their cameras on us I thought this would give them something to keep our legend going."

"You noticed them, did you?"

He laughed. They knew he never missed much. "I thought this would show them we are happy together."

She touched his face. "My heart, when you do things like this it shows the galaxy how much we mean to each other, and you know it doesn't matter what they think. Only what we think."

"I know, but I wouldn't be a very good mate if I didn't try to keep you and those you hold dear happy." He had reached the top of the gangplank. Stopping for a minute he released her legs and wrapped his arms around her waist to hold her against him. His mouth claimed hers just as the doors closed on those watching.

Storm brought her onto the bridge before pressing her up against the wall. He continued to kiss her, their tongues danced, lowering her defenses and raising her need. When he broke the kiss, he leaned his forehead against hers. "They will want us to move this ship right away, won't they?"

"Yes." Heather's voice was a little breathless. "But it might take a while before we're able to lift off once we request to take off. This is a busy port."

"Then let's get this ship ready and hope we'll have enough time to satisfy each other before takeoff."

———

Skye held Sam's hand as their ship approached Vespian space. The last time they tried this they were turned away. He got a ping from Vespian security as they crossed into it, but no one stopped them. He smiled. He aimed his ship toward where Bert's command ship was before. It had better be there now.

"There's Bert's ship." Sam reached out for his hand. "We did it, didn't we?"

"It sure looks like it. Let's find Bert and see if there is anything small we need to tweak." He squeezed her hand. "But looks like we're finally home."

"I just hope what we did worked. I'm not sure I can handle another altered reality."

"It will be okay, Sam." Skye landed the ship and shut it down. He ran through his post-flight checklist then escorted Sam off the ship.

"You're here." Bert met them in the bay. "I have run the numbers, and we are very close. There are a few anomalies, but I believe it is your parents causing it."

"Why?"

"Because those anomalies started on Earth, where they are right now and radiates out to one section of space and I'm guessing that is where Susan is."

Sam heard the squeals of children. She turned to see her twin siblings come flying into the bay.

"Sam!" they shouted in unison.

She knelt and took them into her arms. Tears came to her eyes. Thank goodness they were here. That was something she had feared hadn't been fixed. "I have missed you."

"Where was everyone?"

Sam looked at Bert. "Dian and the people we rescued from Reasta's ship were here when the timeline changed so they weren't affected, but the ship was. It went into a limbo of sorts. They lost all newsfeeds and couldn't contact any of us so had no idea what was going on. The timeline basically disappeared for them, and they had to wait until we fixed it."

Sam nodded as she focused back on the twins. "Mom and Dad should be here soon."

"Are you leaving?" asked Zunni. Her large violet eyes showed fear.

Sam knew she didn't want to be left alone.

"No. We just got here, and I haven't had any time with you." She ruffled her little sister's hair. She needed to distract them to wash away their fears. "I can't wait to see Mom and Dad too and hope to spend some time with everyone. So, what have you two up to?"

"Dian taught me to draw." Zunni clasped her hands in front of her. "Would you like to see?"

"Of course."

Zunni took her sister's hand and pulled her toward the doors.

"Why don't you go and get it and bring it here?" asked Sam. She didn't want to leave Skye's side. With all the changes they had been through she felt a little like her sister and needed his strength.

"It's too big."

Really?" She turned to look at Skye.

Bert was the one to speak up. "We have to wait until your mother and father get here so why don't we all go. I've been curious, but she wanted to wait until you saw it."

Sam let her little sister pull her along to their day room. On one wall was a giant mural. The images were gorgeous, so life-like. She smiled. It showed the twins playing at the feet of their parents. She and Skye were there as well. Pumpkin was even in the picture. "Bubbles this is beautiful. You captured all of us perfectly."

Zunni gave her bright smile.

"How long did this take?" asked Skye. He studied one section of the mural.

"About a week of constant work," said Dian, who had entered the room after them. "It is beautiful, is it not?"

"I've never seen anything like it. Zunni have you done others?"

"Yeah, but they're not as good." She scuffed her feet on the floor.

"Can we see them anyway?"

Zunni nodded.

"She's brilliant. Her ability with a brush, pen, pencil, and computer is amazing. Does Heather have this talent?"

"Probably, but she never had the desire to draw or paint," said Bert. "She loves the sciences and that is what she focuses on when she has some free time."

"Which is not often," added Sam.

Zunnie came running in with a pad and an old-fashioned notebook. Sam flipped through the notebook, looking at the sketches she did. They were beautiful. Images of their mom and dad, individually as well as together. There was one of Bear that made her laugh. It showed him scolding someone. There was one of her and Skye at some ceremony. "What is this one from?"

"Oh, I don't know, but I think it is a naming ceremony."

"Was it yours?"

"No. You're wearing the gown mommy wore at ours."

Sam looked at Skye. Was her little sister seeing the future like their mom? "So are you saying this is something that hasn't happened yet?"

"Have you made me an aunt yet?" Zunni turned her pad to another image and handed it to Sam. "That is what he will look like."

"He? I'm going to have a boy?" Sam looked at the face of the young man her sister drew. He looked like Skye but had her mom's eyes.

Zunni nodded. She skimmed her finger over the surface to flip the page. "I saw this, too."

It was the cave they had converted into their command center on Vespia. "You need to show these to Mom."

"I know."

———

Heather and Storm didn't sit on the tarmac as long as they had hoped. Heather had just slid down his length when Cim told them they were being contacted by flight control. She went to move off him, but Storm wrapped his hands around her waist, keeping her in place.

"Only show her face, Cim."

"I can't do this." She had to be the one to talk to control since she was the one from the planet, but she would be far too distracted to do what needed to be done if she stayed in this position.

"My heart, you can do this. I promise not to move or arouse you while you speak to them." He slid his hands up over her stomach, but you're not moving off me. That is not the Vespian way."

Heather wasn't sure about this and knew he was pushing her, but he never pushed her into doing something she couldn't do. She took a deep breath and adjusted her body on Storm's. She heard him growl as she settled herself on him. "Put them on Cim."

"Commander, you are now cleared for flight." He paused for a moment. "Where is the ambassador?"

"He is lying down right now. Do you need to speak to him?" She was trying so hard to keep a straight face. At least she wasn't lying. He was lying down. No one needed to know it was beneath her.

"Oh, no." The guard she spoke to did seem nervous though.

"Is there a problem, Lt.?" His comment worried her and made her tighten her muscles against her mate.

"No ma'am. You are to follow the flight plan loaded into your system until you clear the galaxy."

"Thank you, Lt." Heather felt Storm's hands caressing her legs. "I'll be signing off then."

"Um, Commander, you haven't given us your flight plan."

"Oh, sorry. Sending that over right now." She was so worried they'd figure out she was naked and impaled by her mate she had forgotten to do that. That was why the guard was nervous too. Storm was the one who normally sent the data needed over.

"Got it, thank you Commander." He smiled, showing his relief. "Have a safe flight."

"Thank you." Cim closed communications and she melted onto Storm.

She heard his laughter. "That wasn't funny."

"Oh, yes, it is. You lost control for a moment, and we haven't done anything yet."

"You know I don't like talking to strangers while trying to hide our intimacy." She brushed her hair out of her face as she shifted so she could look at him. "It breaks my focus."

"I know, my heart, and you did wonderfully. I'm very proud of you." He slid his hands up her thighs and around her derrière. "What I loved the most was the way your muscles rippled against me as you tried to act professional."

Heather could feel the heat from a blush fill her cheeks.

"Now why are you embarrassed? No one knows but me, and I would never complain about something so exquisite. I wasn't sure if I could maintain when it kept happening."

"Kept happening?" She only remembered it happening once. Storm opened his mind to her and shared how she rippled against his length the entire time she spoke to the lieutenant. "Oh, my."

"Oh, yes." The glow in his eyes brightened. "Then there was one very tight squeeze you gave me that was almost my undoing."

Heather knew better. He never climaxed before her and there had been times when she expected him to. Tried to get him to, but he never did. Whether it was pride, or part of Vespian DNA, he always made sure she was boneless before he joined her, and she wasn't about to complain.

She pushed herself up from where she was lying on Storm. His hands went to her breasts the moment they could, cupping her then he gently brushed the pad of his thumbs against her nipples. Once she was sitting up, she looked down at him. The glow in his eyes filled her with joy. She had missed that wonderful glow when he was aroused. The fact it was back gave her hope that they had fixed the timeline.

With her being on top she had all the control, but she wasn't sure how long that would last if she did what she wanted to. Storm had created this chair for their comfort on missions, so she knew she'd end up on her back if his desire became too strong. She smiled at the thought. Pushing him to lose control was something she loved to do. He did it to her all the time so being able to turn the tables made her happy. Time to tease her mate a little.

"Like this one?" She tightened her muscles against him and watched in satisfaction as he shuddered.

"You are not playing fair."

"Like you do?" She pulled up then slid back down, contracting her muscles all along the way.

Storm growled. "Heather."

"Yes, my heart?" She started moving, sliding up and down his shaft as delicious tendrils of excitement filled her.

He moved his hands to her hips, helping her maintain the pace as she got lost in the sensations. Heather closed her eyes, allowing herself to just feel. Each stroke had her pushing toward her release. She wanted it bad. She picked up the pace, but it seemed to be unreachable. Her muscles created a vice grip between them which had them shaking. She was losing it.

Wrapping his arms around her, Storm pulled her toward him. He flipped them over and took control. He drove into her, each time had her wanting to moan her pleasure, but she couldn't speak. Couldn't utter a sound.

It was so close she could feel the beginnings of her climax surround her. It started in the pit of her stomach, racing through her bloodstream, and flinging her out to the stars. She felt nothing but the heat of her mate's body as he continued to pound into her and the euphoria that filled her.

Storm pressed soft kisses against her forehead.

Heather looked up at him, satisfaction filling her.

"You are glorious."

"And you are magic."

―――――

Storm had the ship's cloaked setting activated as they approached the ship Susan was on. He turned to face his mate. "I'm not happy with you going on that ship. Too much could go wrong. I can bring her aboard without anyone knowing."

"I know, my heart." Heather tapped the side of her head, reminding him that she could hear his thoughts. "But I can hide myself from view so I could stand right in front of them, and they wouldn't be able to see me. Besides, we don't know how they are tracking her movements. If we were to make Susan disappear and set off their sensors, Bear would know what we did. We can only do this if we don't get caught."

"I still don't like it." He crossed his arms over his chest.

"I promise to be careful, and you'll know if there is any danger or the moment I am done." Heather smiled. He hadn't come right out and said no.

He frowned. "You are my mate and need to be safe."

"And I will." She had on her Vespian uniform and was attaching the gloves when they started talking.

He came up to her and wrapped his arms around her. "This is very risky, and we could wait until Bear is done with her."

"We don't know what she remembers. If she does remember everything and the government puts enough pressure on her that she talks, she could get us all in trouble. I'll get in and out. You know I can do this." She brushed her fingers against his jaw. "Every time, you worry, but I always get the job done."

"Be safe, my heart."

"I will and I'll be back as quickly as I can." She snapped on her helmet.

Storm sent her over to the other ship, close to where they believed Susan was being held. She went to the interface on the wall once she materialized and overrode the security system, blocking her presence from any scan that might pick her up. Once that was done, she searched for Susan's location. It was a few cells down the hall. Heather opened her mind and searched for any guards who might be in the area, but luckily, no one was there.

Moving quietly, she inched her way to the cell Susan was in. She triggered the door and slipped in. The camouflage setting on her uniform kept her from Susan's vision. Susan was sitting in a chair in the center of the room, her movements restricted by soft straps restraining her. What did she do to make them want to tie her down? Normally she would have been locked in the room and left alone. The restraints showed she was a risk.

Heather stepped up to Susan and took off her helmet. She crouched down in front of the woman. Pulling her glove off, she touched the side of Susan's face, connecting their minds so Susan wouldn't cry out.

Shock filled Susan's face, but she remained quiet. Heather had stopped her voice in time. She stood. *Hello Susan.*

How are you doing this? Susan pulled against her restraints. *Why are you here?*

I am here to make everything right.

I thought you already did that.

Susan did remember. How? Heather closed her eyes and focused on what she needed to do. Deep calming breaths helped her.

I need you to relax, Susan. Open your mind and allow me in.

And let you hurt me? I don't think so. She fought against the straps once more.

Even though Heather could just push until she reached her goal, she didn't want to cause any damage to the woman's mind and knew she had to get Susan to trust her before she could do what she needed to do.

Have I ever hurt you, Susan?

You never showed any emotion, like a little robot. That hurt. I tried to break through that. Tried all kinds of things, but none of them worked.

You never tried kindness, Susan. I was a freak, remember? Showing any cracks in my armor would have been my undoing. You would have found a way to exploit it. The woman was too agitated, and Heather needed to relax her. Normally she used her voice to do it, but she couldn't. This was the first time she had used her mind and wasn't sure if her mind could do the same thing. Heather took another calming breath.

You are feeling very relaxed. It is a light and happy feeling, like you're floating above all your worries. You are safe here. Think back to when you were a child when your father was talking to you.

I don't want to. He was mean to me, always made me feel inferior. Then you came along. No. I won't. Susan shook her head.

Well, that was the wrong way to go. Susan's mind was stronger than others when it came to manipulating it. She had to try another angle. *Tell me about your mom.*

My mom? Why? She died when I was a teenager. Left me alone with him. Daddy said I was the reason she died. That my poor performance broke her heart and forced her to run away. She went away to some small outpost that was attacked and died there. I killed her, Heather. I don't want to think about that any more than I want to think of my father.

Then let's move past that. Heather worked her way through some of Susan's memories. *Tell me about Fred.*

He was the best friend I ever had. A small smile played on her lips for the first time.

That was what she needed. Fred was a pet. A puppy in her memories, but something that loved her back.

He protected you from the pain. Wrap that love around you now. You are loved. You are protected.

Yes.

Now I want you to relax. You're so relaxed you are close to sleeping.

A yawn escaped Susan. Good, this just might work.

You are loved, Susan. What your father felt toward you doesn't matter, what other people thought of you doesn't matter. Only what you think. You're successful and love your job. You get to speak so many unique people. You get to see so many exotic locations.

I do, don't I?

You do. All that hatred you have for me has disappeared. The jealousy has melted away. You don't see me as competition. I was just a girl in school. You were happy with your work and the way you performed in school. You are proud of yourself.

I am proud of myself.

Your desire for Storm is gone too. All those crazy timelines were nothing but a dream. A dream that fades away once you wake up.

A crazy dream...what was it about?

Nothing for you to worry about. Heather sensed something nearby and snapped her helmet back on. She was so close to finishing what she had started and didn't want the interruption. The sound of the doors opening had her ducking behind Susan's chair as she activated her camouflage setting. "Crap." Thank goodness she didn't have the mike on.

"Are you ready to come back?" she heard Storm's voice through her helmet.

"Um, there is a complication. Some guards just came in the door."

"I'll get you out now."

"I'm not quite done. Give it a few minutes. I'm crouched down behind Susan's chair with my camouflage setting on. They can't see me so probably don't know I'm here. You pulling me out could draw their attention so I can't come back."

"You are taking a big risk."

"And if I feel I have been compromised I will tell you. I need a few minutes. That's all."

"I am monitoring."

That meant he'd pull her out the moment he thought she was in trouble. Great. She needed to find out how Susan remembered the different timelines and get the artifact that gave her that ability. In order for this to work, Susan couldn't have anything that might help her remember the other timelines. They needed to be sure the new timeline washed over her. What Heather was doing now was recreating her past so it would be part of her memory. The change in the timeline will be so minute it shouldn't affect what Heather was doing now, but just in case she would be watching Susan to be sure and if she needed to do this again, she'd know what worked the first time.

Heather wasn't sure what would happen when they took off the medallions. It was a question she had wanted to ask Bert but hadn't had a chance to talk to him to learn if any of them would remember when they took them off. She knew one thing, if Susan did have something that helped her remember she wasn't going to leave without it. Whatever it was, it still had to be on Susan. Heather hadn't noticed any jewelry other than what she always wore, but if the necklace had helped her create new timelines, she could be wearing something else to help her remember. Heather wouldn't put anything past Susan. Could the piece be powerful enough to work from a distance? Knowing Earth security, they would have made her remove all jewelry, belts, or anything else she could use as a weapon.

"It's time for you to rest, Susan," said one of the guards.

Susan didn't answer them.

"Susan?"

Heather hadn't had time to release her from the mind control either. She had to make her speak or they might become suspicious. This was something else she had never done before. It took a few tries but soon she had Susan talking.

"But I'm not tired."

"Wouldn't you rather be lying down than sitting in the chair?"

"When you put it that way, I guess I should lie down."

They released her from the chair they had her in and brought her to the bed, reactivating her restraints. As they started to head toward the door Susan stopped them.

"Must you retrain me? It's not like I can go anywhere."

"You're a little too violent for our tastes, Miss Harris, and we've been told not to harm you." With that the guards were gone.

Once they left, Heather moved to Susan's side. *Susan, can you hear me?*

Yes.

How can you remember the timeline changes when no one else did?

You remember.

I have something with me that keeps the timeline from taking my memories over. Did you have something like that?

I don't know.

So she wasn't aware of anything. She had to have been wearing it when the timeline changed, but why didn't it stop working when she took it off? Or did she?

Are you wearing another piece of your mother's jewelry?

No. The guards made me take off all my jewelry. They put them with the rest of my things.

Where are your things?

I don't know.

So they didn't lock it in this room with you? If someone wasn't dangerous, standard procedure was to lock their items behind a panel in the same room. Perhaps it was powerful enough to keep working as long as she was close to it.

Oh. They did put something in a panel over there somewhere. She pointed to the wall opposite of them. *Why? Are you going to take something else of mine?*

I didn't take anything of yours, Susan.

My mother's necklace.

Heather smiled and held out her hand. Once she was sure she had Susan's attention she allowed the necklace to dangle from her fingers so she could see it. *It was always yours, Susan. I just needed to borrow it. Now I want to put it back where it belongs.*

Thank you.

Heather searched the panels and found the one she needed to access. The keypad was a problem though. She didn't know the code and figuring it out wasn't her forte. She smiled. She did know someone who could.

Skye, can you hear me.

Damn it, Heather. I hate it when you do this.

Sorry, but I need your help. I have a keypad in front of me that I need hacked.

You don't want to switch places, do you?

She could feel his distaste at the idea. *It would take several sessions before you would be able to manipulate my body properly. I want to share what I'm looking at with you, so you can walk me through what needs to be done.*

Fine. Let me see what you need help with.

She opened her mind to him so he could see through their connection. Heather had her visor on and had already fixed the settings so he could see which buttons had been pressed the most. What she needed was the sequence. She wasn't sure she could stop any alerts on the deck or in the security office when she tried to open that panel and needed to be off the ship before she could find out. It could take her two to three tries to open it where Skye should be able to open it with the first sequence.

Give me a minute. She could feel his mind running through the calculations. *Nine, three, six, two, two, one, seven, five.*

She knew he would do it. *Thank you.* She pressed the buttons in the order he gave her.

You don't even know if I got it right.

I trust you, Skye. This is where you excel. I don't think you could get it wrong if you tried. Now I need another favor. Susan must have a device like we do because she remembers the timeline changes. Can you ask Bert what I need to look for? She must have worn it. Jewelry or an article of clothing?

Bert says it most likely would be jewelry. A bracelet or ring.

Heather had the panel opened and saw a bracelet on top. She scanned the bag before she dropped the necklace in the bag and took the bracelet, hoping it was the right item.

Alarms went off. They knew the panel had been accessed.

My heart, can you take this bracelet and make a copy?

Heather, they are coming to the cell now. I have to get you out.

How much time do I have?

Seconds.

I need to get this back to Susan. And I have to release her.

You don't have time.

Heather moved to Susan's side. *Susan, focus on my voice. You need to go to sleep. When you wake up you won't remember my visit. You won't remember the different timelines. You will remember the error of releasing your video without clearing it through security and that is why you're here. You're sorry for your actions and will promise to follow the rules from now on.*

I am tired.

Good. Everything will flow the way it's supposed to. You will enjoy your life from this point on. Everything else is a bad dream.

Storm's voice filled her helmet. *I now have the location of her bag and can beam the bracelet directly into it.*

The door opened and three guards stepped in, weapons ready.

And you can pull out anything we need from the bag if this is the wrong piece?

Yes, my heart. I'm bringing you back now.

Heather felt the shift in her awareness before she found herself back on the ship.

"They have raised their shields and are scanning the area." Storm pointed to her chair. "I am going to allow the ship to drift away a little."

"You think they detected us when you had to drop the cloak to beam me back?"

"I doubt it, but since I do not know what type of advancements they might have gained with the timeline changes I want to give us a little space." He sat back in his chair once they started to drift backwards. "You truly push a little too much at times, my heart."

"I had to." Heather removed her helmet. "Susan remembers the change in the timelines. I need to be sure she won't remember when Bert makes the final adjustments to it."

"You just altered her mind, why didn't you change that in her mind as well?"

"I only changed what I felt was necessary." She sat the helmet in a nearby cubicle then detached her gloves. "I don't want to change too much. It's just a little too easy at times. I could have made her my best friend if I wanted to, but I would think part of her would question something that would be against her personality."

"So you haven't turned into the evil person you keep expecting to."

She knew what he was doing. Showing her that she still cared, even when it came to Susan who could have been the one to change her attitude toward her talent. "You are my heart."

He smiled at her. "Let's check to see if that bracelet is the item we need and get back to Bert."

———

Their ship landed at Bert's space compound. Heather was nervous, not sure what she'd find when they left the ship. Bert was the only one who met them.

"My friends, good to see you. The timeline is very close to where it should be. After you left Susan, it corrected itself again." He gestured for them to walk beside him as they headed to his labs. "I think it will be easy to tweak the last few things to get everything back the way it should be."

Heather heard the squeal of her youngest daughter, and her heart leaped. "Bubbles?"

Her children all came around a corner and her eyes filled with tears. This was why she wanted the timeline back. She dropped to her knees and opened her arms as the twins ran toward her. Sam stayed back for a moment before she came to Heather and kneeled as well so she could be part of the embrace. Storm completed it by kneeling with them and wrapping his arms around them all.

"Where were you, Mommy? I couldn't hear you." Bubbles tapped the side of her head. "I still can't hear you."

"I plan on fixing that soon, Zunnie," said Bert. "Let's head to the bridge. Everything is ready there."

Storm stood and picked up their son, Heather picked up Zunnie and held Sam's hand and they headed to the bridge.

"This is where we are." Bert showed them the timeline they were now in. "And this is where we should be based off of the info on Skye's pad."

"What needs to be done to make the last few changes?" asked Storm. He wrapped his free arm around Heather.

She leaned into his strength. Nerves had her wanting to do twenty things at once.

"We need to go to Vespia and merge with the timeline." Bert turned toward them. "We are as close as we can be to the original timeline. Once we reconnect with it, it will start to flow properly."

"And what will happen with the computer we brought from Rolam?"

"I can integrate it into the computers here or we can destroy them."

Heather looked up at Storm. "You never know when you might need something like that."

"True, but Bert has machines like that."

"We could bring them to the planet and hook it up with our systems."

Storm looked at her. "We'll think about it."

She smiled, satisfied they wouldn't destroy them. Heather adjusted her hold on her daughter. "Let's go."

"Only the three of us." Bert stopped her. "The twins never went through the changes. They shouldn't go through this one. Same with Sam and Skye. They were the ones who made us aware of what had happened. After we rejoin the timeline, they should be able to do the same thing without any loss of memory. The alternate realities are part of them."

"What about us?"

"Good question. You altered Susan's mind so she wouldn't remember once this is done. But your mind is so powerful I'm thinking you should remember once I make the last set of changes no matter what. I'm just not sure about Storm and I. I believe we should remember since the change will be slight, but it depends on the shift."

"Haven't you been through something like this before?"

"No." Bert smiled. "I have detected them in the past but never got caught by one. This is new to me as well."

Heather kissed her daughters, then her son. She took Storm's hand. "Let's put everything right."

———

The ship powered down inside the cave that security had converted into a landing site.

Reasta stopped each ship and scanned them, hoping to catch Heather and Storm on one, but they never took a Vespian ship. They always took their private one that had been outfitted with Ancient technology which made the ship unreadable to her. They could be right in front of her, and she would never know it.

She never shot a ship down. Heather figured Reasta didn't want to take a chance of inadvertently killing her, but they hadn't pushed the woman either. They kept their flights to a minimum and never took off at normal intervals.

Storm powered down the ship and opened the inner doors.

They had pulled their necklaces off earlier and left them back on the compound. Once they stepped off the ship, they would rejoin the timeline.

Storm rubbed his knuckles along her jawline. "Ready?"

Heather nodded. She took his hand and focused on the outer doors as they opened. She took a breath and walked out with Storm.

Hundreds of thoughts crashed into her head. She stumbled under the crush.

"You okay, my heart?"

"Yes." She nodded as she pressed the heel of her hand against her forehead. "Just not used to all the voices in my head. We've been out of sync for a while, and I got used to having my thoughts to myself without having to block everyone else's."

"So you remember," said Bert.

Heather nodded. "So do you."

"Remember what?" asked Storm.

Did he not remember? "Why did we come back to Vespia, my heart?"

Fridon stepped up to them at that point, stopping her from questioning her mate. He and Storm spoke quietly for a few minutes which gave her time to get control of all the thoughts bombarding her. First, she pushed away the thoughts of those who were rushing around. They were normally the loudest and most chaotic. Once she was able to rid her mind of those, she felt calmer. Next, she worked with the minds who were looking for loved ones. They could also spike her anxiety when they didn't see who they were looking for right away.

People started to recognize them. She could feel the changes in their thoughts. Awe was the first emotion. Slowly, more and more saw them. Storm was used to the attention, but she still found it overwhelming, especially while she could read their thoughts. Heather inched closer to Storm. He wrapped an arm around her waist and pulled her against him.

The awe turned to love. They showed their happiness toward her and Storm through their thoughts. She felt it down to her toes. Heather didn't mean to cry, but the joy that filled her brought tears to her eyes.

"My heart are you sure you are okay?" he brushed his fingers against a wet cheek. He was always aware of her, even when he wasn't focused on her.

"Yes." She nodded as she swiped at the tears. "I can hear their thoughts towards us. It's beautiful."

"Not as beautiful as you." He bent his head toward hers and captured her lips.

Tears continued to flow as their tongues danced. He tightened his hold on her as he deepened the kiss. When he broke the kiss, he rested his forehead against hers. "How I wish we were in our quarters. I would kiss each of those tears away and show you how you make me feel every day."

She laughed then. "Oh, I think I already know that my heart."

"Now that we have fixed everything we needed to, we need to turn our focus back onto Reasta and stopping her."

"You do remember."

"Yes, my heart. No matter what timeline we're in you are mine." He smiled. "I also had Fridon turn the copy of Skye's medallion off so he would merge with us. We don't need the timeline acting up now that we fixed it."

"Then I shall leave you, my friends," said Bert. "I need to speak to Dian and Ed about our little adventure."

"Thank you for all your help, Bert. I don't think we could have done this without you."

"Skye and Sam are the heroes this time. Without them, we never would have been able to do any of this."

"So now all we have to do is get rid of Reasta then maybe we can live our lives the way we want," said Heather.

"Maybe."

The End

Don't miss out on your next favorite book!

Join the Satin Romance mailing list
www.satinromance.com/mail.html

———

THANK YOU FOR READING

———

Did you enjoy this book?

We invite you to leave a review at your favorite book site,
such as Goodreads, Amazon, Barnes & Noble, etc.

DID YOU KNOW THAT LEAVING A REVIEW...

- Helps other readers find books they may enjoy.
- Gives you a chance to let your voice be heard.
- Gives authors recognition for their hard work.
- Doesn't have to be long. A sentence or two about why you liked the book will do.

ABOUT THE AUTHOR

Writing for Barbara Donlon Bradley started innocently enough, like most she kept diaries, journals, and wrote an occasional letter but she also had a vivid imagination and wrote scenes and short stories adding characters to her favorite shows and comic books.

As time went on, she found the passion for writing to be a strong drive for her. Humor is also very strong in her life. No matter how hard she tries to write something deep and dark, it will never happen. That humor bleeds into her writing. Since she can't beat it, she has learned to use it to her advantage.

Now she lives in Tidewater Virginia with a cat who thinks he owns everything, her husband and daughter.

www.barbaradonlonbradley.com

ALSO BY BARBARA BRADLEY

www.ingramcontent.com/pod-product-compliance
Lightning Source LLC
Chambersburg PA
CBHW031001260626
47169CB00002B/649

* 9 7 9 8 8 8 6 5 3 3 4 0 8 *